ROMANCING

D0384314

An explosion near the royal palace of Montebello sets off a frantic manhunt. One that begins with a confrontation between a proud lord and a mysteriously beautiful woman.

Meet the major players in this royal mystery....

Lord Andrew "Drew" Harrington: Romancing a suspect is not his usual style—but Rose is not a usual suspect.

Rosalinda "Rose" Giaberti: Her visions of fire have saved lives, but it will take a very special man to accept everything she is—and to protect her from others' fears.

Duke Lorenzo Sebastiani: As head of Montebello's Royal Intelligence, he will spare no one's feelings when it comes to keeping the country safe.

Gemma Giaberti: Rose's aunt knows the risks Rose faces. She also knows that, sometimes, taking chances and being hurt is better than always being alone.

Prince Lucas Sebastiani: Montebello's missing prince has found his way home. But his uncharacteristically quiet, brooding silences reveal that something—or someone?—is always on his mind.

Dear Reader,

July is a sizzling month both outside *and* in, and once again we've rounded up six exciting titles to keep your temperature rising. It all starts with the latest addition to Marilyn Pappano's HEARTBREAK CANYON miniseries, *Lawman's Redemption,* in which a brooding man needs help connecting with the lonely young girl who just might be his daughter—and he finds it in the form of a woman with similar scars in her romantic past. Don't miss this emotional, suspenseful read.

Eileen Wilks provides the next installment in our twelve-book miniseries, ROMANCING THE CROWN, with *Her Lord Protector.* Fireworks ensue when a Montebellan lord has to investigate a beautiful commoner who may be a friend—or a foe!—of the royal family. This miniseries just gets more and more intriguing. And Kathleen Creighton finishes up her latest installment of her INTO THE HEARTLAND miniseries with *The Black Sheep's Baby.* A freewheeling photojournalist who left town years ago returns—with a little pink bundle strapped to his chest, and a beautiful attorney in hot pursuit. In Marilyn Tracy's *Cowboy Under Cover,* a grief-stricken widow who has set up a haven for children in need of rescue finds herself with that same need—and her rescuer is a handsome federal marshal posing as a cowboy. Nina Bruhns is back with *Sweet Revenge,* the story of a straitlaced woman posing as her wild identical twin—and now missing—sister to learn of her fate, who in the process hooks up with the seductive detective who is also searching for her. And in *Bachelor in Blue Jeans* by Lauren Nichols, during a bachelor auction, a woman inexplicably bids on the man who once spurned her, and wins—or does she? This reunion romance will break your heart.

So get a cold drink, sit down, put your feet up and enjoy them all—and don't forget to come back next month for more of the most exciting romance reading around…only in Silhouette Intimate Moments.

Yours,

Leslie J. Wainger
Executive Senior Editor

Please address questions and book requests to:
Silhouette Reader Service
U.S.: 3010 Walden Ave., P.O. Box 1325, Buffalo, NY 14269
Canadian: P.O. Box 609, Fort Erie, Ont. L2A 5X3

Her Lord Protector
EILEEN WILKS

Silhouette®

INTIMATE MOMENTS™

Published by Silhouette Books

America's Publisher of Contemporary Romance

Special thanks and acknowledgment are given to
Eileen Wilks for her contribution to the
ROMANCING THE CROWN series.

SILHOUETTE BOOKS

ISBN 0-373-27230-8

HER LORD PROTECTOR

Copyright © 2002 by Harlequin Books S.A.

Visit Silhouette at www.eHarlequin.com

Printed in U.S.A.

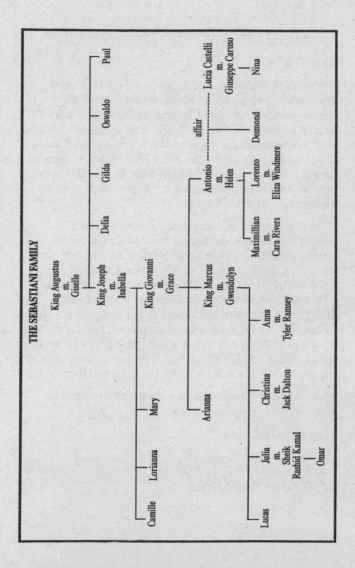

THE SEBASTIANI FAMILY

King Augustus
m.
Giselle

Camille — Lorianna — Mary — King Joseph — Delia — Gilda — Oswaldo — Paul
m.
Isabella

King Giovanni
m.
Grace

Arianna — King Marcus — Antonio ------ affair ------ Lucia Castelli
m.   m.   m.
Gwendolyn   Helen   Giuseppe Caruso

                                            Desmond   Nina

Lucas — Julia — Christina — Anna   Maximillian — Lorenzo
         m.   m.   m.   m.   m.
    Sheik   Jack Dalton Tyler Ramsey Cara Rivers Eliza Windmere
  Rashid Kamal

    Omar

A Note From RITA® Award Finalist Eileen Wilks

Dear Reader,

I've always tended to take on some of my characters' traits while writing about them. When I wrote about a superorganized heroine, I bought a planner and actually used it instead of losing it. While writing about a heroine who was much more traditionally feminine than I am, I developed a passion for the color pink. When a character gets hit over the head, I develop a headache. This is one reason none of my heroines ever suffers from morning sickness—I'm not taking any chances!

So when I started writing about a woman with a mysterious affinity for fires, I decided to avoid wienie roasts, fireplaces and burning candles. Maybe that was excessive, but I'm happy to report that I finished the book without burning anything more than a pot roast. (Though I did burn that thoroughly.) Maybe I only imagined I had more headaches than usual while writing about a hero who suffers from migraines…of a sort. And it was probably a coincidence that, shortly after I wrote about illness forcing Drew and Rose to stay overnight at an airport hotel, something similar happened to me.

But I still don't want to ever give any of my heroines morning sickness. Just in case…

Happy reading!

Eileen Wilks

Prologue

Gretchen Hanson loved babies. It was their mothers she didn't have much use for. "It won't work," she repeated, stubbing out a cigarette smoked down to a finger-burning butt. The noise level in the honky-tonk let her speak flatly, not bothering to whisper. "Midwives don't sign death certificates."

The plump, wide mouth of the woman sitting across from her pursed in a pout. Carnation pink, those lips were to-night. And sulky. "I can't believe you're wimping out on me now, Gretchen. You're always complaining about how dumb those doctors are. If you don't think you can fool one of them—"

"I don't." After all these years, Gretchen knew Ursula Chambers pretty well. Well enough to know that while Ursula's devious plans could lead Gretchen to a life of luxury, Ursula would have no qualms about using Gretchen as her fall girl if they were caught. And she knew how Ursula saw her. Barbie's best friend. The girl who would always and forever be second-string, her only claim to glamour the fallout from her friend's glittery shoulders. In high school, that had been true enough, Gretchen thought grudgingly. But high school was a long time ago. Not that she didn't still play along sometimes, but secondhand glamour wasn't worth risking prison over. "God, girl, get real. There's no way I could slip her an overdose without anyone noticing. Maybe we should rethink this."

Ursula smiled and leaned forward, the tousled fall of honey-colored hair sliding over one bare shoulder. Her blue eyes were bright with mischief. "I've already thought of a way to get her to have the baby at her damned ranch. I'll tell her the apartment is going to be sprayed for bugs—she shouldn't be around all those chemicals, right? You'll go out there with us. She's due any day now, so we won't have to keep her there for long."

The naughty pleasure in those eyes sent a chill up Gretchen's spine. What had seemed like an acceptable plan months ago suddenly felt all wrong. They were talking about murder, not short-sheeting someone's bed. Nervously she pulled out another cigarette and tamped down the end. "There would still be a body to explain."

Ursula rolled her eyes. "There's only a body to explain if we tell people about it."

"You mean…get rid of her. Bury her or something and tell people she left town." Gretchen's breathing turned shallow and fast. "It's a huge risk."

"It's a huge amount of money we're talking about. Remember our plans? Sweetie, we'll never have to worry about money again. You'll finally get out of this stupid town, the way you've always talked about doing. See new places, buy the kind of pretty things you've always wanted. Live the royal life. And don't forget that you'll be able to put that half-wit brother of yours in a good home."

"Gerald isn't a half-wit. He's…" Gretchen laughed.

"He's dumber than a dog, is all. Drives me crazy sometimes. But he does mind me pretty well." As long as he understood what she wanted... "It will be nice to live my own life without having to watch out for him all the time." The possibilities glittered in front of Gretchen's suddenly blank eyes. "But the risk. If I were caught..."

"I've got it all worked out." There was a febrile excitement about Ursula now, as if something was burning her up from the inside. She stretched out a hand and gripped Gretchen's wrist. A ruby glinted, blood-red, on one finger. "Think about that poor baby."

"Huh." Gretchen wasn't so lost in fantasies that she bought that. "As if you care about the baby."

"*You* care, though. Don't tell me you don't. And you know what Jessie has been saying. We've talked about all this, Gretchen. She wants to raise her baby all by herself out on the ranch. The poor little thing will never know his father, never know the life he should have had. She's so selfish, Gretchen!"

"They all are," Gretchen muttered. "They think they're getting some pretty doll to dress up, then when the pain hits they start yelling. 'Get me a doctor,' they say. Like I'm not good enough—but the only reason they want a doctor is to give them drugs. They don't care if it's good for the baby or not. All they think of is themselves."

"They don't care like you do." Ursula's voice was almost a croon. "Jessie sure doesn't. She wants to use the baby, that's what it is. Keep him a secret to pay his father back for dumping her. Is that right? Is that what's *best* for the baby? Letting the poor little thing grow up in a dreary house in the middle of nowhere when he could be living in a palace? He's a *prince*, Gretchen. But he'll never know it—unless you help him."

Gretchen's stomach clenched and her eyes went soft. Yearning ripped through her system like a triple-hit of nicotine. This was how Ursula had gotten her hooked on this scheme in the first place. Oh, she thought about that baby. She thought about all the babies she delivered. All those babies she had to put into other women's arms, all those blithely fertile women who didn't deserve the precious gifts they were given, the innocence, the love....

She cleared her throat and tried to make her voice hard. "He won't be a prince. He'll be a bastard."

"A royal bastard. The only male child in direct line for the throne." Ursula tossed her hair back impatiently. "Trust me, sweetie, I know how these people think. They'll be so delighted this baby exists they'll pamper him, pet him, give him everything a bitty baby could want...and they'll give us what we want, too." She leaned forward again, her voice low, her eyes shining. "I'll be the baby's aunt, so of course I'll live there with him. In the palace. But you know me, sweetie. I don't know beans about babies. I'll need you to take care of him. What do you say, Gretchen? Would you like to be a royal nanny?"

Gretchen's heart began to pound. All those months ago, when she and Ursula had first started scheming, she'd been distracted by the thought of wealth and famous connections. Now an even greater reason to go along with Ursula struck her. She wouldn't have to hand this baby over to some other woman. The idea made her dizzy, almost sick with yearning. "You never told me how you're going to convince the king and queen of Montebello to even talk with you, much less persuade them we've got their grandchild."

Ursula smirked. "I've got connections."

Some man, no doubt. Gretchen reached for her lighter.

"Oh, please don't. Smoking causes wrinkles."

"Causes worse things than wrinkles." Not that there was much worse than wrinkles in Ursula's world. Maybe cellulite. She flicked the lighter and held the flame to the tip of her cigarette, inhaling deeply. "All right. I'll do it."

"Oh, I knew I could count on you!" Ursula was all but quivering with excitement. "I'll get Jessie out to the ranch, but then I'll have to leave. I'll have to go to Montebello to set things up."

"Fine. I'll need some money up front."

"You don't trust me?"

Not for a minute. "I won't be able to work for a while, will I? I'll have to lie low with the baby until you call me." *With the baby.* That sounded good.

It sounded wonderful.

Ursula leaned back in her chair. "You know how strapped for cash I am right now. I wouldn't be in this stupid town if I weren't so broke."

"Broke. Huh! You don't know the meaning of the word. Sell some of the jewelry your back-stabbing ex-manager gave you. If there's as much money in this deal as you say, you can buy more and better."

"I already sold the diamonds Derek gave me." Her mouth drooped. "I hated that, but the ticket to Montebello will be expensive."

"Those diamonds were worth a lot more than the price of a plane ticket. And if you need more…" She grabbed Ursula's hand and held it up. "This ring you've been flashing around has to be worth— Hey, isn't this your sister's ring? The one you're always bitching about because your grandma left it to her, instead of you?"

"Oh, you noticed." Ursula's giggle was light and girlish. She wiggled her fingers. The ring was unusual, possibly unique, with a ruby and a pearl nestled together in an ornate golden bed. "I don't think my dear sister Jessie will miss it, do you? Not where she's going."

Chapter 1

Flames. Orange-hot, sucking the air from her chest, shouting smoke at the sky. Flames, drawing her skin hot and tight over the rapture within, the coiled secret at the bottom of her soul. Flames, calling her.

She fought. Wordlessly she fought, for she was deeply asleep, dwelling in a part of herself sundered from language and reason. But even here she knew the danger. And the draw. Unwilling, afraid, she resisted—yet when fire called, she answered, pulled from safety and darkness into a scene from hell.

Fire crackled merrily over the bones of its prey, a tumbled wreck she saw as dark angles and masses. There were people, too—she saw them as movement, their outlines blurred by possibilities. And there were bodies. They were dark and still and horribly clear.

She shuddered. Along with horror came the stirring of thought, still wordless but gathering focus. What she saw hadn't happened yet. When fire skipped her willy-nilly across time's boundaries, the living always appeared only as blurred, mobiles shapes, each person a small tornado of decisions awhirl with possible fates.

The dead carried no such freight. They lay quiet and dark, their final shapes fixed.

So there was time still. Not much, not when the vision was this clear, the pull of the fire this strong. But it hadn't happened yet, so there was a chance that it wouldn't. She had to think, had to remember what was needed in that other world, the waking world where reality was an orderly march of place and time, cause and effect.

Place and time...where was she? What was the fire eating?

She struggled, fighting the draw of the fire, the great, terrible beauty that called her to dance—fighting the part of her that quivered and yearned and wept with need for the flames. The need to call the fire to her. This time she won the battle, pulling more of reason and the other world into the vision.

She was standing in a smoke-black oven. Air stank in her nostrils and burned her lungs, a poison bath brewed of burning plastic and other man-made materials. People were screaming, crying, though she couldn't see them. A siren wailed in the distance, drawing nearer. And in front of her, the fire. She felt it, heard it, though she could see nothing.

She turned away. There would be no answers nearer the fire, and much danger. When she moved, the fire dragged at her, so that she moved slowly, feeling as if the air itself was reluctant to let her pass. Her movement wasn't quite like walking. Though she saw the floor, she didn't feel it beneath her feet.

The floor. Yes, she could see it now—the smoke wasn't as thick. A tile floor, vaguely institutional.

Think, she commanded herself. A store? Or, dear God, a hospital?

A shape loomed up out of the darkness, gasping—a person, blurred by smoke and possibilities. He or she stumbled past, going the wrong way. Toward the fire. Instinctively she reached out, trying to grab the other. Her hand passed through a barely seen shoulder. A shock of feeling shuddered through her—*his* feelings. Terror, shrill and desperate. Pain. The sobbing need for air.

Then he was gone. Gone, heading for death, and she had no way of stopping him.

It hasn't happened yet, she reminded herself, and pushed on.

Light ahead. Not the red glow of fire, but a thinning of smoke that allowed something like normal vision. A long, low shape with other shapes on it…she moved closer. Suitcases! Suitcases on a conveyor belt—*baggage claim.*

The airport. Dear God. Where had the fire started? Swiftly she aligned her knowledge of the airport's layout with the other sense, the one that knew where the fire was—but in turning her attention to the fire, she opened to it again.

Flames, orange-glow-heat-life, loving, eating, devouring, freeing—flames dancing there, *dancing* here, *inside her—* Shaken, she pulled back, but the call was so strong. Like a lover, fire entranced, compelled—*come, come dance, taste my richness, join. Join.* A rhythmic compulsion, heat of blood and beat of heart matching the wild cadence of flames, drawing her closer, drawing—

Terrified, she yanked her attention away from the fire. And stood once more in swirling smoke, lungs straining, desperate for air, desperately tired. And bereft.

She was no longer near the baggage claim. She didn't know where she was, but it was hot, so hot she thought her skin might split. She had to leave, had to summon the will to wake herself…

Coolness. In this hot, breathless place she felt cool air

waft over her, and the novelty distracted her. She turned. A shape moved toward her out of the smoke. A human shape. Startled but not frightened, she watched the blurred form come closer. A man, she thought, recognizing something in the movement or the shape, something that was wholly male.

He stopped in front of her, almost as if he could see her. And reached out a hand. And she *saw* it. Saw it clearly— a man's hand, large, with a broad palm and long fingers. Pale, northern skin, kissed to a light tan by the sun, nails short and well tended. There was a small white scar on the little finger just below the second knuckle.

Tendons stretched along the back of that shockingly visible hand as it reached for her. Fingers closed, cool and living, around the hot flesh of her upper arm.

Her eyes flew open on darkness. Cool night air moved over skin still hot and tight. Her chest heaved as she sucked in air. Intimate muscles clenched around a throbbing pulse. And her heart was pounding, pounding.

Her hand shook as she reached for the phone beside her bed.

Heat rolled off the tarmac in waves. Much of it, though, was the trapped heat of the sun, released now into a soft June night, rather than the heat of fire. Emergency lights had been rigged to help the eighteen men who labored under the direction of a construction engineer, working to dig out the rubble at the west end of the Montebello International Airport. The fire hadn't reached far—firefighters, mobilized and ready, had put the blaze out quickly. But the blast itself had brought down part of the second floor.

No one knew for sure if there had been anyone left in that section when the bomb went off.

Sweat trickled down Drew's forehead, making the cut on his temple sting. His shirt clung to him, damp and clammy.

His shoulder muscles strained as he heaved yet another ragged chunk of concrete off the pile of debris that was all that remained of Gate 22.

A little over an hour ago, he'd been one of the passengers who had deplaned at this gate.

"Watch where you're throwing your toys. I'd hate to have to arrest you for assault."

"Lorenzo." Drew straightened, wiping the back of his hand across his forehead as he turned. "I rather thought you'd show up. I didn't muss your pretty shoes, did I?"

"I'm nowhere near as mussed as you are," his cousin retorted. Lorenzo was one year younger than Drew, one inch taller and twenty pounds lighter. He had a tricky right, a fondness for good wine, secrets and handmade Italian shoes. He also had a new wife.

Lorenzo shook his head. "You look like hell."

"Explosions will do that to a man."

"Especially if he insists on playing hero."

Drew turned and snagged his jacket from the ground. He was far from being any sort of hero. "I'm glad you're here. There's a little wart of a police captain scurrying around, acting official. Please have him flogged."

"Captain Mylonas." A smile played over Lorenzo's thin, clever mouth. "He's not happy with you."

"I'm not too bloody happy with him. He's detaining fifty people who have already been through hell. He wants to question them. Some of them have small children." He wiped his forehead again. The cut was smarting. "The man's a toad."

"You're smearing the blood around. Here." Lorenzo handed him a folded handkerchief. "He did give you permission to leave, I understand."

"Of course." Drew's lip curled. "Toads don't like to offend the queen's nephew."

"You put him in a difficult position when you refused to leave until he released the other passengers."

"That was the idea." Smoke drifted over from the area that had been hit by fire, irritating Drew's raw throat. He cleared it. "The captain isn't one of your men, but this is your investigation." Lorenzo was head of the Royal Montebellan Intelligence team. "You could release the passengers."

"I will, just as soon as we're sure none of them is aware of anyone still missing."

Drew glanced at the pile of debris and wondered if some poor soul's body was trapped beneath it. "But Mylonas isn't questioning them about who might be missing. He's hunting for his blasted terrorist among the victims. He'd like to show you up."

"The captain was confused about his priorities. I clarified them for him."

Ah. Drew nodded, satisfied.

"Aunt Gwendolyn's worried about you."

His eyebrows lifted. "She knows I'm all right. I—" Annoyingly, a cough chose that moment to rattle its way loose.

"Refused medical assistance, from what I hear."

Drew mastered the coughing fit and straightened. "Medical assistance—for a small cut and a sore throat? Don't be ridiculous."

"The cut's still bleeding. And you swallowed a fair amount of smoke when you went back in to drag that old man out after the blast."

"I've always disliked your habit of knowing everything."

Lorenzo chuckled. "But it pays off, in my line of work. Now, if you're finished flexing your muscles, I'm under orders to tuck you into a limo and send you to the palace. The king's orders," he added. "Uncle Marcus doesn't want

Aunt Gwen worrying. I think they can find another un-
skilled laborer to take over for you.''

Since he'd gotten what he wanted—the other passengers
would be allowed to leave, too—Drew didn't object. ''Give
me a moment to let the crew boss know I'm leaving.''

When he returned, he and his cousin fell into step together. They skirted the firefighters still watching the smoldering wreckage of the gate and entered the main terminal
through a service door on the ground floor. The interior
was eerie, with the west end of the concourse tinted the
smoldering red of emergency lighting and the east end normally lit. The hot air stank of smoke.

Uniformed men were stationed at every entrance, most
of them in the colorful blue-and-gold uniforms of the capital's police force, some in the crisp khakis of the army.
The uninjured civilians had been herded to the far eastern
end of the terminal, where more police officers were stationed. Most of them were quiet, although a few voices
drifted down the empty concourse. A child was crying.

Drew didn't see as many children as there had been earlier. Good. A few of the families must have been released.
''I did make sure word was sent to the palace that I wasn't
hurt. It's not like Aunt Gwen to fret without cause.''

''The past year has been rough on her.''

So it had. Several months ago his aunt's oldest son, Lucas Sebastiani, prince and heir to the throne of Montebello,
had disappeared when his plane went down over the Colorado Rockies in the United States. Searchers had turned
up no sign of him, and eventually the royal family had been
forced to accept that he was dead. There had been little
Drew had been able to do to help, either with the search
or with the family's grief. Still, he'd come here often in the
past months. He might not have known what to do for them,
but he could at least be here.

Of course, he hadn't been the only one to offer the support of his company. Lorenzo's half brother, Desmond Caruso, had practically haunted the palace. Drew had never been able to tolerate much of Desmond's company or understand why others didn't pick up on the stink of jealousy and ambition Desmond gave off.

Last month, Lucas had found his way out of the darkness of trauma-induced amnesia and returned home. "How is Lucas?" Drew asked quietly. "I've spoken to him on the phone. He insists he's all right, but…" Drew shrugged, unable to put his worries into words.

"I don't know. He's quieter. Broody."

Drew chewed on that a moment. God knew Lucas had been through enough to justify a little brooding, but he couldn't shake the feeling that more had happened during Lucas's missing months than his family knew. Or maybe his past was making him paint the other man with his own troubled colors. "The king is proceeding with his plans for the ceremony, I understand."

"Yes. The country needs to see Lucas officially installed as heir."

"Do you think the bombing is connected to the uncertainty about the succession? Tamir—"

"Good Lord, Drew, the last thing we need is to sling a fresh batch of accusations at Tamir! We barely made it through the last few months without a war."

"Yes," Drew said shortly. "I know."

"Sorry." He rubbed a hand over his head. "It's been…difficult."

"I was about to say that Tamir, however unwittingly, did play host to a number of those Brothers of Darkness fellows. Nasty bunch. They aren't what they once were, thank God, with their leaders either dead or in prison, but there must still be some isolated cells operating. I heard they're taking credit for today's fireworks."

"And just where did you hear that? We don't know who

called in the—yes?'' Lorenzo's attention swerved to the uniformed officer who approached.

"Pardon me, Your Grace.'' The young policeman looked nervous and excited. "Captain Mylonas would like to see you. He's detained a suspect.''

Drew's eyebrows rose. Either Mylonas had gotten very lucky, or he was hassling some poor Tamiri visitor who'd been in the wrong place at the wrong time. After Drew's encounter with the captain, he was betting on the second possibility.

"Where?'' Lorenzo said tersely.

"In the security office off the atrium.''

Lorenzo started moving. "Your limo's out front, Drew.''

"If you don't mind, I'll go with you. If there's anything to this, His Highness will want to know. I can brief him when I reach the palace.''

Lorenzo acknowledged the sense of that with a nod.

Montebello's airport was no Heathrow, but it was a fair stretch of the legs to reach the security offices, located slightly west of the center but not in the bombed section. Drew was tired. His head had started to pound and his lungs were issuing warnings of another coughing fit by the time they reached the office where Captain Mylonas had sequestered his suspect.

Who was not at all what Drew had been expecting. He stopped in the doorway.

"Your Grace.'' The captain practically clicked his heels together when Lorenzo entered. Mylonas was a small man with a small, round paunch. His mustache was so black and precise it looked inked on—a forlorn attempt to add distinction to a bland face. "I am pleased you could come so promptly.''

"You have a suspect, I understand.''

"He has heatstroke,'' the suspect muttered. "Or maybe

his mother dropped him on the head as a baby. *That* would explain it.''

Good Lord, Drew thought. Her voice was as perfect as the rest of her.

Mylonas's suspect had skin the dusky olive of the Med-iterranean. Her face was oval, the features imbued with that fluid sensuality some Italian women possess. Black hair rippled down her back like wind-rumpled water. She was dressed plainly enough in a red T-shirt and khaki shorts, but the T-shirt was tucked in at an absurdly small waist, the shorts revealed legs that made him clench his teeth, and that soft red cotton clung with intimate favor to what might be the finest pair of breasts he'd ever seen.

Or mostly seen. The T-shirt wasn't as tight as he might have wished.

''Your name?'' Lorenzo asked crisply.

''Rosalinda Cira Giaberti. Call me Rose. And you are?''

The sweet insolence of her tone had Drew smiling. This was a terrorist?

''Lorenzo Sebastiani.''

A blink cleared some of the boredom from those fine, dark eyes. ''Pardon me, Your Grace, for failing to recognize you. You seem to have left your coronet at home.'' When she glanced at Drew her brows lifted in haughty inquiry. ''You aren't a Sebastiani.''

''No. Call me Drew, Signorina Giaberti.'' His smile suggested that if she didn't call, he would. Soon. ''It *is* signorina, isn't it?'' There was no ring on her left hand.

Her mouth twitched in amusement. ''And if it isn't?''

''Life is seldom fair, but rarely is it that absurdly malignant.'' For some reason his bantering tone slipped, as if he'd spoken nothing more than the truth.

She tipped her head, curious, and met his eyes.

The hairs on his forearms stood on end. He looked into those dark eyes and he knew—he was going to have her.

When and where didn't matter. He would have this woman naked and damp and crying out for him.

Her eyes widened. A small, alarmed jerk of her head snapped the contact.

"Signorina Giaberti called in the bomb threat," Captain Mylonas announced with relish.

It took a second for Drew to throw off the odd spell and understand what the man had said. When he did, his stomach contracted in quick, hard denial. But however his body rejected the implications, his mind knew very well that lovely packages could hold ugly surprises. Yet he still wanted her.

How far had he sunk?

The woman was unimpressed by the implicit accusation. Her glance at the captain was annoyed, no more. *"Madre di Dio.* It was a warning, not a threat. You might consider thanking me."

"Thanking you? For attempting to kill hundreds of innocent people?"

"I tried to kill no one. If I hadn't called, the building wouldn't have been evacuated and the fire—" She broke off suddenly. "I warned you about the bomb. I didn't threaten you with one. The distinction may be subtle to one of your intelligence, so I will give an example. If I say that looking at your smug, shiny face might cause me to lose my supper, that is a warning. If I say I'm going to vomit all over your pretty uniform unless you go away, that is a threat."

Drew choked on a laugh, then doubled over as another coughing fit hit.

Lorenzo took a step towards him. He waved his cousin back, stepping out into the hall so he wouldn't interfere with the interrogation while his body tried to eject the lining of his lungs. He ended up leaning weakly against the wall, eyes watering as he dragged deep breaths through his raw throat. His head pounded, a hard, hot throb of pain. He blinked the moisture back.

One of the police officers was staring at him. Bloody hell. In another minute he'd have the fool over here asking if he needed medical attention. He made the effort to straighten, glancing down at the scuffed white tiles of the floor...

And the world slipped behind a wall.

Sounds, color, vision—all were still there, but removed. Distant, as if everything had slid behind glass. The pain in his head went from a throb to a long slice of agony.

Not again—please, not now. Not again.

But his plea was as trapped as the rest of him. As if someone had taken a grip on two corners of the world and pulled, the square tiles of the floor stretched into parallelograms. Pain became pressure, livid, explosive, almost living, as if it could burst out of his skull and splatter his brains on the white, elongated tiles. He tried to move, to at least close his eyes. And couldn't. He could only stand frozen while the tiles melted and the beast behind his eyes rose in a huge wave—

As suddenly as it had come, it was gone. The tiles dragged themselves back into their proper shapes, the pressure receded, tidelike, leaving him cold and clammy and weak. Last to go was the wall, the glassy barrier that muffled everything...

"...all right, sir?"

He looked up. The officer he'd seen earlier was standing in front of him, looking very young in a soot-smudged uniform. Those spaniel eyes hadn't yet learned a cop's detachment.

Drew dredged up a reassuring smile. "Afraid I inhaled too much smoke earlier. I'll be fine."

As fine as a man could be, that is, when he was losing his mind.

Chapter 2

Montebello was a tiny island with a long history. Conquered, traded, overrun and reconquered, its 3,100 square miles—less than half the size of Wales, smaller than forty-eight of the United States—held detritus from more than two thousand years of bloody civilization. A farmer's plow might turn up Roman coins, an Assyrian ax head, Egyptian pot shards or a handful of spent casings from a machine gun used by Mussolini's occupying army. As Drew's limousine climbed the stubby mountains that separated the airport from the capital city, it passed goats grazing in a tumble of hewn rocks that had once been the walls of a Byzantine monastery.

The Turks had destroyed that monastery after the fall of Constantinople in 1453. Beneath the highway's smooth modern paving lay earth once tramped by Roman legions, who had brought law and the cult of Aphrodite to this small, fertile island. Muhammad's followers had walked here, proclaiming the oneness of God with curved scimitars while their mathematicians brought to the world new ways to measure its bounds. The militant Knights of St. John and the secular knights of Richard I arrived with their straighter swords a century later, housing God in different architecture. They also brought to the island those practical mysteries of commerce and government that supported the growth of a new class—a middle class.

Soon, though, they lost the island to the Doge of Venice. The local nobility didn't fare well in that change of power, but the growing class of artisans and traders prospered under a ruler entranced with the glittering possibilities of commerce. The Venetian branch of a northern Italian family, the Sebastianis, invested heavily in the island and eventually moved there.

Not until Napoleon overran Europe did the little island taste autonomy. The French Emperor claimed it along with his Italian territory, but he had no troops to spare for so distant a possession. The local mechanisms of government persisted, but no one was truly in charge—at least, no one the locals could agree on.

A small, prosperous island without a strong defender wouldn't be allowed to dabble in sovereignty for long. Augustus Sebastiani, by then a Duke, stepped into the temporary vacuum and by a combination of trickery and economic clout made himself the de facto head of state. He forestalled any violent courtships by Montebello's acquisitive neighbors with a series of canny trade agreements and marriages. One Sebastiani daughter went to France, another to a Spanish prince, while the oldest son took a noble English bride.

This hedging of bets through arranged marriages proved wise when, after Waterloo, Europe divided the spoils and England acquired Montebello and held it in a loose and friendly grip. In 1880, either from altruism or a lack of interest, Great Britain bestowed the island upon its people in the person of King Augustus Sebastiani, who promptly married an English noblewoman with ties to the British throne.

The Sebastianis had ruled ever since. In some ways the family personified the results of the island's long and bloody history—a mingling of races, religions, tongues and cultures that had produced a people both passionate and pragmatic. Over the years the ties with England had been strengthened through commercial and political agreements—and once more, thirty-seven years ago, through marriage. Montebello's ruler, King Marcus II, had married an English noblewoman connected to the British throne—Lady Gwendolyn Sebastiani, née Peterson. Drew's aunt.

In the quiet, cushioned luxury of the king's limousine, Lord Andrew Harrington passed through the outskirts of the capital without seeing the lights, the old buildings leaning at age-settled angles or the new ones, briskly upright.

He was counting.

Exhaustion had hit the moment the spell passed, a great, gray, sucking swamp that experience told him would eventually drag him down. Once he gave in he would sleep for hours, sleep so deeply he might as well be unconscious, doped or dead.

Drew hadn't come here to scare his relatives to death by arriving unconscious. Nor did he want to be admitted to the hospital for a malady the doctors wouldn't be able to identify or remedy. He might not be able to avoid the gray tide entirely, but he could postpone it. This, too, he'd learned the hard way.

...ninety-eight, ninety-nine, one hundred.

Sweat stood in suspended drops on Drew's forehead as he released the muscles he'd held mercilessly taut in his left calf, then clenched those of his thigh. And began counting again.

Movement helped stave off collapse. Concentration

helped, especially when turned to the cool realm of business. But he couldn't move in the confines of the limo, and his laptop and briefcase had been left behind, with his luggage, at the airport. So he substituted a slow counting while isolating and tightening the muscles of his body. Holding each clenched set of muscles to the point of pain before he released it and moved on to the next.

Pain, too, helped.

At last the elongated luxury of the limo was climbing the cobblestone road to where the palace waited, pale and pristine in the moonlight, at the top of the cliffs capping the northeastern tip of the island. When Drew stepped out of the limo, the night air covered him, freshened by the ocean and the distinctive smell of northern Montebello, where oregano and thyme grew wild. The spicy scent mingled with the headiness of his aunt's roses.

He wished he could pass through the gardens instead of the palace, take the rocky path down the cliff and walk along the beach, alone with the sea and the night. He wished, in fact, he could go anywhere but through the ornate doors at the top of the stairs. Once inside, he would have to deal with the people he loved. His inadequacies in that area were always painfully obvious. But even if he'd been willing to play the coward, the tide that waited to drag him under made that a foolish choice. Drew didn't care to delight the paparazzi by passing out on the beach. He'd sold enough copies of their rags for them in his younger, wilder days.

Grimly he started up the steps. There were thirty-two of them.

Rudolpho, of course, waited at the door to admit him. "If you are not too tired, my lord," the old man said in his excellent English, "the king wishes to see you before you retire. He and the queen are in their quarters. Shall I send up some refreshments?"

"Coffee would be welcome, thank you." Drew preferred tea, but an extra jolt of caffeine might help. "And if you could locate a clean shirt, I'd appreciate it. My luggage is still at the airport and I'd rather not present myself to the king stinking of smoke."

"You can have one of my shirts," a voice said from the grand staircase. "We're nearly of a size. A clean pair of pants wouldn't hurt, either, from the look of you. But why is your luggage held up? I trust no one became so carried away by some notion of duty that he refused to release it to you."

The unconscious hauteur of that last statement pulled a small smile from Drew as he turned to face his cousin. Lucas was a very approachable prince—but he was still a prince. "I didn't want to take the time to dig through the piles to locate my bags tonight. Things are rather a mess still."

Lucas's face hardened. "No doubt." He glanced at the majordomo. "I'll see Lord Andrew upstairs. You may send his coffee to my father's rooms."

Lucas looked much the same, Drew thought as he joined his cousin on the stairs. Thinner, perhaps, but fit. No shadows of illness, no obvious marks from his ordeal showed…yet there was a change. A certain guardedness about the dark blue eyes and around the fine, wide mouth. It reminded Drew of what he saw in the mirror every day.

Something had closed that used to be open. Silently, privately, he mourned the loss.

"You can stop searching my face for signs of imminent collapse," Lucas said dryly.

"Sorry. I didn't realize I was being obvious."

"You're never that." Lucas started back up the steps.

Drew followed. What did you say to a cousin you'd grieved as dead? How did you tell him what it meant to have him back? Drew counted stairs, hunted for words and came up dry. "It's good to see you, Lucas. Good to have you back."

Lucas glanced over his shoulder, and for a moment the tightness around his eyes eased. "I hear you've been a frequent visitor in my absence."

Drew shrugged. "For whatever good it did, yes."

Lucas didn't reply. Drew struggled to find a pleasant topic. "How are your sisters?"

"Fat and happy. At least they're all happy and two out of three are on their way to fat, though they aren't showing yet."

"Two?" Drew stopped near the stop of the stair. His legs seemed to weigh at least ten stone apiece. "I knew Anna was expecting. Christina—?"

"Yes, she's a finalist in the baby sweepstakes, too, and so delighted we keep having to yank her back down off the ceiling. Her husband, Jack, too. She's due to reach the finish line a month after Anna." Lucas's hesitation was brief. "It's wonderful news, of course."

"Of course." But not, Drew thought as he started walking again, a completely happy subject for Lucas. In the months the prince had been missing, one of his sisters had become engaged and two had married, and Lucas didn't know any of the men. In some ways, his family had moved on without him. Though he gave a decent impression of his usual upbeat manner, his heart wasn't in it.

By the time they reached Lucas's room on the second floor, Drew had had enough. "For God's sake," he said as he shut the door behind him, "would you quit working so hard at being cheerful? It isn't necessary, you know."

Luke swung around to face him. "I suppose it interferes with your plans to pry the lid off my skull and lap up the contents."

"Quite a gruesome turn of phrase you've developed." Drew observed, unbuttoning his shirt. "No doubt your recent trauma has given you a fascination with cracked skulls and addled brains. Didn't you promise me a clean shirt?"

Lucas's mouth twitched. "Good old Drew. Same chilly bastard you've always been. It's nice to know some things didn't change while I was gone. I'll see what I can find." He opened the door that led to his dressing room.

"I suppose the rest of the family has been tiptoeing around you." Drew followed, tossing his filthy shirt into the hamper just inside the dressing room. "When they aren't hugging you."

"Lord, yes. Everyone's so blasted careful with me…you won't bother with that, at least. You'll just stand around not saying much until I spill my guts." Lucas handed him a pale-blue shirt. "It's quite a trick. I've often wondered how you do it."

"So have I." Drew had never understood what about him prompted confidences. Lord knew he didn't have any special wisdom to offer, nor any great warmth. Yet people told him things. Private things. Griefs and guilts and choices made or unmade, all the aching questions that can trouble a soul when the night is dark and lonely. This compulsion to confide, to confess, was alien to Drew. He couldn't imagine willfully violating his own privacy that way. Yet often those who breached their privacy with him seemed to feel better for it afterward, the way one does after a splinter is removed or a bad tooth has been pulled.

And sometimes, afterward, they avoided him. Drew slipped on his cousin's shirt and stepped out of his slacks—which were, as Lucas had noted, much the worse for wear.

His unwanted knack for eliciting confidences had been the one thing he could offer his aunt and uncle while their son was missing, and later, when they thought him dead. He wondered if they would be uncomfortable around him now, if they would avoid him. He told himself it didn't matter. Or not very much, anyway, not as much as helping them had mattered. If he had helped. "Why do people answer questions I don't ask?"

Lucas, rummaging through the hangers, turned around holding out a pair of slacks—gray, clean, faultlessly pressed. "I guess it's like dropping stones in some dark pit. There's the assurance that any foolishness we let fall won't come back at us. Lord knows nothing else does. Clams have nothing on you."

"Hmm. Vanessa compared talking to me to howling at the moon or going to confession. Except, of course, that I don't hand out penance."

Lucas's mouth turned up wryly. "Sisters can be the very devil, can't they? They know us too well and spare us very little. Here. These won't be a perfect fit, but at least they won't leave soot on the upholstery. Speaking of sisters, one of mine is upset with you."

"Which one?" He stepped into the slacks, which were a trifle long—Lucas was six-two to Drew's six-one—but were a major improvement otherwise.

"Anna. Have you offended Julia and Christina lately, too?"

"Probably. I'd better go see your father now that I'm decent." Before he collapsed. Fatigue was lapping at his defenses like a flood-swollen river. He started for the door.

Lucas fell into step beside him in the wide hall. The king and queen's private suite occupied a separate wing that lay an achingly long distance away, from Drew's current perspective.

"So why is Anna mad at you?" Lucas asked as they crossed the picture gallery.

"She didn't care for the way I treated the last candidate she sent me."

"Candidate? But what—no, she didn't. Surely she didn't decide to play matchmaker. Not with you. I know she was very successful with your brother—"

"It went to her head." Briefly Drew's expression softened. His brother Rafe had settled into marriage as if he were made for it—and perhaps he was. As long as his partner was Serena. "The last bit of bait Anna trolled across my path was a pretty blond bundle of innocence named Theresa. I gather I was supposed to have been struck by the contrast she made with my usual fare and collapsed, smitten, into matrimony. Or at least come down with a mild case of honorable intentions."

"Ah. What did you do? Or maybe I don't want to know."

"Probably not."

Lucas held his tongue through the picture gallery and into the green sitting room. "I take it you aren't feeling any overriding impulse to unburden yourself."

"You sound very American. Another result of your trauma?"

"Dammit, Drew—*was* the girl an innocent? And just what did you do?"

"Nothing extensive, though I'm afraid the tour I offered her wasn't exactly what your sister had in mind. Don't worry," he added drily. "I may have done more sightseeing than I should have, but I don't tour virgins."

It was easy to see Lucas didn't approve, but then, Sebastiani males were born with a hair-trigger impulse toward chivalry. "Was that really necessary?"

"It seemed so at the time. She wasn't the one I was trying to discourage."

"You wanted her to run crying to Anna so she'd stop matchmaking."

"Yes." He paused. "I suspect my mother had been encouraging her."

Lucas didn't respond, a courtesy Drew appreciated. It was well-known within the family that Drew and his mother were, if not estranged, at least at odds. Her Grace

did not approve of her son's lifestyle. In time-honored female fashion, she considered that the cure lay in finding
the right woman—kind, gentle, well-bred and as close to
untouched as possible.

Drew often wondered how a woman as perceptive as his
mother could read her own son so poorly. "You haven't
asked me about the bombing," he observed.

"No need for you to go over everything more than once.
I think I should warn you—oh, hell, that's presumptuous
of me, isn't it? You've been here." Bitterness bit down on
the last words. "I haven't."

"You've been here for the last three weeks."

"But not for months before that. What that did to
them…I've never seen age sit on my father the way it does
now. It worries me. I'm trying to help, to take over some
of the responsibilities—but dammit, why did he stay up to
hear from you tonight? It's past one o'clock. He might have
trusted me to find out if there was anything urgent. Or even
to act on it myself."

They'd reached the double doors that led to the king's
suite. Drew stopped. "It isn't about you, you know. Marcus
doesn't lack confidence in your ability or your dedication,
but letting go doesn't come easily to a man accustomed to
rule."

Lucas stared at him, grim and silent, then gave a quick
bark of laughter. "God help me, you did it again. You're
like a bloody stage magician—no matter how closely I
think I'm watching your hands, you still pull secrets out of
my hat." He slapped Lucas on the back harder than was
necessary. "Go on, go in there and talk to my father before
I tell you about the time I lost my virginity."

"You told me that years ago. Not long after it happened,
as I recall, though the disclosure was more along the lines
of bragging than confessing. You were—"

His cousin opened the door and shoved him through it.

When Drew passed through those doors again forty minutes later, he was alone. The suite reserved for the Harrington family lay in yet another wing. By the time he turned into the second-longest hall on his route, he was weaving, and after a while he realized he'd stopped moving altogether. Instead, he was leaning against one wall, staring at the paintings hanging on the other.

A Monet and one of Segatini's rural scenes. He remembered them, but he couldn't see them. *It's not my eyes,* he thought. There were shapes, forms, colors. His brain had simply stopped processing the input.

A vague mental image of a sofa, brocaded and plump with pillows, rose in his mind. He wouldn't have to stagger all the way to the bedroom. The sofa in the sitting room would do. Or the floor.

But not this floor. He was still in the hall. Blinking, he managed to focus, push away from the wall and take a few steps.

"Drew? Are you all right?"

Lorenzo. Turning his head, Drew saw his cousin about twenty paces away. Had Lorenzo seen him propped drunkenly against the wall? No, he decided. If he'd seen that much, he wouldn't ask if Drew was all right. It would be all too obvious that he wasn't. Drawing on the stubborn dregs of his pride, Drew shut the fatigue away once more, closing up the part of him that knew how few minutes remained before he collapsed. "I'm fine," he said curtly. "More tired than I'd realized."

Lorenzo started toward him, frowning. "You look like hell."

"I've been running short on sleep the last few days, that's all. It's caught up with me."

Lorenzo stopped in front of him. "You shouldn't have stayed at the airport so long, flexing your muscles."

Drew couldn't penetrate the fog well enough to read the

other man's expression. God, he wanted to be alone. Like an injured animal dragging itself back to its den, he craved the closed door that would shut out the rest of the world. "I was hoping for a medal. Something tasteful to wear on state occasions."

That earned him a grin, but it was perfunctory. "Yeah, such a glory hound you are. I'd intended to talk to you after reporting to Marcus, but maybe I should ask you now. You don't look as if you'll be upright much longer."

True. Though he was apt to go horizontal more dramatically than his cousin expected. "Ask me what?"

"About the woman Captain Mylonas found. Signorina Giaberti. Mylonas is an idiot, of course, but he may have accidentally turned up a decent lead. We don't have any evidence against her, nothing that links her to any known terrorist groups, but she's involved somehow, or she's protecting someone who is. God knows her story doesn't hold water."

It was hard to follow a thought long enough to reply sensibly. "What's her story?"

He snorted. "She's psychic. Saw the whole thing in a dream."

Drew pictured her, the knowing eyes and amused mouth. The body, lush and firm and inviting. A small, distant flicker of sexual interest arrived with the image, along with a tinge of disgust. "As lies go, that one sucks."

"It's nonsense, of course, but there's a certain superficial credibility. Her mother was burned as a witch."

"Good God, Lorenzo, this isn't the sixteenth century!"

"Not for you and me, maybe, but in some ways Montebello is one big village, and time moves differently in the village mind. Never mind that now. I can fill you in on her history tomorrow, if you agree."

"You haven't asked me anything yet."

"I noticed a certain chemistry between you and the *si-*

gnorina. I'd like you to pursue that. See her socially, get her to trust you. Talk to you. You're good at that.''

So he was. He couldn't keep the distaste from his voice. ''Pillow talk?''

''If that's what it takes. I don't want another bomb going off. Drew…'' Lorenzo's hesitation was brief. ''You know what a powder keg we've been sitting on the past few months. The king kept us out of war by sheer force of will, but you'll have seen what a toll it's taken on him. Now that he considers the danger over, he's…not as clearheaded as usual. I'm not going to tell him what I've asked you to do.''

''He wouldn't stand for it, would he? Too bloody unchivalrous.'' Colors were starting to fade as the gray at the edges of his vision blurred into the rest. He could scarcely think beyond the need to be alone. ''Of course I'll do it. Why not?''

Chapter 3

The flame was blue-white with heat—but tiny. Small enough to be safe. The woman guiding that flame wore a canvas apron over pink chinos and tinted safety glasses. No jewelry, no makeup. Her black hair was tied in a rough knot at her nape, though curly bits escaped to frisk around her face.

The worktable she was bent over was cluttered. Tongs, tweezers, wire cutters, a two-inch nail and a tiny hammer, spools of silver wire and several thin golden squares crowded the surface directly in front of her. Small wooden and plastic boxes lined the back of the table, and more tools hung on the pegboard on the wall behind it. A draftsman's adjustable light was clamped to the table's edge. A vise gripped a silver arm cuff, three inches wide and partially worked, at the front of the table.

The little soldering iron kissed the air beneath the bit of wire Rose held, kissed and retreated in a butterfly's insubstantial salute. Silver beaded and fell, directed by a subtle flick of her wrist.

"Natala Baldovino is at the market," Rose's aunt Gemma announced gloomily from the doorway.

"I thought you were watching the shop." Rose released the button on the little soldering iron. The flame died.

"I needed pancetta for the carbonara sauce, and some olives. Pietra offered to go. I think she has her eye on the youngest Christofides boy."

"Pietra has her eye on both Christofides boys, along with any other male who crosses her path. She doesn't mean anything by it. Nothing serious, at least."

"I'm not sure the young men realize that. She said Natala Baldovino had already made the rounds."

Rose studied the way silver swirled over gold in a stylized, intricate yin-yang design on the arm cuff and nodded, satisfied. "I suppose Signora Baldovino is allowed to buy olives."

"If that had been her purpose, I'd have no objections," her aunt observed in a fair-minded way. "But you know it isn't. You know what she's saying."

Rose had a pretty good idea. She also cherished some hope of finishing the cuff—and avoiding the lecture Gemma had been trying to deliver ever since the police released her yesterday. She loosened the vise, turned the cuff and tightened it again. "I'm thinking of using mother-of-pearl here, for the moon."

"Very pretty, dear. It reminds me of that new ring."

"What new ring?"

"Didn't I tell you? A rather flashy young woman brought it in yesterday morning. An American."

"You bought a ring for the shop." Rose inhaled a slow breath for patience as anxiety bit. The shop did well normally, but this summer hadn't been normal. The possibility of war with Tamir had discouraged tourists, sales were half what they'd been last year at this time, and her bank balance hadn't been this low since she'd first opened the shop.

Now it might be in the red. "You didn't check with me. You *know* you have to check with me before you buy anything."

"How could I? You were in jail."

Defeated, Rose swiveled on her stool.

Her aunt stood in front of the desk Rose used when she couldn't avoid paperwork any longer. Gemma Giaberti was a small woman, plump and firm as a pear, with black hair coiled high on her round head. She had cow's eyes—big, brown and placid, with extravagant eyelashes. Her skirt was long and full, the color of moss. Her blouse was white and embroidered. Today she wore only two necklaces, a baroque locket of about the same age as her house, and an intricately worked chain her niece had made for her two years ago.

"I wasn't in jail," Rose said, studying those placid eyes with suspicion. "I spent hours at the police station because Mylonas is an idiot, but they didn't put me behind bars. How could they? They have no evidence of any wrongdoing."

"Of course not, but that isn't stopping Natala Baldovino from passing around her version of events."

"Maybe the gossip will bring people into the shop." When her aunt just blinked at her in polite skepticism, Rose grimaced. "I know, I know. They're more likely to put a rock through the window."

"Oh, surely not. No one's done that in years, have they? Except for the Peterson boy, and really, I don't think he counts. He threw rocks through everyone's windows until he went into the army." Gemma clucked her tongue. "Rose, your head is hurting. You forgot to eat lunch again, didn't you?"

"I had a big breakfast. Do you by any chance remember how much you paid for this ring?"

"I'm sure I wrote it down. I know you like everything

to be accounted for...the receipt book?'' Her forehead, smoother than a woman her age had any right to have, puckered now as she considered the matter. ''Yes, that's it. I asked her to give me a receipt for the money, and she did. She signed it and—'' Gemma finished with triumph ''—I had her put her address below her signature.''

''That will help—if it's her real name and address.''

That brought a moment's silence. ''I suppose I should have asked to see identification. A passport or something.''

''It might have been a good idea.'' Rose stood and stretched, unkinking stiff muscles. How long had she been bent over her newest design? A glance at the clock informed her that Gemma was right. She had forgotten lunch. ''Just think how happy it would make Captain Mylonas if we bought stolen goods and he found out.''

''Bah. He's a worm.''

''A worm with a badge.'' Gemma had been right about something else, too. She had a headache. Nothing vicious, more like a tired child whining for attention. Rose reached up to loosen her hair and rub her temples. ''I'll need to give the police a description of the ring so they can check their list of stolen property, just in case. Is it in the stockroom?''

''I put it with the receipt book, I think. In the cash drawer.''

''The cash drawer? No, don't tell me. I'm sure it made perfect sense at the time.'' She untied her apron as she walked briskly to the door. ''What does the ring look like?''

''Not terribly old, but unusual. A ruby and a pearl set in a thick band. I'm sure you'll like it. After all, the pattern is the same as the one you're making now, so that proves it, doesn't it?''

Her apron went on a hook on the back of the door. Her hands went to her hair, finger-combing it quickly. Fruit, she thought. Or maybe some nuts. A little food would cure the ache in her head. She pushed open the door to the shop.

Her spirits lifted. The shining counters, the shelves and display cases full of the beautiful, the fanciful, the unique— this was hers. Her aunt helped, certainly. So had the bank. But persuading a banker to take a chance on a young, un-married woman—one who lacked the convenience of a fa-ther—had been as much of an accomplishment as finding the stock, teaching herself bookkeeping and building a cli-entele and a reputation.

A different reputation, that is. The one she'd been born with had its drawbacks.

She turned the key in the cash drawer. First the receipt book… The figure she saw entered in Gemma's rounded handwriting made her mutter something in German. Rose considered German the best language for cursing, partly because of all those clacking consonants. Partly, too, be-cause her aunt didn't understand it.

"Where's the ring?" she demanded. "Is this it?" She held up a small glass box, her eyebrows raised. "Glass, Zia?"

Gemma smiled vaguely. "It seemed best."

Wonderful. She was going to have to use almost all of her savings to cover a check written because her aunt re-fused to stop meddling. Rose scowled and snatched off the lid. "This had better be…"

"Yes," Gemma said softly from Rose's shoulder. "I thought it was the same, and it is."

Executed in miniature on the band of the ring was her own yin-yang design—a design that had come to her in a dream. She gave one quick, irritated shake of her head. "Damn. I'd better see why it showed up, then." She reached for the ring.

"Rose, wait until—"

Too late. She'd closed her hand around the ring.

Seconds later her knees went soft. She swayed.

A plump arm closed around her shoulders, steadying her. The ring left her hand, breaking the connection. Her eyelids lifted. "My God."

"Are you all right?"

She blinked. Gemma had put the ring back in its glass box, shielded once more. "You might have warned me."

"I tried to," Gemma said tartly. "Though I had no idea it would hit you so hard."

"You put it in glass. You knew it needed warding."

"I knew it was for you to see, that's all. Psychometry isn't my Gift." She released Rose's shoulders. "What did you feel?"

Her aunt's voice held all the crispness it usually lacked. Rose responded automatically. "Grief. Wild and deep...whoever she is, she's hurting."

"You're rubbing your stomach. Is she in physical pain?"

Oh. So she was. Rose stopped rubbing but kept her hand on her stomach, turning her attention to the echoes of feeling still trembling inside her. "Not physical pain. Emotional. An empty womb." Her voice went flat and bleak. "Whoever she is, she's lost a child. Miscarriage, maybe..." Rose shook her head, throwing off the traces of someone else's heartache. "I don't understand why the connection was so strong. Aside from the ring being made of metal, there's no link to fire—"

"Are you sure?"

She glanced at her aunt, impatient. She knew what Gemma wanted. The same thing she always wanted—for Rose to explore her Gift, to learn it, use it. That was why she'd bought the ring. "I couldn't very well miss that. I didn't recognize her."

Gemma patted her arm. "You will next time, dear."

"No."

"The ring came to you. There's a reason for that, even if—"

The chimes above the door rang. "Later, Zia." Rose tucked her hair behind her ear, turned to the door—and froze.

It was him. The man from the airport. The one who'd been with His Grace, Duke Lorenzo Sebastiani, nephew of the king and head of Montebello's intelligence service. His clothes were cleaner and more casual today, but just as expensive. His face was hard, lean. Not a lovely face, but the sort a woman remembered. And the eyes—oh, they were the same, the clearest, coldest green she'd ever seen.

So was the quick clutch of pleasure in her stomach. "What are *you* doing here?"

"Rose." Gemma's tone was repressive.

"Your store is open, isn't it?" He had a delicious voice, like melted chocolate dripped over the crisp consonants and rounded vowels of upper-class English.

Gemma moved out from behind the counter. "Pay no attention to my niece. Missing a meal makes her growl. Did you have something specific in mind, my lord, or would you like to look around awhile?"

My lord? Well, Rose thought, that was no more than she'd suspected, and explained why he seemed familiar. She must have seen his picture sometime. This man wasn't just rich, he was frosting—the creamy top level of the society cake.

She, of course, wasn't part of the cake at all.

"Quite specific," he said. "About five foot seven, I'd say, with eyes the color of the ocean at twilight and a sad lack of respect for the local police."

Rose lifted one eyebrow. "Are you here on Captain Mylonas's behalf, then...my lord?"

"I never visit a beautiful woman on behalf of another

man. Certainly not on behalf of a fool. I asked you to call me Drew.''

Ah. Now she knew who he was. "So you did, Lord Andrew.''

His mouth didn't smile, but the creases cupping his lower eyelids deepened and the cool eyes warmed slightly. "Stubborn, aren't you.''

"Do pigs fly?'' Gemma asked.

"Ah...no, I don't believe they do.''

Rose grinned. "Aunt Gemma has a fondness for American slang, but she doesn't always get the nuances right. She enjoys American tabloids, too. And Italian tabloids. And—''

"Really, Rose,'' Gemma interrupted, flustered. "His lordship can't possibly be interested in my reading habits.''

"No?'' Rose's smile widened as she remembered a picture of Lord Andrew Harrington she'd seen in one of her aunt's tabloids a few years ago. Quite a memorable photograph—but it hadn't been Lord Andrew's face that had made it so. His face hadn't shown at all, in fact. "I'm afraid we don't sell sunscreen. If you're planning to expose any, ah, untanned portions of your body to the Mediterranean sun, you'd do better to shop at Serminio's Pharmacy. They have a good selection.''

"Rose!'' Gemma exclaimed. "I'm sorry, my lord, she didn't...that is, she probably did mean...but she shouldn't have.''

The creases deepened. "I'm often amazed at how many people remember that excessively candid photograph. Perhaps my sister is right. She claims the photographer caught my best side.''

His best side being his backside? Rose laughed. "Maybe I do like you, after all.''

The door chime sounded again. Tourists, she saw at a glance—a Greek couple with a small child. She delegated

them to her aunt with a quick smile. To her surprise,
Gemma frowned and didn't step forward to welcome their
customers.

Her *zia* didn't approve of Lord Andrew Harrington? Or
possibly it was Rose's flirting she didn't like. Ah, well. She
and Gemma had different ideas about what risks were
worth taking. She answered her aunt's silent misgivings
with a grin, and reluctantly Gemma moved toward the front
of the shop.

Lord Andrew came up to the counter. "Perhaps you
could show me your shop."

How odd. She couldn't feel him. She felt something, all
right—a delightful fizzing, the champagne pleasure of at-
traction. But she couldn't feel *him*. The counter was only
two feet wide, which normally let a customer's energy
brush up against hers. Curious, she tipped her head.
"Maybe I will. But I'll have to repeat my aunt's question.
Are you looking for something in particular?"

"Nothing that would be for sale. But something special,
yes."

Oh, he was good. Rose had to smile. "We have some
very special things for sale, though, all handmade. Necklaces, earrings…"

He shook his head chidingly. "I'm far too conventional
a fellow for earrings—except, of course, for pearls. Pearls
must always be acceptable, don't you think?"

"Certainly, on formal occasions," she agreed solemnly.
"I'm afraid we don't have any pearls, however."

He looked thoughtful. "I believe I have a sister."

She was enjoying him more and more. "How pleasant
for you."

"No doubt she will have a birthday at some point. I
could buy her a present. In fact, I had better buy her a
present. You must help me."

"Jewelry, or something decorative?"

"Oh…" His gaze flickered over her, then lifted so his eyes could smile at her in that way they had that didn't involve his mouth at all. "Something decorative, I think."

"For your sister," she reminded him, and left the safety of the counter. Quite deliberately she let her arm brush his as she walked past, and received an answer to the question she couldn't ask any other way.

Nothing. Even this close, he gave away nothing at all.

Rose's skin felt freshly scrubbed—tender, alert. Her mind began to fizz like a thoroughly shaken can of soda, but she didn't let her step falter as she led the way to the other side of the store, away from her aunt and the Greek tourists.

Here the elegantly swirled colors of Murano glass glowed on shelves beside bowls bright with painted designs. Colors giggled and flowed over lead crystal vases, majolica earthenware, millefiori paperweights, ceramic figures and crackle-finish urns. Here, surrounded by beauty forged in fire, she felt relaxed and easy.

A purely physical reaction. That was all she felt with this man. That and curiosity, a ready appreciation for a quick mind. She turned to face him and she was smiling. But not like a shopkeeper in pursuit of a sale. "What is your sister like? Feminine, rowdy, sophisticated, shy?"

"Convinced she could do a better job of running my life than I do." He wasn't looking at Rose now, but at a shiny black statue by Gilmarie—a nymph, nude, seated on a stone and casting a roguish glance over one bare shoulder. He traced a finger along a ceramic thigh. "I like this."

The nymph was explicitly sensual. Rose's eyebrows shot up. "For your sister?"

"I have a brother, too."

"No doubt he comes equipped with a birthday, as well."

"I'm fairly sure of it. I'm not sure I want this for him, though. I like the look on her face. The invitation." His eyes met Rose's then. There was no hint of a smile now. "Any man would."

What an odd thing a heart was, pumping along unnoticed most of the time, then suddenly bouncing in great, uneven leaps like a ball tumbling downhill. "She's flirting, not inviting."

"Is there a difference?"

"To a woman, yes. I think of flirting as a performance art. Something to be enjoyed in the moment, like dancing. Men are more likely to think of it as akin to cooking—still an art in the right hands, but carried out with a particular goal in mind."

The creases came back, and one corner of his mouth helped them build his smile this time. "I am a goal-oriented bastard at times."

So they knew where they stood. He wanted to get her into bed. Rose hadn't decided yet what she wanted, but thought she would enjoy finding out. She didn't doubt for a moment that the decision would be hers. She smiled back. "Are you a patient bastard, too? Even when you don't get what you want?"

"I can be. Have dinner with me tonight."

She tipped her head to one side. "Where?"

"Why don't I surprise you?"

"I like surprises. But somewhere with people around, I think."

"A reasonable precaution. Perhaps I should mention that while I may be goal-oriented, I play by the rules."

"You did say something about being conventional. But then, there's your hair." It was too long, too curly. It contradicted the hard face and remote expression, hinting at sensuality, even exuberance. The color was a pure, pale ash-brown. She wanted to touch it.

Impulsively she did. "Soft...and hardly businessman-short. It doesn't fit the rest of your image, does it?"

His face tightened. "I'm not a soft man. Just a busy one. I've been forgetting to get it cut." He caught her hand and drew it between them, toying with her fingers. "You're rough on your hands." He ran a finger along a scabbed scratch on her thumb.

"I—" She glanced to where he held her hand in his. And stopped breathing.

After a moment, unsteady, she said, "I make jewelry. Little nicks are inevitable."

"Is some of the jewelry here yours?"

"Most of it."

"You have talent." He carried her hand to his mouth and placed a kiss, almost chaste, on the tips of her fingers. "Be ready at seven. Where should I pick you up?"

"Here. We…my aunt and I live above the shop. Use the stairs at the side of the house. Will you be wearing your pearls?"

"It will be a dressy sort of surprise, but not formal enough for pearls. You would be lovely in black."

She said something and he didn't stare at her as if she were crazy, so she must have sounded reasonable. Then he left. She managed to respond appropriately when two more tourists, both female, wandered in while her aunt was ringing up a purchase for the Greek family. Rose sold her tourists a bracelet, three postcards and a beautiful ivory vase.

But all the while her mind was whirling. She'd recognized his hand. She'd seen it quite recently. For the first time, the only time, she had been touched while walking a fire dream. Touched by *his* hand. While around them the airport burned in a vision that now—thank God—would never come true.

Rose had no idea what it meant. But the slamming of her heart against the walls of her chest felt very much like fear.

Chapter 4

Rose wasn't surprised when her aunt joined her that evening while she was getting ready. "I had hoped you would take another look at that ring," said Gemma, settling on the edge of the tub.

"I haven't decided yet." Rose leaned over the sink, shut one eye and stroked color on the closed lid.

"You didn't pick up any feeling of urgency when you held it?"

The hopeful note in Gemma's voice made Rose smile. "No. And you ought to be ashamed of yourself, wishing danger on some poor woman so you can coerce me into working with my Gift."

"I never would! But there must be some reason the ring came to you. You need to find out what that is." She cocked her head like a curious parrot. "You aren't wearing *that* to go out with Lord Andrew, are you?"

Rose grinned, studied the smoky color on one eyelid and applied herself to making the other match it. She was wear-

ing black, as Drew had suggested—a skinny silk swish of
a dress with straps thin as spider silk. "Don't you like it?"

"What there is of it. I hope you know what you're doing."

"Where would be the fun in that?" She dropped the eye
shadow in the caddy that held her play-pretties and dug
through the brushes, boxes, tubes, crayons and pencils.
Rose didn't always bother with makeup, but when in the
mood to indulge, she did enjoy her paints.

Red lipstick, she thought, but not siren red. More of a
mauve, maybe...then she saw her aunt's face and paused,
creamy color dialed but unapplied. "Zia? What's wrong?
This isn't exactly the first time I've gone out with a man."

"This one is different."

Rose couldn't deny that, since it was his difference that
intrigued her. Quickly she smoothed color over her lips. "I
like him."

Suddenly vehement, Gemma stood. "It isn't him you
like, it's his silence. You thought I hadn't noticed? My Gift
may be small, but I'd have to be spirit-blind not to notice
that nothing at all comes from Lord Andrew Harrington. If
you were to close your eyes when he kissed you, you
wouldn't know he was there. And *that's* why you're going
out with him."

"Well, yes." Rose turned, a smile tugging at her mouth.
"But trust me. If he kisses me, I'll know he's there."

Gemma tossed her hands in the air. "Rose, this man is
trouble. Even if he weren't wild...oh, the stories I've heard
about him! I'm sure they can't all be true...but some of
them must be, and his birth, his family—you must see how
impossible it is. Lord Andrew is looking for fun and games,
love. A playmate, nothing more."

"Maybe I want to play. Have I shocked you?" She put
an arm around her aunt's plump shoulders. "Surely not.
You know what it's like. If anyone knows, you do."

Gemma's eyes were troubled as their gazes met and held. "You mustn't think that because I'm alone, you will be. You're only twenty-seven. There's time."

"I suppose. But—" the twist Rose gave her mouth landed between a smile and a grimace "—I don't think I'm made for celibacy."

Gemma turned and put her hands on Rose's shoulders. "So, you want a fling? With that man? *Bambina,* I didn't raise you to be stupid."

"Is it stupid to go out with a man I find attractive? Whatever happens, it will be my choice. I want—oh, just to be normal. For once, to be normal." Too much bitterness colored that last statement. She moderated her voice, dug deep and found amusement. "I don't have my heart set on a flaming affair. I may have hopes, but no definite plans."

"That, I gather, is supposed to reassure me." Gemma's voice was tart. "You are going to be hurt."

"Hey." Rose dropped a kiss on her aunt's soft cheek. "I'm supposed to be the seer around here. No dire predictions, please. I don't expect to be hurt, but if I am, what of it? Most women my age have stumbled in and out of a few heartaches."

"Bah. I don't know why I try. Once you have your mind made up, there's no reasoning with you. Oh, here, you're going to be late if you don't hurry." She gave Rose a little push, turning her to face the mirror again, picked up a hairbrush and began drawing the bristles firmly through Rose's hair. "I'll braid it for you."

"Thank you, Zia," Rose said meekly, then, "Ouch! Do you mean to discourage Drew by making me bald before he gets here?"

"It wouldn't pull if you'd hold still. At your great age you should be able to stand quietly a few minutes... Did you want me to use the clasp you have out? No, hold on to it a moment, I'm not quite ready. No one is born blocked, you know. Somehow, sometime, he was hurt.''

Rose's heart felt suddenly larger as it filled with warmth for this dear woman who could no more hold on to anger than she could add a column of figures and come up with the same answer twice. ''Now you're worrying about him.''

''I'm quite capable of worrying about more than one person. And I'm ready for the clasp…thank you. I don't know when I've seen someone so completely blocked— well, there's my cousin Pia, poor soul. And old Arturo Domino, but he's crazy.''

Amused, Rose said, ''I doubt that Drew talks to aliens on a regular basis. He has a solid feel to him, don't you think?''

The busy hands gave one last tug to Rose's braid, then Gemma stepped back. ''How would I know? How would you, when he keeps himself fully to himself?''

''A hunch?'' She turned, smiling mischievously.

''Where would you find a hunch when you can't read him, not at all? Sitting out on the stoop, waiting for you to pick it up? Unless… Rose, have you dreamed him?''

''No. How do I look?''

''*Mia felicitá.*'' Gemma's eyes were moist. ''So beautiful. Maybe I should be worrying about Lord Andrew. Tonight, you could break a man's heart.''

So of course she had to hug Gemma. ''If you make me cry, my mascara is going to run.''

''It would serve you right. Oh, go on, finish getting ready.'' Gemma pulled away. ''You don't have your shoes or your purse, and he will be here any minute. I suppose you had better borrow my Spanish shawl. It won't keep you warm in *that* dress, but it will look pretty.''

Gemma hurried out. Rose went to get her evening bag and heels from her room, her steps slowed by guilt. The shawl was one of her aunt's chief treasures, a lacy extravagance purchased on a long-ago trip. Gemma had been twenty and still hoping to find a man, the right man. For the women in their family, there was only ever one man. Gemma's mother had traveled with her to Greece, Italy and Spain. So had her younger sister, who eventually became Rose's mother.

Gemma had found love on that trip. And lost it. He had died before they could marry, this man Gemma seldom spoke of but had never forgotten. Yet the shawl held only happy memories for her.

I didn't lie, Rose told herself as she stepped into her heels. Not exactly. True, Drew had appeared in her vision, but the sending had been about the bombing, not the man. But she didn't want to tell Gemma about the hand that had touched her during the time that wasn't. Gemma would fuss, wanting Rose to enter into a fire-trance to find the truth. She would assume Drew was tied somehow to Rose's Gift.

In a sense, he was. Because of her Gift, he might be the only man she would ever be able to go to bed with.

Summer days were long in the southern Mediterranean. At seven in the evening the air was warm as a baby's bath, the light slanting but still rich. Voices called greetings and chatted in high-speed Italian or the musical English that was the island's official tongue, punctuated here and there with German, Greek or Spanish from tourists wandering from shop to shop.

Not as many tourists as usual. Fear had kept many away, a situation that wouldn't be helped by the recent bombing. Drew was considering the economic consequences as he strolled along with the tourists and the natives. It was easier than thinking about what he planned to do that night. And the woman he planned to do it with...or to.

Sex was a mutual activity. Deceit wasn't.

It was hard not to like her. That was a problem he hadn't anticipated. He reminded himself that she wasn't, couldn't be, what she seemed. She'd known about the bomb before it went off, which meant she was connected, somehow, to the Brothers of Darkness. Maybe she wasn't really part of them. She might have heard of the attack through a lover or a friend—but if so, she hadn't given the investigators the name of that friend or lover. Whether her silence came from complicity or misguided loyalty, she was guilty of protecting killers. And his own guilt was misplaced.

Drew returned his attention to the street and the people on it. He'd had to park a few blocks away. Rose Giaberti's shop was on one of the old streets, tight and twisty, that made no provision for such modern intrusions as automobiles.

There were streets like this in England, narrow and crowded by buildings leaning comfortably into old age, but the light was different. So were the faces—smiling, frowning, emotions flowing freely, with hands gesturing to support a point or touch a friend. People stood closer to each other here. This communal urge toward intimacy might have made a man like him uneasy. Instead, in Montebello he relaxed as he seldom could at home. Here, he was known to be different—British, and therefore foolish about some things. His reserve, therefore, was a national trait, not a personal failing.

Her shop was still open, he noticed when he reached the two-story stone building. A girl with a pretty smile and short, shaggy hair was ringing something up on the antiquated cash register as he passed the big window. As instructed, Drew climbed the stairs on the side of the house. The balustrade was wooden and old. The steps were much older, and stone.

At the top of the stairs was a small balcony and a yellow door, which opened at his knock. The aunt invited him in without apologizing for her home, which he liked. Her parlor was modest and colorful, not terribly neat, and a fierce, inexplicable wish suddenly split him, leaving half his mind making sure he said what he should while the other half longed to sit in the faded blue armchair and talk with this warm, silly woman. Just sit and talk, in comfort.

Foolishness.

Rose, she said, would be ready in a moment. She made proper if slightly scattered conversation and offered him a seat, but she didn't sit down herself, so courtesy kept him standing. He didn't find out if the blue armchair would welcome him as this woman, however polite, did not.

Gemma Giaberti might be silly, but she was no fool. She didn't trust him. Maybe he should have tried to charm or reassure her, but that particular deceit was beyond him. The woman was right to worry. He would almost certainly hurt her niece.

Some small noise must have alerted him. Or maybe it was her scent, sensed but not consciously noted, that made him turn to look at the doorway just as she reached it.

She wore black.

For once Drew's inability to show his feelings was a blessing. His reaction couldn't be concealed entirely, of course—there were some things no man could hide—but his dress slacks fit loosely enough to offer some concealment.

"I'm sorry I kept you waiting," she said, coming forward with a smile. "Last-minute emergency. I couldn't find the right purse."

"For results like this, I would have happily waited much longer." He didn't offer his arm. Instead, acting on impulse, he held out his hand.

Her palm was warm, her clasp firm. The contact felt obscurely right, and he didn't want to analyze his motives or consider consequences. She gave her aunt a kiss on the

cheek, her aunt gave her a lacy black shawl, and he left the
house with Rose's hand in his.

The air felt like silk on what little bare skin it could
reach. Drew found himself regretting the way he'd chosen
to entertain her tonight. It demanded far too many clothes.

On his part, at least. He glanced at the woman beside
him. There was a great deal of her skin available to the
evening air. Perhaps he hadn't made such a bad choice,
after all.

Dammit. He had no business regretting or enjoying his
plans for the night. Rose was a beautiful woman, but more
than that, she was vivid—sensual, unexpected, brimming
with life. He couldn't help responding and needn't apologize for it. But tonight wasn't about him and his unruly
libido. He needed to remember that.

"Am I allowed to know where we're going?"

"First to the car. I had to park a few blocks away. Then,
I'm afraid, to pick up my cousin." That startled her. And
didn't please her overmuch, he thought.

"Which one?"

"Lorenzo. It's his car. Is it my imagination, or are we
attracting more than our share of attention?"

She chuckled. "What did you expect? I didn't tell anyone I was going out with the queen's nephew, but I did ask
my assistant to close the shop for me tonight—after you'd
come to see me this afternoon. That would be all it took to
start the gossip moving. They're probably disappointed you
didn't pick me up in a limo."

He raised his eyebrows. "Do you know all the people
who have been staring at us, then?"

"Don't you know most of the people in the village near
your family's estate?"

"Montebello isn't a village. The population of the capital
alone is over two hundred thousand."

"But there aren't two hundred thousand people on my street. I've lived in the house we just left for seventeen years."

He was reminded of what Lorenzo had said about Montebello and the village mind. "Most of our admirers seem to be smiling. They must approve. No, wait. The woman standing in front of the pharmacy you recommended to me for sunscreen is scowling at me. No doubt she reads the same magazines your aunt does."

"Natala Baldovino." She sighed. "It isn't your reputation that puts a scowl on her face. It's mine. She probably thinks I've put a spell on you and is trying to decide which authority to report me to. Maybe I should warn her not to bother telling Captain Mylonas. He doesn't go in for all that psychic nonsense."

Startled, he said nothing.

"Look." She stopped, pulling her hand away from his, and faced him. "We may as well get this out of the way. How did you get my address?"

"From Lorenzo," he admitted, since it was obvious she'd guessed that much.

"That wouldn't be the only information he gave you about me. Your cousin, whose car you borrowed, thinks that either I'm responsible for the bomb at the airport or I know who is. He would have told you that. You must have decided to give me the benefit of the doubt, and I appreciate it. I don't appreciate being manipulated."

"I beg your pardon?"

She made a small, disgusted noise. "This business of picking up your cousin because you have his car. His Grace owns more than one car. He could catch a ride with a dozen other people, not counting the police or his own staff. But you've arranged things so that I have to face a man who thinks I'm in league with the—oh, I don't have any words bad enough for them. With the Brothers. That's a surprise, all right, but not the kind I was expecting when you asked me out."

Her perception of him shook him—but she didn't really know why he'd set things up this way. She'd guessed part of it, but not all. "I'm sorry."

"Judging by the expression on your face, that much is true."

His face wore a readable expression? "I didn't think you'd realize Lorenzo held you in suspicion. He did arrange for Captain Mylonas to let you go."

"Because there's no evidence against me, not because he doesn't suspect me. I'm not an idiot. He's probably having me followed, though I haven't spotted anyone lurking behind us yet. I understand why your cousin is suspicious, but that doesn't make him pleasant company for me."

Best, he decided, to speak as much truth as possible. She was too bright to swallow a comfortable lie. "I'm afraid you're right. Lorenzo believes you know more than you've admitted. He insisted I arrange things this way tonight. I think he wants to reassure himself I haven't fallen under your spell." He captured her hands. "Not the kind of spell your Signora Baldovino has in mind... I'm not sure I'll be able to convince him, though. I'm not sure it isn't true."

She studied him for a long moment before pulling one of her hands away. "She's not my Signora Baldovino," was all she said, but she left her other hand in his as they started walking again.

Neither of them spoke again until they reached the car, a silver Mercedes Benz. For Drew, the silence was a relief. Concealing facts and feelings came naturally. Deceit, he was learning, wasn't the same as concealment.

He reached across her to unlock her door, but paused before opening it. "Do you see the man in the blue shirt who just rounded the corner? We need to give him time to reach his car, but it's me he's following, not you."

She stood so close, almost within the circle of his arms, that he could see the dark rims around her irises, like midnight encircling the ocean. "Why is he following you? And why do we want him to?"

"I refuse to go everywhere flanked by bodyguards. My cousin refuses to let me wander around Montebello without them. The gentleman in the blue shirt is a compromise."

Her eyes widened. He could feel the warmth from her body calling to his. She smelled of roses and something darker, a hint of musk and secrets. "You're a target because of your relationship to the Crown. I...hadn't realized."

"Not a primary target. Maybe not a target at all, now that Lucas is back and war seems unlikely, but kidnapping remains a possibility. My uncle wouldn't deal with terrorists, no matter whom they held hostage, but we can't be sure they believe that. It's only fair that you be aware of this. I wouldn't have asked you out if the danger was great, but there is some risk. There's also some loss of privacy."

Her smile came slowly and her voice, when she spoke, was light. Deliberately so, he thought. "As long as the gentleman in the blue shirt doesn't find it necessary to peep in windows, I'm not worried about the loss of privacy. My neighbors will be watching us much more keenly than he will, believe me. As for the danger...we'll just have to hope I'm a good enough seer to keep us both out of trouble, won't we?"

Something complex and silent seemed to pass between them, a communication he lacked the understanding to translate. Heat, yes—that was there. It was the other message he didn't have words for. But he felt it.

He looked away before she did and opened her door. She slid inside.

How could he keep from respecting her courage? Drew had no answer for that as he settled behind the wheel.

"So where will you, me and your suspicious cousin be eating dinner?"

"Didn't I tell you?" A smile touched his lips as he clicked the seat belt in place. "At the palace. With my other cousin, Prince Lucas. And his parents."

This time, he noted with slightly malicious pleasure as he pulled out into traffic, she was the one startled into speechlessness.

Chapter 5

At thirty-five minutes short of midnight Drew headed for Lorenzo's new home on the palace grounds. It was ironic, really, Drew thought. For years Lorenzo's half brother had been jealous because Lorenzo lived in the palace, while Desmond had to settle for a house on the grounds. Now that Lorenzo was married, he'd casually relinquished what Desmond wanted so fiercely, preferring the privacy of a separate dwelling.

Drew doubted that the move had done anything to ease Desmond's envy.

Lorenzo's new wife, Eliza, let Drew in and showed him into the study, then withdrew discreetly.

Lorenzo was sitting at his desk with a map of the palace grounds spread before him, anchored at the corners by a book, a half-full decanter, a chunk of quartz and a .9-mm pistol. "If you'd like some brandy," he said without looking up, "the glasses are on the credenza."

Brandy sounded entirely too civilized. "Not now," Drew

said, sitting in the chair across from his cousin. Lorenzo had been pressed for time that morning. He'd briefed Drew quickly on what they knew about Rose Giaberti, and he'd given him some instructions. Tonight Drew meant to learn more—and make a few suggestions of his own.

"I hadn't expected to see you back quite so early." There was a gleam of amusement in Lorenzo's dark eyes.

"If you're expecting regular reports on my sex life, you're doomed to disappointment."

Lorenzo leaned back in his chair. "No. I wasn't expecting you to be this prickly, either."

He hadn't even kissed her good-night. She'd been angry when she learned he was taking her to the palace and on her guard when he took her home. That was one of the reasons for his restraint. There were others—he preferred not to do the expected. Her aunt had been waiting for her behind the yellow door at the top of those stairs. He wanted her to trust him, and quick, hot sex wasn't the way to build trust.

But those reasons were garbage. He knew that, just as he knew that, wary or not, she'd wanted his kiss. But he remained unsure of his real reason. "Have you any evidence that a cell of the Brothers of Darkness remains intact here? Any names you can give me, descriptions, anything like that?"

"I'm afraid not. There were indications in the records we recovered after the raid on their headquarters that there had been a cell in Montebello at one time. Nothing to identify its members. We don't even know for sure it still exists, though the bombing at the airport makes that seem likely. If so, it's operating on its own now."

"I don't think she'd have anything to do with the Brothers."

"You've reached that opinion based on one evening? An evening spent in the company of others?" He shook his head. "I don't see how even you could have coaxed any confidences from her in between salad and chicken piccata."

"Logic," Drew said dryly, "is sometimes more useful than waiting for people to tell me secrets. First, the Brothers are exclusively male. Their beliefs about women wouldn't allow them to admit a woman to their councils. At most she might be a friend or lover of one of the terrorists, but that doesn't fit. This isn't a woman who would waste time on a man who wanted to put her in purdah."

Lorenzo gestured impatiently. "People kill for love, for money, for more twisted or obscure reasons—hatred, revenge, even social advancement. We can't assume she has no reason to cooperate with the Brothers just because we don't know what it is. She could be part of some other group that's climbed in bed with them for their own reasons."

"If that's the case, why isn't she dead?"

"Because she tipped us off about the bomb, you mean? Trust me, that has occurred to me. She's being watched. But it's possible they don't know who called in the tip."

Drew drummed once, twice, on the arm of the chair. "Your Captain Mylonas detained her for questioning at the airport, then took her to the police station. If the Brothers are too stupid to figure out what that means, they aren't much of a threat."

"Please. Mylonas is not one of my men, which he made quite clear. The idiot wouldn't turn her loose until I persuaded his superior to override him. As to why she's still alive…you have to remember that we're dealing with a small, isolated remnant of our old enemy. The Brothers had resources in terms of arms, information and men that these people lack. They may not have enough men to risk exposing one of their number by trying to kill her right now. They'll know we're watching her."

It was some consolation. Drew's heart was pounding too hard, and there was no reason for it. None. He steepled his fingers. "It's also possible that she isn't tied to the Brothers in any way. I'm going to proceed on that assumption."

Lorenzo's eyebrows snapped down. "You want to tell me why?"

"Because that's the most useful assumption for me to make." Not because he found it impossible to believe otherwise. Though that was true, it was subjective and proved nothing. "I won't be much help if she's connected to the Brothers. She isn't going to open up to me about that. But if she heard or saw something she wasn't supposed to, she might have decided to use this psychic nonsense as a way of tipping you off without admitting she can identify one of the Brothers."

"I see what you mean. She'd be afraid of what they would do to her if she identified one of them. But she may trust you enough to tell you the truth." Lorenzo nodded. "All right. You work with your assumption, but don't forget that's all it is. Watch yourself."

"Of course. You want to tell me why you had me bring her to the palace tonight?"

"Because I'm hoping like hell your assumption is wrong." Lorenzo stopped suddenly, as if mastering whatever emotion had his jaw so tight. "We had another tip."

"And?"

"There may be an attempt on the prince's life at the Investiture."

"Holy hell." The Investiture was a centuries' old ritual in which the king officially named his heir, who was then installed by the island's elected body as the Crown Prince. "If they smuggle in another bomb..."

"They could wipe out most of the government."

Drew sat in bleak silence a moment, absorbing the implications. "How reliable was your tip?"

Lorenzo shrugged. "Hard to say. It came from a petty criminal who sometimes turns informant. His information has been reliable in the past, but he's never given us anything of this magnitude before." Lorenzo paused. "He's since disappeared."

"Dead?"

"Or gone into hiding. The information he gave my man was vague. We're trying to corroborate some of it. No luck so far, but it's early yet."

"You've told the king, I assume. He intends to go through with the ceremony?"

"I tried to talk him into postponing it. He refused. He's convinced it's necessary to hold the ceremony as soon as possible, both to secure the succession and as a symbol for the people. Hell, he may be right. My job, as he pointed out, is to make sure he can do his job."

That sounded like his uncle. "And the prince?"

"Lucas knows. The queen hasn't been told."

"I still don't see why you had me invite Rose to the palace tonight."

"Like I said, I'm hoping your assumption is wrong. If she's one of them and seems to have easy access to the palace—to the prince—they may decide to make their attempt through her. It's easier to guard a single, known quantity than to prevent attack from an unknown direction. And if she does try something—" his left hand closed into a fist "—then we'll have her. And through her, the rest of them."

Drew's temples were beginning to throb with the dull precursor of a headache. He needed to finish up and leave. "I have a suggestion. Ask her to help with your investigation. Police departments do occasionally work with psychics."

Lorenzo's chair creaked as he leaned farther back. He laced his fingers together over his stomach and spoke mildly. "I'm sure you have a good reason for suggesting we work with a suspect."

"Her value to you is as a conduit to others. You need her alive, so you need to convince the Brothers they have nothing to fear from her. If she is working with them, this might help persuade them to make the next attack through her, as you said. They'll think you trust her. If she's an innocent witness, let it be seen that she's sticking to her story of seeing visions. The Brothers will have a good laugh at us for believing that psychic nonsense and put less of a priority on silencing her."

Lorenzo considered that for a long moment. "And if they believe in that psychic nonsense? We could be making her more of a target than she is now."

"If they actually believe she can peer into her crystal ball and identify them, she's as good as dead now," Drew said flatly. "Unless you lock her away somewhere for her own good."

"I need her alive and where they can contact her. And dammit, I need to know what she knows and hasn't told us. All right. We'll try it your way and see how it goes. Not that I plan to believe a word she says, you understand. Here's how we'll play it."

They talked for another ten minutes. Drew was on his feet, about to leave, when Lorenzo said, "One more thing." He moved the chunk of quartz and picked up the pistol, letting the map roll up in a quick shudder of paper. He held out the gun. "From now on, I want you armed whenever you leave the palace."

Silently Drew accepted the weapon. It was a Glock automatic, the model he'd learned to shoot with on the firing range below the palace more than ten years ago. "Your memory is remarkable. I'm still better with a rifle, but a rifle would be hard to tuck under a jacket. I'll need a shoulder holster."

"That could be awkward. Not that I'm asking about your sex life, mind. But she's apt to notice it."

"Not a problem." Drew slid the gun into his jacket pocket. It was heavy, the weight obvious. "I pointed out my tail earlier and gave Rose a brief explanation. She might be surprised to discover that I'm armed, but she'll associate it with the threat of kidnapping."

"You pointed out Roberts?"

"She would have spotted him sooner or later. Chances are she'll spot whoever you have on her, too, but that's okay. She's expecting it. And no," he added, smiling at the expression on Lorenzo's face, "I didn't tell her you would have her followed. She told me. She's bright, and not one to play ostrich when life gets nasty. Will palace security be alarmed by the bulge in my pocket?"

Lorenzo didn't look happy. He stood. "I've notified them. Find some time to visit the shooting range. I doubt you're in practice. You know, Drew, if it were anyone but you, I'd be worried. This woman is smart, she's sexy, and you sound as if you admire her. Maybe it's just as well you came home early tonight."

Anger hit, making Drew's head throb. "But you know better, don't you? If I were capable of losing my head over a woman, I'd have done it long ago." He nodded curtly and left.

The night was warm and quiet, the noise of the city cushioned by the trees that rimmed the grounds. From somewhere nearby a nightingale called, its song rising in a liquid crescendo. Drew hurried along the path that led to the palace, wanting to be in his room, alone, as soon as possible.

It might be a normal headache. Probably it was, and a couple of aspirins would prove that. In the past year he'd had six crazy spells, none of them closer together than four weeks. But the interval between them had shortened, and a headache was the usual precursor.

Still, this particular ache could be the product of pure sexual frustration. He'd been very ready for Rose when he didn't kiss her good night. Alarmingly so. And maybe that was the real reason he hadn't kissed her—on some level she frightened him.

No. No, that was absurd. He might fear losing control, but he wasn't afraid of the woman.

For once Rudolpho, the majordomo, wasn't on duty, and if the guards at the palace door noticed the bulge in Drew's pocket, they ignored it. He took the stairs quickly.

He'd done what he could to protect her. He wouldn't apologize for wanting to. Drew thought of the way she'd discussed the economic consequences of the bombing at the dinner table with four royals, himself and Lorenzo, and smiled. She'd been nervous, but she hadn't let it show.

What made him think she'd been nervous? He frowned as he crossed the picture gallery, unable to remember an expression, an awkward word, anything but his simple certainty. Maybe he'd imagined it, or assumed—

Between one step and the next, it hit. All at once this time—the glassy separation, the slicing agony in his skull, the dislocation of his senses. Walls melted into floors, colors ran together, and chaos chuckled in the hollow space between self and madness. He lost touch with his body— was he moving, falling, frozen in place? Was he *anywhere?*

He still *was*. He was *here*, dammit, even if he couldn't find *here* in the swirls of colors and jutting angles, the walls that moved and traded places with floor or ceiling. Even if he couldn't feel his body, he still existed in his mind. Desperate, he began to count, then switched to long division...

"...get help? Drew, answer me!"

He blinked. He was standing in the hall near the royal suite. His skin was clammy, chilled. And his aunt's face was looking up at him, the patrician features tight with worry. Her hand clutched his arm. He felt her fingernails, dulled by the cloth of his sleeve, digging into his flesh.

He felt. The reliable witness of his senses had returned. Dizzy with relief, he tried a smile. "Sorry. Didn't mean to worry you."

"Never mind that. Are you all right? I haven't seen you look like that since you were a boy. Those migraines you used to get—"

"Yes." Gratefully he seized on the explanation she'd unwittingly offered. "I'm afraid they've come back."

She released his arm, but her worried frown didn't ease. "Are you sure that's what this is? You look ill. Have you seen a doctor?"

"A neurologist, actually." Amazing how easy it was to deceive while speaking the truth. "He put me through any number of indignities and didn't find anything wrong. No bleeding, tumors or other abnormalities." No traces of drugs. No explanations at all.

"Now, that scares me almost as much as your pallor did a moment ago. The headaches must be severe for you to give in and see a doctor without being nagged into it. Unless…oh, your mother must have—"

"She doesn't know," he said quickly. "I hope you won't tell her. You know how she worries."

"Oh, Drew." She caught her lower lip with her teeth. "It doesn't seem right to keep something like this from her."

"Aunt Gwen." He took a deep breath, then let it out slowly. The exhaustion was already sweeping over him, making his thoughts sluggish. *I can't hold it off this time.* Panic and adrenaline turned him light-headed even as they plundered the last of his reserves. How long did he have? Minutes? "You know why I had migraines as a boy. Mother doesn't deal well with reminders of that time."

The queen was still chewing on her lip. "It was terrible

for all of us, but worse for you. If the migraines have come back, is it because of Lucas's disappearance? Oh—I'm so selfish. That never once occurred to me. We did think at first he might have been kidnapped, and I never stopped to think how that might affect you."

"Don't." Drew had to get away. Now. But he took a moment to put an arm around her shoulders and squeeze quickly. "You had no reason to think about that. You were sick with fear, then grieving. I didn't want you to worry about me. I still don't."

Her mouth turned up wryly. "I know that well enough. But I reserve the right to worry about the people I love."

"I'm fine," he told her with every bit of sincerity he could muster. "Aside from being more of a sorehead than usual. I've got some medicine for it in my room, if you'll excuse me."

Hearing that, of course, she sent him on his way.

When the door to his suite closed behind him, he locked it, closed his eyes and leaned against it. He was shaking.

This time had been different. He'd been in the hall leading to the wing that held the Harrington suite when the spell hit. When he came back to himself, he'd been near the royal suite. This time, he'd continued walking after the spell hit. That had never happened before.

Fear bit deeply. What else might he do while out of his senses?

He straightened and pulled the gun from his jacket pocket, staring at it with a chill that cut partway through the exhaustion dragging him down. Maybe he shouldn't carry it. Tomorrow…tomorrow he would decide. Weaving slightly, he made it to the desk, opened a drawer and shoved the gun inside.

Seconds, now. It was all happening much faster this time. He had only seconds left.

Lorenzo was right to worry about him, though he had

hold of the wrong reason, Drew thought as he stripped, his clothes falling in a ragged trail to the bedroom. He wasn't losing his head over a woman. He was losing his head, period. Or his head was losing his body.... And as the darkness closed in, taking him to a place where thought stopped, there was time for one image to float through his mind—a woman's face, her lips moist and parted, her eyes smiling, her skin as soft and smooth as every unbroken promise ever made. Rose's face, tilted up to him as it had been earlier, inviting his kiss.

There was time, too, for the flash of fear that followed him down into the waiting darkness.

Chapter 6

Rose woke all at once the way she had when she was a child. The air was warm, the light pure, as if it had been born fresh for that day. But this wasn't her birthday or a holiday....

Then she remembered. And smiled. Rose had never been one to hold on to anger. It flowed hot when it hit, but then it flowed on. And Drew had been so charming.... *No he hadn't,* she thought grinning. He was far too direct for charm. He'd been courteous, certainly—holding doors, taking her arm—but beneath the courtesy had been something much headier.

He'd been focused on her. Even when speaking with the others, he'd been aware of her, as he'd shown in a dozen small ways. Turning to her just before she spoke. Asking her opinion of a new trade treaty. Catching her gaze with his when the prince told a joke, that secret smile in his eyes.

It had been a magical evening. The palace had been

splendid—a little overpowering maybe, but the king and queen had been warm and gracious, and the prince, truly charming. And if Cinderella had had to return to her garret, well, it was a very nice garret, made even nicer this morning by lovely memories.

And the hope of making more and even lovelier memories. Unable to lie still a moment longer, Rose climbed out of bed and stretched.

No wonder she'd woken up anticipating something wonderful. It wasn't likely to happen today, though. Drew hadn't even kissed her last night, though she'd let him know she would welcome his kiss.

But he'd wanted to. She walked the short hall to the bathroom with her clothes folded over her arm and her blood humming. Turning on the shower, waiting while the pipes banged and the old hot water heater labored to rise to the occasion, she smiled as she remembered the look in his eyes.

They'd been standing in front of her aunt's home, after all. Not much privacy there, and he was a man who valued privacy, she thought. He was also a man who liked to plan things. She slipped out of her nightgown and under the shower, tilting her face into the warm spray to savor the pleasant shock of heat hitting night-chilled skin.

The question was, should she allow him to plan her seduction? Or should she plan his?

By the time he called her later that day, she had some ideas about that, and a plan of her own.

The *fioreanno* of the eldest daughter of Cletus Anaghnostopoulus was a great success. On every table the flowers were fresh and bright. Laughter rang freely and the little café was satisfyingly crowded, while in the piazza across the street a band played—the same one the Calabrias had engaged for their daughter's wedding and really quite good, though the trumpet player had started playing jazz after a few drinks, and who could dance to that?

Among the friends, neighbors, relatives and well-wishers attending were such important people as Adolfo Oenusyfides, Commissioner of Roads; Signore Calabria, who owned three fishing boats, as well as the café where the celebration was held; and several members of the Vinnelli family headed by old Porfino, whose son was a doctor and whose niece had married a rich American and lived in Los Angeles with the movie stars.

If Cletus was inclined to congratulate himself rather too often on the success of the party, his friends overlooked this while their wives complimented his wife on having had the foresight to ask Signora Serminio to stand as godmother sixteen years ago. For a *fioreanno* is always given by the child's godmother, and Signora Serminio was herself a person of importance now, the owner of a fine pharmacy and the mother of a son with a promising career at the palace.

And if a few people glanced at one of the guests and muttered under their breath, most were more tolerant. Maybe Rose Giaberti was *una strega,* maybe not. Her mother had been, but young Rose did not sell charms and potions and fortunes as her mother had done, and if she didn't attend Mass as often as she ought, what young person did? Certainly she was lively and friendly, with good manners. And she always brought a nice gift to a *fioreanno*.

She had brought more than a prettily wrapped box with her that night.

"You should try the *souvlakia,*" Rose said, indicating the spicy shish kebab, one of many offerings on the groaning buffet table. "Emil—he's the cook here—has a wonderful way with lamb."

Obediently Drew placed one on his plate, but slid her a wry glance. "I think you just want to see me dribble sauce on my shirt."

She grinned. "No, I wanted to see if you'd eat it with your fingers or struggle with a knife and fork."

Rose had brought Drew to the *fioreanno* after giving him the same amount of notice as he'd given her last night. None. She'd told him something of what to expect on the way here, assuming that, while he might have heard of the *fioreanni,* he wouldn't have attended one. The upper classes didn't. A *fioreanno* was like the *quinzeñero* celebrated by young Mexican girls, or the coming-out ball given young ladies of his class in England. His sister, she supposed, would have been presented to society. This was much the same thing.

She'd also given him a hint of how to dress, since he'd done that much for her. Casual, she'd said, and for herself she'd chosen a sleeveless sundress, full-skirted for dancing, baticked in the deep colors of a dying sunset. She wore one of her favorite necklaces with it, a copper-and-brass design of her own.

Of course, what passed for casual with Drew stood out in this company every bit as much as she'd failed to blend with royalty at the palace last night. He looked every inch the relaxed aristocrat in khaki chinos and a shirt of un-bleached linen that had probably cost more than her favorite little black dress.

They carried their laden plates to one of the tables that spilled out onto the sidewalk. A short, middle-aged man sat alone at a nearby table—Drew's bodyguard. He'd followed them here in a tiny Fiat and was looking everywhere except at them.

He was the only one who *wasn't* watching them. Amused, Rose sat at the little table. "Will you dribble sauce on yourself, do you think?"

"Undoubtedly, if there's a photographer from the *Tattler* or *Le Stelle* within flashbulb range. Otherwise I may manage to muddle through. Which brings up a question," he said, putting down his plate so he could draw out her chair. "Why did you introduce me to our host and hostess as Drew, no last name? You said your neighbors all know who I am."

"This way they can pretend they don't. More comfortable for everyone that way. Rather like the way your aunt, uncle and cousins pretended last night that they didn't know that I am, at best, that crazy woman who claims to be psychic. Or at worst…" She lifted her eyes to his as he sat across from her at the tiny table. "The worst would make me something unspeakable."

"I don't believe the worst," he said quietly. "As for what my family believes, Lorenzo asked me to—"

"Please." She put her hand on his wrist. "I shouldn't have said anything before we've had a chance to taste Emil's *souvlakia.* I didn't intend to. If His Grace asked you to convey some message to me, you can tell me after the party, all right? For now, let's eat too much and talk about our neighbors and enjoy ourselves. That's what a *fioreanno* is for."

He didn't respond right away. She wouldn't have known what he was thinking, what he was feeling, if her fingers hadn't been resting on his wrist, where his pulse beat. It had picked up when she touched him.

As had hers.

"All right," he said, but it was his mouth that carried his smile this time, not his eyes. "Tell me about your neighbors, since none of mine are nearby to gossip about."

So she did. While they ate *souvlakia*—he did use his fingers and didn't get any spots on his shirt—she told him brief, amusing stories about some of the people she knew in the crowd. And insisted he uphold his end by talking about people he knew back in England. You could learn a lot, she knew, about a person by the way he spoke of others.

At first he resisted. "I'm not asking for secrets," she

told him severely, spreading *melitzana* on a slice of crusty bread and handing it to him. "Or anything hurtful. Just the sort of thing that everyone knows already. You know... who's been married five times, who is getting married— and why, if possible. That makes it more interesting. Who collects Elvis memorabilia, or better yet, thinks she's spoken to Elvis recently."

Amusement softened his face and made his green eyes bright. "The sort of thing they'd put in the *Tattler,* if the *Tattler* were ever to do an edition about normal people?"

"Exactly. Though you can omit the candid photos."

Though his stories were short, they revealed a dry wit and tolerant acceptance blended with a good deal of perception. She listened, she chuckled at times, and she watched the strong bones of his wrists and the way the candlelight gilded the messy curls of his hair.

Impulsively she asked, "Why do you wear your hair long? I like it, but it doesn't seem to fit."

If her question surprised him, it didn't show. But for a second, she thought he looked uneasy. "I don't like getting it cut. It's childish, of course. As soon as I'm told to sit still and behave, I get restless."

It was easy to forget that he wasn't a handsome man or a charming one. He was too self-contained for charm, and his face was too long, his shoulders broad but too bony for true masculine beauty. But there was something in the way he moved that drew the eye, something compelling in the way those uneven features were knit together, something in even his silences that fascinated...and then he smiled. He smiled, and you forgot whatever silly ideas you'd once held about what was and wasn't beautiful.

They were interrupted a few times. Drew watched their latest visitor—an old woman with a mustache and a black cane—hobble off. "Amazing. I don't think I've ever been quite so thoroughly interrogated without being asked a single question."

Rose chuckled. "It would be rude to question you, since everyone knows you're here incognito."

His gaze flicked back to her, the creases beneath his eyes deepening. "Everyone knows? As in, one of those things everyone already knows and part of the stories making the rounds tonight?"

She grinned. "You and I are being discussed and speculated about with almost as much interest as is given to what all this cost. And that, you know, is a matter of great importance. You noticed the compliment Signora Lorenzi paid just now to the florist who provided the flowers?"

"You told her you would pass it on to someone named Adrian."

"That was to let her know that Signora Serminio probably got her floral arrangements wholesale. Adrian is a florist. He is also a second cousin of Signor Anaghnostopoulus, our host. I'm expected to pass on some of these details, since my shop is across the street from Serminio's."

"Who sells sunscreen." A smile tugged at the corner of his mouth. "You didn't share these important financial details about your neighbors with me."

"Somehow I didn't think you'd be interested." She smiled, shrugged. "We're a nation of merchants. It's how we've survived all these years in spite of conquerors, imperialists, Nazis—and now, terrorists. We bend, we accommodate, we compete with each other and we help each other. It's why we've been content to remain a monarchy. Let the Sebastianis do most of the hard work of government and leave the rest of us free to pay attention to important matters."

"Such as how much Signora Serminio paid for her goddaughter's *fioreanno?*"

"Exactly. Oh, look—we have to be quiet now. Speech time."

The father spoke first. He had a long list of people to thank, rather like an actor at the Oscars who feels obliged to mention every member of his family, every friend and friendly influence—including, but far from limited to, his third-grade teacher—as well as the Almighty and various business acquaintances. Then the priest blessed the young girl, her family and all those attending, closing with a special prayer for the guidance of the king in "these difficult times." At last, to everyone's relief, the talking was over and the band started playing once more. Some of the guests began drifting across the street for the dancing, while others headed for the bar.

Drew commented, "The priest is Orthodox."

"Of course. The family is Greek."

"But many of the guests are Catholic. That's typical of Montebello, though, isn't it? There isn't much religious friction here, though you have Orthodox, Catholic and Protestant churches. Not to mention the mosques."

"And if we could get our Muslim neighbors to come to more *fioreanni,* there would be even less strife. They're wary of the dancing and the naked faces and opinions of the women at these affairs, but I have been to *fioreanni* that had Muslim guests. This is how we make it work, you see. We remind ourselves how much we have in common, how much we need each other."

Drew was frowning, but not in skepticism. More as if he was trying to understand. "By giving coming-out parties for your young women?"

"All this—" she spread her arm, indicating the café, the piazza, the people "—it's really about connections. I've made you think the money is what counts, but by itself the cost of a *fioreanno* means nothing. Anyone who spends enough could give a good party, but that alone wouldn't make them an important family, one that other families want their sons or daughters to marry into. It's the connections that matter.''

''So while the cost of the flowers is interesting, the second cousin who's a florist is more important?''

She smiled, pleased with him. ''Exactly. This, tonight, is how Signor Anaghnostopoulus says, 'Look at my family. We are stable, settled. We know how things work. We know these people in the merchant community, these in government, these in the Church. And maybe, if you are lucky, your family can join with mine through this, my beautiful daughter, and our connections will grow and we will all prosper.'''

For the first time that evening he touched her deliberately, taking her hand. He played idly with her fingers and looked at her, and she wondered if he could feel what happened to her pulse the way she'd felt his change earlier. ''Did you have a grand *fioreanno* when you were sixteen, with fresh flowers on every table?''

She didn't let her smile slip. ''I'm afraid not. A father is necessary for the occasion, you see, even though it's the godmother who gives the party.''

He still held her hand. ''You are an orphan?''

What she saw in his face wasn't as trite as sympathy—more like a vast, incurious acceptance, as if he couldn't be moved to shock, pity or any intrusive emotion, no matter what she said. As if it was safe to tell him anything. ''My mother never married. I don't know who my father was. And that,'' she said, smiling brightly, ''is one of those things that everyone knows, but such old history it won't have been part of many of the stories told tonight.''

''I think we've exchanged enough stories for now.'' He stood and drew her to her feet. ''I'd very much like to dance with you.''

* * *

The moon was mostly full, a child's lopsided white circle painted on a charcoal sky. Cyprus and oak filtered the lights and sounds of the street on three sides of the piazza. On the fourth side the band stood on its modest platform with the curved wall at the back, designed to catch and reflect the music outward. Later, when mostly young people remained, they would probably try out more modern music; now they played the old songs. So far, the trumpet player was behaving himself.

The dancers were all ages, from nine to ninety. Drew led Rose to the edge of the square, where she slipped into his arms as easily as if they had danced together a hundred times before. A waltz was playing...and oh, the man knew how to waltz.

He held her correctly, one hand warm at her waist, the other clasping hers lightly, with the prescribed distance between their bodies. And he looked into her eyes as they moved in smooth, swooping circles, their bodies joined by movement rather than touch, the lilt of the music riffed now and then by laughter.

Did he know how seductive this graceful courting was, when her body learned to follow his while still separate and sovereign, so that each turn became an act of surrender?

She smiled up into his eyes. He knew.

After the waltz came a lively country tune that invited the dancers to romp. To her surprise and delight, after watching the others for a moment he abandoned formality and spun her around the crowded square as if he'd been dancing like this since childhood. There followed another quick country dance, which left her breathless and happy.

Then they played "Moon River," and he pulled her close.

Her head fitted his shoulder perfectly. His shirt smelled faintly of starch. His skin had its own perfume, which passed like a secret through her senses, and her heart beat fast and hard.

So did his.

They circled slowly now, gliding together in a dark, closed space bounded by music. She felt the movement of his legs and the way the linen moved over his body as she stroked her hands from his shoulders to his waist. The skin beneath the thin cloth was heated, slightly damp. Already, an ache had begun, growing larger as they drifted—easy, langorous, important.

It didn't occur to Rose to hide what she felt from him. She was sweetly, dreamily aroused. She wanted him to know. She lifted her head so she could look in his eyes and let him see hers.

What she saw on his face wasn't sweet or dreamy. His jaw was taut. His focus on her was so intense, so complete, her breath caught in her throat. He lifted a hand and traced the side of her face with his fingers carefully, as if all he knew of the world must be drawn to him through his fingertips. She shivered. He bent his head, and she glimpsed his eyes before her own closed—the lids heavy, the pupils dark but gleaming from some fugitive reflection.

His lips touched hers, a quick shock of feeling, then retreated. His fingers tightened along the side of her face and his mouth came back, firmly this time, to join hers.

Heat. A rushing—in her head as her blood answered a new tide, making her ears echo the ocean like shells. In her body, as if her center were suddenly lost and, dizzy, she spun without moving. His tongue painted promises on her lips, her hands dug into his waist…a sudden tremor in his left hand, the feel of her skin beneath the fingertips of his right hand, need growing, loins aching, flesh rising to press against cloth, her heart pounding, his heart pounding, our *hearts*—

Hands dug into her shoulders, thrusting her back. Air

moved, cool, along her heated body. And she stood alone in the small space left them by the shifting bodies of the other dancers. Alone, body and mind and heart, staring at his face, where there was no expression at all. And at his eyes, where she saw a deep and consuming horror.

Drew turned and started walking. It wasn't a conscious decision. There was nothing in him capable of reasoning or deciding at that moment. He walked, that was all. Away. Quickly.

There were too many people. People everywhere, their voices and faces blurring into a crowd—pressure he couldn't tolerate. Instinctively he sought darkness, privacy. A moment later trees loomed around him, and as the press of people grew less, thought began to return. He remembered to watch for traffic when he crossed the street, almost running now.

No headache, not yet. But it would come. The sliding disorientation, the loss of reality—there was no mistaking that. It had hit while he was kissing her, dear God, while she was in his arms....

But the rest of it hadn't hit. His steps slowed, stopped. For the first time the spell, once begun, hadn't taken its terrible course. He was in control, body and mind. In control, and standing in a dark, dead-end alley beside a garbage can. Somewhere behind him, the band swung into a cheerful rendition of ''Tequila.''

The world hadn't left him.

Neither, he realized as footsteps approached and stopped, had she.

''Drew?''

What the hell did he say? Excuse me, didn't mean to run off, but I just remembered I left the water running somewhere?

God. He ran a hand over his head, front to back, ending

with his fingers squeezing the base of his skull as if he could press out an answer.

His head didn't hurt. The terrible exhaustion wasn't hovering, waiting to drag him down. He was pathetically grateful to be spared that, along with the rest of it, even if he had no idea why he'd been spared. But he couldn't try to figure it out now. Now, he thought, bitterly aware of the irony, he had to persuade Rose he wasn't crazy.

"I'm sorry," he said without turning. "I don't have a good explanation."

"You don't have to explain. I've never... It scared me, too."

Relief poured in. She thought he'd been frightened by—what? Passion? Excessive emotion? It didn't... No, he realized, shamed. It did matter. If she'd been frightened by what she felt when they kissed, he couldn't let her go on thinking he felt...whatever she thought he felt. "Rose," he said, turning, unsure how to make himself clear without hurting her.

She stood three feet away. Worry or strain wrinkled her forehead. "Why didn't you tell me you're an empath?"

He stared. She was as crazy as he was.

"Oh. Oh, Lord." The hand that pushed her hair back was shaky, but her mouth shaped a rueful smile. "You haven't the foggiest idea what I'm talking about, do you? I don't suppose you believe in all that psychic crap."

Carefully he said, "I try to keep an open mind."

For some reason that set her off. She laughed so hard it doubled her over. He was about to grab her, thinking she was hysterical, when she straightened, gasping. "An open mind. Yes, I'm sure you think so." One last chuckle escaped, then, when he reached for her, she stepped back. "Hands off, I think, for now. Things have changed."

He took a deep breath. Still no headache. Otherwise,

things were pretty much all mucked up. "All right. If that's how you want it."

"If I knew what..." She sighed. "Never mind. I'm sure you think I'm a nutcase. Maybe it's time we talked about it—about my claim to be psychic, I mean."

He wouldn't have a better opening. "Maybe we should. But not here. Let's go back to the party." Where they'd be surrounded by plenty of nosy people.

His head might not hurt, but he damned sure ached elsewhere. He would need all the help he could get to follow her blasted hands-off policy.

Chapter 7

They made their way back to the café in silence. A light mist began to drift through the air, the droplets fine as dust motes. The dampness didn't discourage the dancers in the piazza, but it had chased those at the sidewalk tables into the shelter. The little café was crowded, loud with cheery voices. Roberts was there. He looked relieved when he saw Drew. Drew was relieved, too, though for a different reason. Apparently his bodyguard had lost him in the crowd. He hadn't seen Drew race off like a frightened rabbit.

They didn't go in. There was a tiny bistro three doors down, away from the noise and curious faces. Music and mist floated in the open door, but the narrow room was dark and quiet, with lights over the bar and candles on the tables. A few customers were talking, their hands flying in occasional counterpoint or emphasis.

Drew went to the bar for their drinks, leaving Rose staring moodily at the fat, red candle on the table. Roberts found a spot at the end of the bar.

Drew wondered if the story of his flight from the dancing was making the rounds back at the café. So far, he'd bungled the evening badly. He wanted to get this next part right, but wasn't sure how to procced.

Rose was still studying the candle as if it held all sorts of secrets and solutions when he returned. She didn't look up when he set her wine in front of her, sat down and spoke. "I mentioned my cousin Lorenzo earlier."

"You said something about having a message from him."

"He'd like you to work with him."

Her head jerked up. "What?"

"Police departments work with psychics sometimes. He needs leads. He's willing to try this."

"I'm not."

She sounded very definite. Drew studied her. Her lids were lowered, the lush eyelashes screening whatever was happening in those expressive eyes. She started digging little fissures in the softened rim of the candle with a fingernail, letting the melted wax escape in lavalike runnels. As the pool of wax went down, exposing the wick, the flame grew larger. "Why not?" he asked.

"You don't know what you're asking." Now her eyes lifted, meeting his. Her eyebrows were drawn in an uncompromising frown.

"Explain it to me."

"Just like that?" She gave a half laugh. "Drew, you don't even believe in psychic phenomena."

"My belief or lack of it doesn't determine reality. People once believed, based on good evidence, that the world was flat."

"That open mind of yours." This time she didn't laugh. She just looked tired. "Maybe you're willing to change your mind if I can prove you wrong, but I'm not interested in proving anything."

"I'm not asking you to. Listen." Impatient, he claimed her hand. Her palm was very warm. "If Lorenzo is willing to give you a chance, why can't you try? Don't you want to see the bastards caught?"

"Oh, unfair. Of course I want them caught. But I'm not…" She sighed and pulled her hand back. "I'll try to explain. I doubt you'll accept what I say, but I'll try. First, I use the word *psychic* because that's the term you understand, but I was raised to think of myself as Gifted."

"I see."

She chuckled. "No, you don't. You're trying not to let on that you think I'm a few bubbles shy of a full bath, and my family must be weird, too."

"I can accept that what you say is fact to you."

"Good enough." She sipped her wine, her brows drawn slightly in thought. "I won't begin at the beginning, because that goes back a little too far—more than twenty generations. The women in my family have always been Gifted, you see, some only slightly, some…quite strongly. Of course we aren't the only ones. The Gifts—psychic abilities—appear in people all over the world, and I suspect that almost everyone has some trace of them. But because they have appeared so consistently and strongly in those of my blood, they have been studied. We know a great deal about how these abilities work, how to nurture and train them. And how to protect ourselves from them."

"There is some danger in these, ah, Gifts?"

"The stronger the Gift, the greater the danger. Especially if the Gifted is unaware and untrained." The delicate skin around her eyes tightened and she looked away. Once more she started playing with the softened candle wax, this time pushing the sides in toward the wick, forcing the melted wax higher on the wick. The flame retreated, diminished, until it was a small, stubborn bubble of fire, nearly drowned.

It was obvious she believed utterly in what she was saying. Drew thought of the *fioreanno* she hadn't had, the father she'd never known and the way she'd smiled so brightly when she told him her mother had never been married. His throat ached with pity. There was a great deal she hadn't said, a great deal he knew from Lorenzo that he had no business knowing. Such as how her mother died.

Yet she understood and applauded the strengths of the society that had made her an outsider. Was it surprising, then, that she would cling so fiercely to a set of beliefs, however bizarre, that gave her a heritage? That sense of belonging may have been what gave her the strength to reject bitterness.

"You're trained, though, I take it?" he said carefully. "And certainly not unaware. Wouldn't that lessen the danger?"

"Yes, but…the nature of the danger varies according to the nature of the Gift, which is fourfold—what you would call telepathy, empathy, healing and prophecy. We name them Air, Water, Earth and Fire. My Gift is Fire. I see visions."

He didn't want to know any more. The tally of her delusions was already troubling. But she posed a threat to people who liked to deal with their problems by killing. He had to persuade her to cooperate with Lorenzo. "And what is the nature of your danger?"

She raised her eyes to his. Some trick of the light reflected the tiny candle flame there, twinned. "Burning, of course," she said. Suddenly she breached the candle wall with one finger, spilling the liquid wax. The flame leaped high, higher. And she set her hand, flat-palmed, atop that flame.

He seized her wrist and yanked her hand away.

The wick smoked, dead and black, filling the air with

the pungent scent of a just-snuffed candle. He turned her hand over.

Her palm was unmarked. There was no reddened spot, no sooty residue. Nothing.

His gaze flew to her face. Her expression was clear, remote, smiling. "A little fire like that can't hurt me. It's the big ones I fear."

It had been a trick, of course. The candle must have been extinguished before her palm touched it. "That's why you won't help?"

She pulled her hand away. "I *can't* help. From what I can tell, psychics who work with the police—the ones who aren't charlatans, that is—are empaths or telepaths. I'm not. I can't slide inside a terrorist's mind that way."

She was too calm. He didn't think she was lying, exactly, but she was holding something back. "What aren't you telling me?"

"All sorts of things. It would take rather longer than you and I have to pass on the accumulated lore of the last thousand years." She stood. "I think, for me, the party's over. It's time I went home."

He shoved his chair back and stood, too, reaching across the table to grab her wrist—as if he had to anchor her to keep her from vanishing as suddenly as the snuffed candle flame. "A thousand years?"

When she lifted her eyebrows that way, she reminded him of his grandmother, who was capable of depressing pretension at twenty paces with just such an expression. "Roughly that. Twenty-seven generations, to be precise, traced through the female line. I could recite my begats for you."

"Twenty-seven generations' worth?"

"I had to memorize them as a child. Look, Drew, this evening hasn't gone as either of us intended. I think it's best I saw myself home."

"That isn't happening." He moved around the table, transferring his grip from her wrist to her hand. "Does your aunt believe all this, too?"

"Of course. She taught me a good deal of the lore." Rose didn't protest his hold on her hand as they left the bistro. She ignored it.

The mist had deepened, thick enough now to dampen his face when he stepped outside. Overhead, the sky was lost in the drizzling darkness; on the street, lights from shops, cafés, the piazza and lampposts were draped in gauzy drifts. It was still early, barely ten o'clock, and the weather didn't seem to have discouraged anyone. The sidewalk held plenty of others with their own goals for the night.

Drew wondered at himself. Why did he keep seizing her hand? It would have been reassuring to put the urge down to desire, but it wasn't a woman's hand he usually wanted to hold. "Does your aunt have one of these Gifts?"

"Yes, though hers isn't strong. She's Earth-Gifted—a healer, among other things."

"What other things?"

"Oh, children and puppies adore her, plants grow for her and she loves to cook. She can take a headache away, ease a fever or speed the healing of cuts, breaks, burns, scrapes or scratches. She also acts as my...but that wouldn't be of interest to a confirmed skeptic like you."

The way she cut off whatever she'd been about to say left Drew a bread-crumb trail he intended to follow. When they reached the street corner, though, where an awning kept the mist out, he stopped. "The car's about four blocks away. Why don't you wait here while I get it?" She'd be safe. He'd glimpsed Roberts in the crowd, hanging back in an effort to be unobtrusive. He'd tell the man to stay with her.

"But there's no need for that!" Rose tipped her face up

into the dampness, letting it dew her cheeks. "This feels good."

"Your affinity for fire doesn't make you dislike getting wet, then."

"It doesn't work that way. I enjoy the ocean." She started walking again, so he kept pace with her.

The street beside them was busy with buses, bicycles, cars and taxicabs, but traffic in Montebello was leisurely compared to the frenzied battle of Italian streets. For the most part the people, too, ambled along with a lack of haste typical of this city, an easy flow of workers in wrinkled cotton, young men in neatly pressed shirts with their arms around women in bright dresses, teens of both sexes in jeans and Reeboks, old men in stiff shoes and black pants, and old women with shawls and full skirts. Here and there he saw a uniform—police or army. Most of the faces held the sun-kissed duskiness of the Mediterranean peoples, though a few were tourist-pale or African-dark. He didn't see a single umbrella.

"So you like the water?" he asked after a moment.

"My family's lore says that a Fire-Gifted who fears or dislikes water is out of balance. It's rather like the Chinese system of *feng shui,* in which the elements have a constructive and a destructive or balancing cycle. Fire without water to cool it becomes purely destructive."

"I've heard of *feng shui,*" he said neutrally. He wasn't interested in it, any more than he was in fortune-telling or numerology. But people told him things. "The astrological signs are divided along similar lines, too, aren't they? And, ah, what's it called—the witchcraft religion. It refers to earth, air, fire and water, too, doesn't it?"

"Wicca, you mean? There are similarities in most of the mystical or magical systems, probably for the same reason religions all over the world value the same qualities—like love, kindness, courage, loyalty, honesty. Some things are universal. As for astrology... Drew, you don't believe that nonsense, do you?''

He delivered his line with appropriate shock. ''You mean you don't?''

''I don't mean to criticize anyone who does believe in it, but it seems silly. Though I suppose a half-awake seer might be able to use horoscopes to tap into her abilities,'' she conceded. ''It can't be worse than using a crystal ball.''

''You don't believe in astrology or use a crystal ball. My illusions are shattered.''

''You're teasing me,'' she said resignedly.

''So why don't you use a crystal ball?''

''Real crystal can be useful, but those glass globes people call crystal balls aren't of much use, except as a neutral focus. Glass is a psychic insulator. Drew, do you really want to hear all this? I feel as if I'm delivering a lecture in Psychic Studies 101.''

''I want to hear it.''

''All right.'' Her attention seemed fixed on the sidewalk in front of her, or else on an interior landscape. ''Many materials hold psychic impressions. Some contain or insulate them, some disperse them, like water or salt—that's why they're used in cleansing rituals. Gemstones intensify whatever is impressed on them, which is probably why they've often been thought to have magical properties. Being Fire-Gifted, I'm especially sensitive to the emanations of materials that have been through fire, such as metal or pottery.''

''I see. Your abilities aren't limited to visions.''

Her sudden tension revealed itself in the way her fingers tightened, then relaxed in his, telling him he'd followed the trail correctly. ''I do pick up impressions from objects sometimes. From animals and people, too. But not the way an empath or telepath would, so I don't see how I could help.''

"What kind of impressions do you get from people?"

"I feel their *èsseri*—call it their essence, or their auras. When I'm close to someone, it feels as if the air is denser, slightly resistant. And I get a sort of blunt sense of who this person is. Like a smell, I guess. Just as dogs recognize a person by scent, I recognize people by the way their auras feel."

"But you don't pick up actual thoughts? I can see why you didn't think you could help. But," he added thoughtfully, "I don't understand why you were so reluctant to tell me about this."

"Don't you?" Her mouth twisted. "But then, right now you don't believe any of this is real. Think about how you'd feel if you did believe it, or just started wondering if it was true. Would you want to be around someone you thought could read your mind?"

"I suppose not. But this business of feeling people's auras isn't like reading their minds."

"No. I don't pick up thoughts. Sometimes I can tell when someone is lying, if I'm close enough. Well—almost always," she corrected herself reluctantly. "But a lie detector does the same thing, and that evidence would be admissible in court. My testimony wouldn't."

"And is what you pick up from objects similar? A unique 'scent' from those who have handled them?"

She shot him an annoyed look. "You're persistent. If I didn't know better, I'd think you were taking this seriously."

He took it very seriously. He didn't believe it—hell, he'd lied to her consistently and successfully. But her life might depend on his finding the right argument. "If you could pick up a residual aura from fragments of the bomb, you might be able to identify the person who planted it."

She bit her lip and looked down. The sidewalk here was old and canted as it climbed a hill. It glistened damply in the red-and-blue light from a neon sign on the store they were passing. So did her hair, black and lustrous.

Hunger bit, and frustration. He wanted his hands in her hair, his mouth on hers again. And didn't dare touch her.

"It's called psychometry," she said quietly. "And yes, it might work. I hadn't thought of trying to trace the bomber that way. Are the fragments metal?"

He had no idea if they'd even recovered any fragments. "I'll have to check with Lorenzo about that. Will you do it?"

She nodded slowly. "I'll try, anyway. Tell him not to expect too much. Even if I do pick up a clear impression, I won't be able to identify the person it came from unless I already know who that *èssere* belongs to."

"Good." Satisfaction filled him. At least he'd done one thing right tonight. As for the rest of it... He stopped, facing her and putting his hands on her shoulders.

Her skin was slick from the mist, but warm, not chilled. His thumbs moved, savoring the softness. "What I say next has nothing to do with Lorenzo or anything he wants from you. This is just from me." It was true. True enough to worry his security-minded cousin. Hell, it worried him, too. "I want to see you again."

The dim light made secrets of her eyes, and her voice was too low to give anything away. But her shoulders were tense beneath his hands. "How long will you be in Montebello, Drew? A week? Two?"

"I haven't decided. My business..." He shrugged. "It's flexible. I can handle a great deal of it from here."

A small smile. "I thought you were an international playboy. That's a job with duties you could fulfill pretty much anywhere."

"You've been reading your aunt's magazines."

The smile widened. "I look at the pictures sometimes."

He thought of the one picture he knew she'd seen—him,

bare-bummed on a nude beach on the Riviera. The woman
he'd gone there with hadn't been in the photograph, but
there'd been several coy references to her in the accompanying article. "There was a time when I worked hard to
earn my reputation. I've grown up some since then, but no
one wants to read about my real-estate investments for
some reason." His thumbs moved over damp, warm skin.
"Is that a problem for you? My reputation?"

"No. But you aren't going to be here long." She paused.
"I didn't think that would be a problem, before...before
you kissed me. Now...I don't know what I want now."

He knew what he wanted—to follow the heat that moved
between them, see where it led. He wanted his hands on
her, and his mouth, and he wanted to know what sound she
would make when he drove inside her. And if they had
been alone, if only they'd been somewhere private right
now, he was almost sure he could have found out.

Unless, of course, he went crazy on her. That would be
a real mood spoiler. "You said you liked the ocean. Have
you ever been snorkeling?"

"A few times. But—"

"Come with me tomorrow. There's a private beach at-
tached to the palace grounds, a little cove that's perfect for
snorkeling."

Tartly she said, "I'm not royal or noble or rich. I can't
close my shop on a whim to go play."

"You must close it sometimes." He moved closer, thinning the space between them until he could catch her
scent—roses and musk, an unexpected blend of the culti-
vated and the wild. Like her. His fingers curved around her
arms, rubbing lightly. "When can you get away?"

"I haven't decided to get away with you. Or even to see
you again." Her expression was haughty, like a cat that
hasn't given permission to be petted. But her breath was

hasty. "I need time and space to make that decision. I want you to back off."

"That would probably be the smart thing to do." Her hair turned frisky when it was damp, he noticed, losing its sleek gloss to curls. He pushed it back with one hand, tucking those wayward curls behind her ear so he could see her face better. Neon light, filtered by mist, fell rosy and soft on the curve of her cheek and jaw.

He really should back off. She'd asked him to. But maybe it would be best to find out if he was going to lose more than his control every time he kissed her.

Bending, he claimed her mouth.

Her lips were warmer than the skin he'd caressed. Her hands flew to his shoulders—maybe to push him away, but she didn't. Instead, her fingers dug into his skin. Held on. Hunger twisted through him, smoky and treacherous.

He wouldn't lose control this time. If he took it slow, held back, maybe he'd be safe. Maybe he could go on kissing her, holding her.

He fitted her into the curve of his body. She felt perfect there, held tight against him. She made a small sound. His arms tightened, and his mouth took. But the hands that had been kneading his shoulders were pushing against him. She was trying to end the kiss, to stop him—and he didn't want to stop. Instead of letting her go, he held on more tightly. *I can make her accept my kiss, accept me…*

The thought echoed in a suddenly empty mind. He was thinking of forcing her? Shaken, he loosened his arms.

She tore herself free. Her chest was heaving. Her hands were clenched into fists at her sides. But it wasn't anger he saw in her eyes. It was fear.

Appalled, he could only say he was sorry, that he had never meant to frighten her. Then he thought he should have kept his fool mouth shut, because a woman with her pride wouldn't like being accused of fear.

She took a steadying breath, met his eyes and said something that made no sense. "I know. But you can hardly help scaring me." And she turned and walked away.

He stayed with her, of course. In silence. In silence they climbed into his car, and neither of them spoke for several blocks. He told himself he was being ridiculous—he'd grown up knowing how to make social small talk. This silence shouldn't be hard to fill. But she was the one who spoke first.

"I suppose you'll tell His Grace that I've agreed to help, if I can."

"I'll let him know." They'd left the busy streets behind. Here, near her shop, the street was almost empty. He could see Roberts's little Fiat in the rearview mirror. "I've screwed things up, haven't I?"

"It's not you. Or rather, it is you, but it's me, too." Her laugh was shaky and short, but genuine. "And if you understood that, please explain it to me."

"You're confused about what you want. There's a hell of a lot I'm not too sure of myself, but I know what I want." He double-parked in front of her shop. "I'll walk you upstairs."

"There's no need. Truly." She turned in her seat to face him. "Once you've had time to think it over, you'll probably be relieved things ended between us when they did."

The muscles along his shoulders tensed. "You said you needed time to think, not that you were refusing to see me again."

"Drew." She shook her head slightly. "I'm confused, yes, for a lot of reasons, but mainly because I had a psychic moment."

He smiled, relieved. If that was her main objection, he could find a way to reassure her. "Is that what happened?"

"Can you honestly say you're still interested in me? A woman who thinks she has visions?"

"Oh, yes. I want to see a great deal more of you. And I mean that in every way, including the one that worries you."

Her expression was calm, but her fretful fingers told another story as they slid the pendant back and forth on its chain. "That's honest, at least. I'm not sure it's flattering, since you think I'm nuts."

"I think you're brave and smart and lovely. Will you go to the ocean with me as soon as you can take some time off?"

"I...no, I don't think so."

"You pick the place, then."

She grimaced. "Pushing me to make a decision won't get you the answer you're looking for."

He wanted to push her, to make her agree, but some sliver of conscience or common sense held him back. "Just a minute," he said, and got a business card from his wallet. He scribbled a number on the back of it and handed it to her. "That's my cell-phone number, so you won't have to go through the palace switchboard. Call me. Day or night, whenever you decide, call."

She turned the card over, studying it as if it held a mystery more significant than a private number. "All right."

When she got out, he didn't stop her. He watched as she climbed the stairs, forcing himself to sit in the car instead of seeing her to her door. The drizzle had stopped, leaving the air clear, the shadows stark. A car moved slowly around him.

No doubt he was blocking traffic. He couldn't bring himself to care. He watched as she opened the door, watched as it closed behind her. And still he sat there like a fool with nowhere to go, feeling as alone as he ever had in his life.

Chapter 8

Rose knew her aunt had waited up for her before she reached the top step. Strains of an aria from *Carmen* drifted out through the walls and door, and the window nearest the door glowed.

Damn. Rose wasn't sure she wanted to talk about what had happened tonight. Not yet. She jabbed her key in the lock and twisted.

"Couldn't sleep?" she asked dryly as she closed the door behind her.

Gemma was curled up in the big green recliner reading a magazine. Her hair was braided for the night, as usual. The long braid hung over one shoulder of her powder-blue robe. She looked absurdly young. "I'm thinking of diversifying a little more," she said placidly. "There's an interesting article in the *Economist* about utility bonds."

Rose shook her head. Gemma sometimes had trouble with simple addition. She had no problem with esoteric economic principles, however, or investment strategy. Her portfolio wasn't large, but it was as healthy as her herb garden. "Well, you can stay up and read if you like," she said lightly. "I'm for bed."

"That's fine, dear," Gemma said, putting the magazine down and uncoiling her legs. "I'll make you some tea. Chamomile, I think. You'll need a little help sleeping tonight."

Rose's breath huffed out in exasperation. "How do you *do* that? I know darned good and well you aren't reading my mind."

Gemma padded up to Rose and patted her cheek softly. *"Cara mia,* I know you. I don't need telepathy to know when you're hurting. Maybe valerian would be better than chamomile?"

Abruptly Rose's eyes stung. "Aunt Gemma, he's an empath. A very strong, completely blocked empath."

"Oh, my dear. I'm so sorry." She blinked as her eyes, too, filled. "That poor boy. But he can't be completely blocked, can he? I really don't think he's homicidal."

Her laugh was ragged. "No. No, Drew isn't a sociopath. I exaggerated. His shields are thick and strong and utterly involuntary, but there must be some leakage I can't detect. Maybe another empath could, if we could find a strong Water-Gifted who isn't nutty."

"There's my cousin Pia...well, no, I suppose not. She's strong, but..."

"Nutty," Rose said wryly. "She's blocked, too."

"Her shields are voluntary," Gemma said chidingly. "But I suppose she wouldn't be very helpful. She doesn't process what she receives well. There's Cousin Gerald, too, but he only has a thimbleful of the Gift...and Gerald's daughter is only seven, so I don't think she..." Gemma sighed. "I'm not sure how much it would help to have another empath try to read Drew, anyway. He isn't likely to cooperate. Unless he's had some training?'' she ended hopefully.

"He's completely unaware, from what I could tell. He doesn't believe in psychic nonsense.''

"Still, you were able to get past his shields at some point. You must have, or you wouldn't know he's an empath.''

"His shield slipped.'' She hugged herself, thinking of the split second when he'd been unshielded. He'd been kissing her...such a tiny slice of time to change her world so completely. "Just for a moment, it slipped. And scared him half out of his mind.''

"I'm sure it did, since he doesn't believe in any of this. Though he can't have been so completely blocked all of his life, surely. He seems to function very well.''

Silence fell. Rose thought of all the ways an untrained empath could fail to "function well.'' The Water-Gifted were in danger two ways—from the deluge of emotions their Gift exposed them to, and from blocking that Gift. It was impossible to predict what damage a blocked Gift would do, but Rose thought of it like water backed up in a dam. The results varied depending on where the dam was located, but one effect was inevitable: the conscious part of the blocked empath slowly dried up, becoming parched of emotion, while behind the dam the power built. And built. Until eventually no dam—no block—could hold it.

The solution was shields, not blocks—soft, layered shields that were flexible and porous, allowing some leakage. Shields the empath controlled. Shields that were acquired, learned, from childhood on.

Rose didn't know an adult empath with Drew's power who hadn't been trained from childhood. Because without that training, they generally went insane.

"There's something...'' A faint wrinkle formed in

Gemma's smooth, round forehead. "Something I can't quite bring to mind. I read it a long time ago..."

"Something you read about Drew?"

She nodded. "Not about any of his affairs or that woman he was engaged to. This was long before that." She sighed. "Oh, well. I suppose it will come to me eventually."

"He was engaged?" Rose asked, startled.

"Oh, yes, years ago. It ended quite sadly—the poor thing wasn't very stable, apparently. She tried to kill herself."

"Dear God."

"Of course, the tabloids printed a lot of nonsense about it. You know I don't take the things they say seriously."

"Of course not," Rose murmured.

"And it was all very one-sided, making Lord Andrew sound like a beast. I remember feeling sorry for him. It can't be pleasant to be accused of driving your fiancée to attempt suicide—assuming, of course, he *isn't* a beast, and I don't think he is."

But she didn't sound sure, and Rose knew why. "I'm going to wash and get into my nightgown," she said abruptly.

Gemma patted her arm. "I'll make your tea."

All evening Rose had been calling up everything she remembered of the lore as it applied to the Water-Gifted. It wasn't encouraging. She creamed off her makeup and tried to be realistic.

Most people had a touch of empathy, just as many were brushed lightly by the other Gifts—dreams did sometimes come true, close friends or lovers sometimes knew what the other was thinking, and nurses, mothers and doctors often did bring comfort with a touch. In small doses, the Gifts were normal and human. They didn't become troublesome until they reached a sort of critical point, when the Gift was too strong to remain unnoticed.

Empaths were the least stable of the Gifted when the Gift

was strong, for obvious reasons. A strongly empathic baby didn't distinguish between its feelings and those of others. It never developed much sense of self.

The Gifts didn't usually show up in babies, of course. But an empathic toddler still suffered. Even the most loving of mothers had moments of anger, exhaustion, frustration, times when she just wanted her screaming or whining darling to shut up and go away. Such perfectly normal feelings didn't damage most children, and actually helped civilize the little monsters. They learned that temper fits didn't get them what they wanted.

An empathic child, however, *felt* its mother's anger and knew itself to be the object of that anger. This didn't make for a healthy child, or a healthy adult.

It all depends, Rose reminded herself as she slipped her nightgown over her head, on when Drew's Gift first appeared. The more powerful the Gift, the earlier its arrival—that was the maxim. But sometimes a Gift didn't manifest fully for years. Unfortunately her family's lore was confusing, even contradictory in places, about why or how a Gift's full strength might be delayed.

Gemma's cousin made that point quite adequately. Poor Pia. She'd been identified as a Water-Gifted soon after she was born, thanks to Rose's mother. Elenore Giaberti had been Fire-Gifted, like her daughter, and so able to touch the baby's *èssere.*

The members of Pia's family had done everything they could. It hadn't been enough. Oh, Pia wasn't damaged in the way an empathic baby in an unaware family might have been. But her Gift had been so strong. Pia had never been able to process the welter of emotions she received when unshielded, so she spent most of her life cut off from her Gift—with decidedly peculiar results. She was a gentle soul, mildly paranoid and convinced she talked to aliens.

But at least she'd been guided in developing her shields.

Some empaths developed shields naturally. And those who shielded too completely, from too young an age, felt no connection with their fellow humans. They became sociopaths.

Drew's Gift couldn't have shown up when he was still a baby, Rose thought as she sat on her bed and began brushing out her hair. If it had, he wouldn't have such a strong sense of self. And she couldn't, she *wouldn't*, believe he was sociopathic. She'd touched his *èssere*...

Her hand stilled, the brush, her hair, the room and everything else forgotten as she remembered. Such a tiny slice of time...

"Here's your tea, dear."

Rose stirred and put the brush down. She hadn't even noticed Gemma come in. "Yes. Thank you." The woodsy scent of chamomile soothed her. She took a sip.

"What are you going to do?"

She found a reassuring smile. "I'm a big, soggy, confused mess right now, but I'll be all right."

"That wasn't what I asked." Gemma's eyes were troubled. "I know what the lore says about one way to help a Water-Gifted release his shields. But it isn't a sure thing."

Gemma knew her too well. "I realize that."

Like a mother checking for fever, Gemma laid her hand on Rose's forehead. "Be gentle with yourself, *mia cara*."

She left. Rose took her cup and saucer over to the window and pushed the curtain back. The city sparkled at her, lively with lights in the darkness. She couldn't see the palace from her window, not even the hill it rested on. And she wanted to. If she could just look at the place where he was, maybe she wouldn't ache so badly.

Her eyes closed. She rested her forehead against the cool glass. Ah, this was bad, worse than she'd ever thought it might be. She could reach him. She knew how to send her *èssere* out, how to seek—

Gasping, she straightened and turned away from the window. Had she lost all sense? Send her *èssere* out, without a Ground to protect her? Send her essence out in search of Drew and encourage her Gift to grow, to strengthen? Did she *want* to burn?

She shivered, put down the cup of tea, now cold, and climbed into bed.

There were several ways that a blocked empath might be helped to release his shields. Most of them involved a long teaching process and a high level of trust on the part of the empath. Certainly the person being helped had to believe in the powers he'd blocked.

Drew wasn't going to be in Montebello long. He didn't fully trust her, and he certainly didn't believe either of them was psychic. Which left only one way for her to help him.

In sex, the barriers went down. Usually. Not always, but his shield *had* slipped when he was kissing her. If it went down all the way, even once, the backed-up pressure would be relieved…but with what results? If the shields went down when they made love, she'd be with him, bodies joined, èsseri touching. She'd be able to help him when the flood hit, but would she be able to help enough? She wasn't a healer. That wasn't her Gift or her training.

Rose shivered, pulled up the sheet and hugged her knees to her chest.

What was she going to do? She didn't know. But as she sat in the bed she'd slept in since she was eleven, feeling desperately alone, she remembered once more that moment when she'd touched all that Drew was. She remembered the one word that had come to her then.

Mine.

There were no windows in the bedroom Drew always used in his family's suite at the palace. The only light came from the glowing red numbers on the clock by his bed, which clicked over from 12:42 to 12:43 while he watched, keeping a methodical tally of his sleeplessness. He was nude beneath the sheet, and achingly awake.

He hadn't reported to Lorenzo in person this time. He'd left a message on his office phone, instead. The deceit was beginning to leave a foul taste, one he had no intention of exposing to his cousin. He could no longer believe Rose had anything to do with terrorism. She must have heard something she shouldn't.

She thought she had visions. That she could sense people's auras, pick up "emanations" from objects.

He rolled over, turning his back on the accusing numbers on the clock. Weren't hunches the result of the unconscious mind processing bits and pieces the conscious mind missed, leaving no logical trail to follow, only a gut feeling? Maybe Rose's visions were like that. Maybe she had an extremely clever unconscious, and it had resurrected some unremembered snatch of conversation she'd overheard, giving her a dream about the bombing that was all too accurate.

Why did it bother him, anyway, if she thought she was psychic? He'd been with women with odd notions before. That model he'd dated in Paris right after his disastrous engagement, for example. She hadn't gone to bed with him until she'd checked it out with her pet astrologer.

She'd done everything else, though. In the limo, right after they met at a party. He'd been taking her home. Wendy had been just what he needed at the time—hungry, self-absorbed, sure to lose interest quickly—everything poor Laura hadn't been. But Rose was nothing like Wendy.

She wasn't like Laura, either, thank God. She might not have notched her bedpost with the careless abandon of women like Wendy, but she was no fragile innocent, either. Deluded, maybe, when it came to this psychic business…but she'd been raised to believe as she did. And face it—compared to him, she was marvelously sane.

Had kissing Rose for the first time brought on the spell that hadn't quite happened? Or had it somehow averted the spell? Maybe desire was an antidote of sorts. Reality had stayed firmly in place the second time he kissed her.

His cell phone beeped. He'd left it on the table next to his bed. He picked it up without turning on a light, certain whose voice he would hear. "Yes?"

"I'll go to the ocean with you this Sunday after Mass. If you still want to."

Chapter 9

The beach Drew took her to that Sunday couldn't be seen from the palace. They were more than halfway down the path before she caught a glimpse of it. The land curved one slim arm around the little cove, sheltering it from the roughness of the open sea. From this high, the water looked glassy and green.

There was a reef, too, he'd told her. It would be a good place to snorkel.

They each had gear to carry—swim fins, face mask, towel and snorkel. In addition, Drew had a fancy insulated backpack filled with goodies from the palace kitchen. His free hand was wrapped around hers.

It wasn't necessary. She was surefooted and the path was well graded, not terribly steep. But she liked the idea that he wanted to hold on to her. She liked touching him. Her skin felt prickly, sensitive. The gauzy beach robe she wore over her swimsuit was long, slit up both sides, and with every step it brushed against her legs. The sun was hot, the breeze was salty and damp, and life filled her, packed down so tightly she fairly vibrated with it.

He'd been quiet since he picked her up. She wondered if the same thoughts were churning through his system that had her heart beating so fast.

Then he spoke and burst *that* bubble. "Lorenzo tells me you were able to, ah, get an impression from one of the fragments."

"Yes."

"He said you insisted that your aunt be present."

"Aunt Gemma is my Ground." She flicked him a glance. He wore dark-blue swim trunks with a polo shirt in some kind of nubby blend—linen and cotton, she thought. There were buttons. He hadn't buttoned them. The deep, open V-neck gave her a beguiling glimpse of his chest. "That's psychic jargon for someone who helps me keep planted in the here and now. Fire-Gifted have a tendency to wander when in trance. We're easily distracted."

"Is this trance business safe?"

"A lot safer when Gemma is with me."

The bomb had been in a metal first-aid kit. A little terrorist humor there, she supposed grimly. She'd been given a blackened piece of the handle. The traces of *èssere* clinging to it had been slight, almost unnoticeable at first. She'd had to trance deeply to fasten on to those traces, had to resist the pull of the moment when fire had burst free. She'd succeeded, but it hadn't been easy.

"You told him the bomb had been planted by someone who worked at the airport. Someone in a uniform." He sounded skeptical.

Dammit, wasn't he feeling any of the excitement she felt? "Someone who belonged there," she corrected him mildly. "He might be a security guard. He might not. There was a feeling of..." She paused, groping for words. "I didn't get any sense that he was out of place, somewhere he wasn't supposed to be."

"How could you tell? You said you didn't pick up thoughts or feelings."

"Normally I don't. But very strong feelings do become imprinted sometimes, and the fragment they gave me is connected to fire because it went through the explosion. That makes a difference. I went to a particular moment, the last time that object was handled before fire burned everything."

He shook his head. "You're not making much sense to me, I'm afraid."

"Language is built on common referents. I'm trying to describe an experience that took place outside those referents."

He didn't say anything more for a few minutes. The path curved around an outthrust portion of the cliff, and suddenly the beach lay right in front of them—a small slice of perfection nestled at the base of the cliff. The sand was pale and coarse, almost blindingly bright in the sunshine. Near the waterline it was strewn with the usual detritus of the sea—seaweed, shells. Little waves ruffled the turquoise surface of the ocean, frothing gently as they reached the shore, like soda with most of the fizz gone. It was peaceful and lovely...and very private. This beach was connected to the palace grounds. Drew's bodyguard hadn't followed him here.

Her spirits lifted as she left the dusty path for hot sand.

Rose didn't want to discourage Drew's curiosity. The closer he could come to accepting the reality of psychic abilities, the better. But the day was bright and lovely and she didn't want to be weird, different, the odd one who was tolerated, even liked, but never fully accepted. Today, she just wanted to be a woman playing in the surf and the sun with her man.

"You could tell that the bomber was a man, though."

She repressed a sigh. "Sex usually comes through very clearly." So did other things. She remembered the *èssere* of the man who'd handled the bomb, the small, dark, greedy feel of him. "He isn't anyone I know. Your cousin plans to have me meet the security guards and see if I can identify one of them."

"Your hand is cold." He stopped. "I'm upsetting you. I don't mean to doubt you, but this is all pretty strange to me."

"You're skeptical, which I understand. You're also curious, and that I'm glad about." Glad for more reasons than she could tell him or he could accept. "But it was... unpleasant, touching that man's *èssere*. I'd like to put it out of my mind now."

"I didn't bring you here to interrogate you. I'm sorry." He dropped his gear, shrugged out of the backpack and touched her chin, tilting her face up. The creases beneath his eyes deepened. "You've been very patient with me."

"I'm glad you noticed." The sensation of being filled to the brim came bubbling back. "I would have pointed it out myself, but I couldn't think of a patient way to do that."

He grinned.

Rose had seen many different smiles on Drew's face. Often just his eyes smiled. Sometimes only his mouth was involved and the smile never reached his eyes. A couple times his whole face had gotten into the act. But she hadn't seen him grin before. Suddenly there were deep grooves in his cheeks and his eyes were wicked and happy. *Why,* she thought, *his face is made for big, fat, know-it-all grins.*

He bent, brushed her lips quickly with his, then stepped back. "If I don't keep my hands to myself, I'm afraid we won't make it into the water."

"That would be a shame. I bought a new swimsuit yesterday." Smiling mischievously, she dropped her fins and snorkel, kicked off her sandals and squished her toes into the sunbaked sand. Her long beach robe snapped up the front. She took hold of the neckline and tugged, and one by one those snaps parted, letting the gauzy material settle to the ground at her feet.

Her swimsuit wasn't daring, not by the standards he was used to. On some European beaches women went topless, with little thong bikini bottoms covering the very barest of essentials. Rose's suit was red, one-piece and smooth to the throat. But the legs were cut up to her hipbones, and the material was thin. Very thin. And stretchy.

There wasn't much he didn't know about her body now. And from the look in his eyes, he liked what he saw.

He reached for her and she danced back, laughing. "Uh-uh. Let's get wet."

His fiery Rose turned out to be a water rat.

She played. She pounced. She tried to drown him. When they were in the deepest part of the little cove, near the reef, she dived deep, swam underneath him and bit his toe.

The reef was a good distance from the shore, but even before he knew how at home she was in the water, he hadn't worried about that. With the tide out they could walk about half the way, waist-deep in the warm Mediterranean. The sun was hot, his muscles were loose and warm, and the woman beside him was beautiful. And happy. She had her own glow, Rose did, that warmed him in a way the sun never could.

"I should make you carry everything," he told her. "You've exhausted me."

"Wimp." She sounded immensely satisfied. "You aristocrats have no staying power. We peasant women have had to be strong, having all those babies while we're out tilling the fields."

"Done that a lot, have you?" he asked with interest. "It

doesn't show." Her hair hung down her back, sleek and dripping, while her swimsuit... God almighty. *Everything* showed. If she'd painted herself red, it wouldn't have been any more revealing.

He looked away. "I might be able to summon a little energy if you feed me."

"If you wait for me to feed you, you could end up with scraps. I've worked up quite an appetite."

So had he. But he wasn't going to act on it. Yet.

It wasn't conscience or any gentlemanly constraints that held him back. He intended to have her today, here on the beach, with the sun shining down on them. But he had to be careful, stay in control. He didn't think he could stand it if one of his crazy spells hit while he was making love to Rose, and he came back to himself to see fear and pity in her eyes.

So when they reached the dry sand, she spread the light throw that had been in the backpack and he helped her set out the wine, cheese, bread and fruit. He concentrated on conversation while they ate, trying not to glance too often at her full breasts, or her long legs, or the slight roundness of her stomach.

That bloody swimsuit was so snug he could see the indention of her belly button. He popped an olive into his mouth and cocked his leg up to hide the evidence of his interest.

She'd made it clear she didn't want to touch on the heavy stuff anymore, so he avoided anything to do with terrorists or psychic bull. Instead, he asked her about making jewelry and learned that she'd taught herself bookkeeping. He told her about his business. "Why real estate?" she asked at one point.

He shrugged. "For all the obvious reasons, I suppose. I'm a second son—I wasn't going to inherit the family land, so I set out to own as much property elsewhere as possible.

I had a small inheritance from a great-aunt that got me started.''

"Do you like it, though? The whole process, I mean—evaluating properties, buying and selling them. Or is it the end result you like—the money, the ownership, coming out on top?''

The question startled him. He hadn't thought about what he did in those terms. "All of the above, I suppose," he said slowly. "I enjoy having money, of course. But these days I enjoy the game more than the ownership. I discovered I was good at it, and we usually enjoy the things we're good at.''

Somehow from that, he'd found himself telling her about tax laws in Tokyo. Tax laws, for God's sake! Admittedly it was something he knew all too much about, since he currently owned investment properties in seven countries. But it was hardly a subject with which to beguile a beautiful woman. So he asked about her aunt. Before he knew it, she'd turned the conversation to *his* family, and he ended up talking about the paparazzi and what it was like to have his life made into public property.

It was damned disconcerting. Not that he didn't talk with the women he went to bed with. He did. Mostly, though, he listened. He wasn't used to talking about himself and couldn't understand why he was doing so much of it today. Except that he was comfortable with her. It was a strange thing to realize, when he was so aroused that his erection twitched every time she moved.

Was this how people felt with him? he wondered. As if they could say anything, anything at all, and it would be all right?

"That was good." She patted her stomach, then slid her plate into the backpack and pulled out a tube of cream. "We should probably put some more sunscreen on. Wouldn't want your delicate English skin to blister.''

There was a light dusting of sand on her thigh, pale against the dusky skin. He wanted to smooth it off. "You hardy peasants don't get sunburned, I take it."

"I've got more melanin protecting me, paleface." Her finger made a little circle in the air. "Turn around and I'll put some on your back."

He didn't move. "Rose, if you put your hands on me now, I'll have your swimsuit off in two minutes. Maybe less. Is that what you want?"

Her eyes widened. "I didn't— You haven't—" She stopped, frowned and said, "You haven't shown any signs of being overwhelmed by lust."

"I'm hoping to avoid being overwhelmed. I'd like to keep enough control to do a few of the things I've been fantasizing about." He plucked the tube of sunscreen from her lax fingers. "Rose, you're not naive. You've seen me looking at you in that damned swimsuit." Then he did what he'd been wanting to do and brushed at the sand on her thigh.

Her skin was warm and dry. She shivered. He curled his hand around her thigh and looked at his hand on her, looked at all that smooth, dusky skin and the scarlet tease of her swimsuit. His heart pounded. Slowly he dragged his gaze up to her face. Her pupils were dilated.

She liked his hand on her.

The knowledge sent a rush of pleasure through him. "You know why I asked you to swim here, where we would be alone. You know what I want."

Her head moved in a tiny nod.

"If that isn't what you want, you need to say so now."

She didn't answer. Not in words. Instead, she took the sunscreen from him and put it down. Then she slid her arms around his neck. Her fingers teased the hair at his nape. Her voice was unsteady. "You sure there aren't any paparazzi around with telephoto lenses?"

"I can't guarantee anything." He eased her up against him, and everywhere she touched it felt like sparklers going off just under his skin, a thousand tiny flashes of heat. "Not a damned thing, Rose. I wish I could." And he kissed her.

He'd thought he was prepared. But there was no way to be ready for the rush of hunger, the sudden hollowing of his stomach, as if the world had suddenly dropped out from under him. Her mouth was sweet and giving, and it wasn't enough. He needed more. He didn't want her willing, he wanted her wild, wanted her as lost as he was in a strange, high country where the air was thin and the blood pumped thick and hot.

He ran his hand up her thigh, along her hip, finding the dampness of her suit, the curve of her belly. He loved the feel of her stomach, the curves and softness of her. He lingered there a moment, caressing her waist, feeling her muscles shift as she moved, bringing herself more fully against him. Making him shudder.

Cupping her breast with one hand, he pressed her down onto her back. He couldn't make himself stop kissing her. Her taste was like a drug, and much as he wanted to sample her elsewhere, he couldn't tear himself away from her mouth. She made a small sound of approval, her hands eager on his shoulders, his back. His legs moved restlessly.

He tugged on one strap of her swimsuit. When she didn't protest, a fierce exultation seized him. This time she wasn't pushing him away. This time she wanted him.

Then, because he had to see, he pulled his mouth from hers. The damp suit clung to her skin. He needed both hands to peel it down, unwrapping her carefully, stopping when the scarlet clung to her waist.

Her breasts were full, her nipples dark and hard, the areoles large and pebbly. She was breathing quickly. He glanced at her face, wanting her to know how much she pleased him, excited him. Her lips were parted, her eyes swallowed by pleasure, and he knew she liked having him look at her.

"We're going to end up with sand in all sorts of uncomfortable places." Her voice was breathy, happy.

"I don't mind," he assured her, and bent to taste.

She started to laugh, but it changed to a moan when he licked one upright nipple. He licked it thoroughly, then started to suck. She threaded her fingers through his hair, holding him to her.

He was almost sure he was going to last until he could get her out of that swimsuit, but knew he'd better not wait too much longer. He started tugging at it again, and she distracted him by squirming, her hips pushing against him.

He knew what she wanted. Firmly he cupped her, and her quick gasp of pleasure made the delay worthwhile. He massaged her gently, making sure the heel of his hand put the pressure where she needed it.

Her head tilted back, and her low moan sent his blood surging. She clutched his wrist. "Drew...oh. Oh, my. I need to tell you..." Her voice ended in a gasp as he rotated his hand.

He kept his movements small and careful, clinging to the edge of his control, and smiled tightly. "Yes?"

"I...you should know before we go much further...I'm something of a newcomer to this."

He froze. No. No, she didn't mean that the way it sounded. She couldn't. He spoke with the same care and precision he'd been using with his hand. "You're sexually experienced."

"Well—yes. Sort of. But technically, I'm a virgin."

Technically?

He threw himself off her, rolling onto his back. His chest heaved. He stared up at the sky, so angry he didn't trust himself to speak or move. He didn't watch her sit and pull her swimsuit back up, but he knew from the slight sounds, the corner-of-the-eyes glimpses, that she was covering herself.

Then she spoke. "If this is some kind of...of excess of gallantry, you'd better get over it fast."

She sounded nearly as furious as he was. "I do not—ever—seduce virgins." His jaw was so tight he had to grit the words out.

"Here's a news flash—I was the one seducing you, and a hard time I was having of it, too, for a while. So you can tuck your overactive conscience back where it belongs, and—"

"Let me put it this way." He sat up and began slinging the remains of their picnic into the backpack without looking at her. "I don't go to bed with women who don't know the score."

"The score?" Her voice rose. "Is that what this is about—scoring? Are we playing soccer? For God's sake, Drew." She made an effort to smooth the anger out of her voice and put a hand on his arm. "Talk to me. Tell me what's wrong."

He shook her off and stood. "Get your things together."

She muttered under her breath as she grabbed her towel and coverup—first in Italian, then in German. Drew recognized most of the Italian. He didn't know as much German, but he caught a couple of the words she used. His eyebrows shot up. Quite a vocabulary she had.

Anger was good, though, he thought as he yanked up the throw they'd nearly made love on, stashed it in the backpack and grabbed his gear. Anger was excellent. If she'd cried...but Rose wasn't the weepy sort. She'd probably cut off her arm before she let herself cry in front of him now.

He found himself hoping rather desperately that was true. "I wasn't being gallant," he said abruptly. "Or acting on my conscience. I'm a selfish man and I acted selfishly. I prefer experienced women."

The phrase she snapped out was in English this time. He ignored the insult to his mother, silently agreed with her opinion of his intelligence and started for the path.

He'd never set out to infuriate a woman before. It wasn't hard to do, even if it did leave him feeling like something the cat hacked up on the carpet.

She joined him on the path. "Does this infuriating nobility of yours—which I agree is damned selfish—have anything to do with the woman who tried to kill herself?"

"What?" Furious all over again, he made a mistake. He looked at her. "What do you know about Laura?"

Her eyes shimmered with unshed tears. She didn't try to hide them, either, meeting his gaze with stubborn pride. "You were engaged to marry her, and she tried to kill herself. That's all I know."

Something ripped inside him. He wanted to cup her cheek, to kiss the salt from her eyes. But he knew better than to touch her, so he started walking again. "Laura made the mistake of falling in love with a cold bastard who couldn't give her what she needed. I made the mistake of becoming involved with a clinging woman. I won't do it again."

"I'm not that vulnerable, Drew." She kept pace with him. "And I've never clung in my life."

"I've already hurt you. I'm not going to make things worse."

"You want to tell me what a thin little membrane has to do with whether I get hurt or not? Drew," she said, exasperated, "I may not have done the deed before, but I've enjoyed men and they've enjoyed me. I'm not completely inexperienced."

"How old are you?"

"Plenty old enough to make this decision for myself," she snapped.

"All right, I'll guess. You're under thirty, over twenty-five—"

"I'm twenty-seven, if it matters."

She wasn't looking at him now. That helped. "It matters. A woman doesn't make it to the age of twenty-seven with that little membrane intact unless it matters."

When she didn't answer, he knew he was right. Her virginity meant something to her. How could it not, if she'd waited this long to allow a man the final intimacy? She was Catholic, living in a country that clung to that bloody village mind-set he kept being reminded of. Maybe she had done some heavy petting. Maybe she'd done everything except intercourse. The fact remained that she'd stopped short of taking that final step, and there had to be a reason, a powerful one, for a woman as passionate as Rose to stop.

There had to be a reason, a powerful one, for her to decide not to stop, too.

Drew didn't want to think about that, but he couldn't seem to keep fom it. Either she'd hoped to barter her virginity for title, or she felt something for him—something strong, something that might be love.

He couldn't believe the one explanation. He was terrified of the other.

They trudged up the rest of the way in silence, as close physically as they had been when they went down the same path. Except, of course, that he wasn't holding her hand now. He would never hold it again.

Foolishly, it was that loss that burned in him more cruelly than anything else.

The drive back to the shop passed in stiff, miserable silence. Rose was disgusted with both of them. Obviously telling him she was a virgin had been a huge mistake. But she'd seen his face, felt the tension in his body. She hadn't wanted him to drive into her like a freight train. And how could she have known he had such a hang-up about it?

If she hadn't told him, though…he'd been close to losing control. Maybe, if she'd been less worried about a brief physical pain, his shield would have dropped. Maybe she would know what it was to be joined, body and soul, with the only man she would ever want to give herself to.

And maybe, she thought, shifting restlessly, he'd be twice as angry now and still locked tight behind his walls. There was no way of knowing.

When he turned off on her street, she swallowed hard. He didn't intend to see her again. She knew that, and it hurt.

He was such an idiot. She wasn't giving up, but how could she make the stupid man change his mind if she couldn't see him, talk to him?

Since it was Sunday, traffic was light and there was parking along the street. Drew pulled up right in front of her shop. Caught up in her unhappy thoughts, Rose gathered her things without looking at him. She didn't realize something else was wrong until he started cursing.

Her startled gaze flew to his face—and then she saw what he was staring at. Big red letters were sprawled across the window of her shop: *Non soffrirete una strega per vivere.*

Thou shalt not suffer a witch to live.

They'd added a crude drawing of flame, in lieu of punctuation.

So it had started. Rose's heart beat a little too fast and the sour taste in her mouth was more fear than anger. But her voice sounded level enough, at least. "I take it you read Italian."

"Well enough for this." He turned to her, and there was nothing smooth or detached about his face now. It blazed with anger. "I'm calling the police."

She shrugged and reached for the door handle. "It won't help."

"They can question your neighbors. Someone may have seen the son of a bitch who did this."

"And if they catch him, he'll be fined for vandalism. That won't erase the sentiment." She pushed the door open and got out.

She meant to go directly into the shop. There should be some turpentine in the back, and getting this cleaned off as quickly as possible sounded like a very good idea. Instead, she found herself standing right in front of the defaced window, looking at those dripping letters, at the crude, malevolent image of fire at the end of the sentence. Her mind was empty. Her stomach hurt.

She didn't know Drew had gotten out, too, until she felt his touch on her arm. "Rose. Lorenzo told me about your mother. I'm sorry, maybe he shouldn't have, but this... You need protection. It takes a truly sick mind to do something like this."

She couldn't argue with that. "More than one, probably. This sort travels in packs for courage."

"You don't seem surprised."

"I've been afraid of something like this ever since Captain Mylonas made it obvious he suspected I'd had a role in the bombing."

"All the more reason, then, to call the police. Or my cousin. Lorenzo can let it be known that you're cooperating with the authorities. That should reassure people you aren't connected to the terrorists."

She slid him a glance. He really didn't have a clue. But then, she'd been careful not to tell him all the reasons she'd been reluctant to work with the authorities. His cousin probably knew—the Sebastianis understood their people fairly well—but Drew came from outside her world. He hadn't realized what he was asking of her, and she hadn't wanted to burden him with that knowledge.

Probably not one of her brainier ideas. "It won't help. They'll just assume I've cast a spell on your cousin."

"They can't be that stupid."

That drew a short, hard laugh from her. "Never underestimate the power of fear combined with ignorance. Drew, the people who did this don't think I helped anyone plant a bomb. They think I caused the fire all by myself."

"That's crazy."

She didn't say anything. The vandals who had painted their threat across her window were ignorant and vicious and wrong about almost everything. But they were right about one thing, though Drew would never believe it.

She couldn't bespell people, that was true. And she hadn't caused the fire at the airport.

But she could have.

Chapter 10

Evening was stretching shadows behind the slim black rails of the iron fence surrounding the grounds, the sheltering trees and the still figures of the guards on duty at the gate when Drew pounded on Lorenzo's door.

His cousin opened the door himself, took one look at Drew's face and called over his shoulder, "It's Drew. I'll talk to him in the study." Then he stood back.

Drew made it halfway into the quiet room with its comfortably shabby furnishings before the fury in him vibrated out. "I want to know who wrote that obscenity on Rose's window. Don't tell me you don't know."

Lorenzo shut the door behind him. "I take it you're referring to the vandals who left a message on Signorina Giaberti's window today."

"You know damned well I am. And you know who it was. Your man would have seen it done. Not," Drew said, clipping each word off precisely, "that he thought it worthwhile to stop the bastard."

"The men watching her are under orders. They are to observe who comes to the shop, to her living quarters upstairs, whom she meets when she isn't with you. They aren't to reveal themselves unless her life—or yours—is in danger."

It was logical. It was reasonable. It made him want to smash something. Drew took a steadying breath, and if he didn't actually feel any calmer, he reclaimed enough control to act as though he was. "I think I could use a brandy, if you don't mind." He nodded at the decanter.

"Help yourself."

He did. The first fiery sip made him want to toss back the whole shot. This was such an unusual reaction that he stopped and stared at the amber liquid.

Rose had given in to his insistence that they call the police, though more with resignation than outrage. Drew had stayed until they arrived. His name, his connection to royalty, could be a bloody nuisance, but he didn't hesitate to use it when necessary. Making sure the officers understood the importance of this particular investigation had been quite necessary. "Did your man give the police a description of the vandals?"

Lorenzo nodded. "Three men, all under twenty-five. Two of them have been identified, and I expect we'll know who the third one was shortly. Neither of the two have any known connections to the Brothers."

That would be Lorenzo's priority, of course. It wasn't his, not anymore. Drew wondered if he should feel guilty about that, but all he felt was tired. Almost as exhausted as if he'd had one of his spells.

He took another, healthier swallow of the brandy, hoping the heat would translate into energy, however spurious. "I knew she was in some danger from the terrorists. It didn't occur to me she might be risking attack from her friends and neighbors, as well."

Lorenzo frowned, moved to the sideboard and poured himself a shot of brandy. "What do you want me to tell you, Drew?"

"Did I increase her risk when I arranged to have her work with you? Did that help convince the people who threatened her today that she really has magical abilities?"

"It may have increased the risk she'd draw this kind of attention, yes. But she's in a lot more danger from the Brothers than she is from a few superstitious fools."

"Her mother wasn't safe from those superstitious fools."

"Her mother wasn't under a twenty-four/seven watch by my men."

Lorenzo hadn't denied the danger, Drew noticed. His lips tightened and he paced over to the window, which faced west. The drapes were open, letting the ruddy glow of sunset spill onto the carpet in a long, orange rectangle. Outside, the leaves on the trees were fire-tipped, their edges molten in the gaudy light.

Damn her, anyway. He wanted to shake Rose, make her admit this psychic nonsense was just that. Clinging to her heritage was endangering her. His temples started to throb. "What are you going to do about the cretins who threatened her?"

"They'll be arrested, of course. Eventually."

"Eventually?"

"We have to be sure they won't lead us to anyone else. Also, of course, we don't want to give away the presence of my men." His eyes were steady and watchful over the rim of the snifter as he took a sip of brandy. "That doesn't meet with your approval, I take it."

"I see the necessity." But Drew didn't like it. He looked at the dying glow outside, swallowed brandy and thought about fires. And conscience.

Finally, reluctantly, he spoke. "I don't think there's any need to keep your men on her around the clock. Not from your standpoint, that is. She doesn't know anything. But I hope you'll continue to keep her under surveillance. She isn't safe."

Lorenzo stared at him. "You're worrying me."

"Why?" Drew snapped. "Because I formed an opinion?"

"Because you've known her a week, and your objectivity is shot. Next thing I know you'll be telling me she really does have visions."

A week. Drew swirled the last of the brandy in the snifter, releasing the biting aroma. It seemed a great deal longer. "No," he said slowly. "I'm not likely to tell you that."

"Are you going to be able to go on with this, Drew? Without giving away why you're really seeing her?"

"That's the other reason I came to see you, actually." He set the snifter down on his cousin's desk with a little clink. The brandy hadn't done a thing for his headache. "I won't be seeing her anymore."

His head was throbbing by the time he reached his room. He left the lights turned off, removed his shoes and lay down on his bed fully clothed, shutting his eyes against the pain.

Lorenzo assumed he was worried about giving away their suspicions. That was far enough from the truth to be funny—if he'd been able to find anything about this damnable situation funny, that is. The simple truth was, he couldn't continue seeing Rose without taking her to bed.

He'd ruined one woman's life. That was enough. This fixation he felt for Rose would fade. Never before had he been so close to having a woman and had to draw back. Naturally that made him think about her too much...the softness of her skin, the color of her eyes, her beautiful breasts. Her laugh. The sound of her voice.

He knew her voice. As if he'd heard it all his life, instead

of for only a week, he knew the sound of her.... He'd
known instantly it was her when she called last night.

He lifted heavy eyelids. The throbbing had turned to
pounding, hard, vicious blows from the inside out. As if
something in his brain was trying to burst out through his
skull. Soon the pain would hit that white extreme he
dreaded. And the disorientation would begin.

Drew forced himself up on one elbow and reached for
his cell phone. And turned it off.

He was about to go crazy. Again. He wasn't taking any
chances on having her call in the middle of that to tell him
what a bastard he was, or...or anything else.

Collapsing back on the pillow, he shut his eyes against
the coming onslaught. But he couldn't shut out himself.
Pain blurring his thoughts to an endurance marked off second by second, he knew it was fear that had made him turn
off his phone. Just as it was fear that had made him push
her away. He was afraid of giving in to this craving, afraid
of giving in...to something he couldn't name—

The spell hit. His senses twisted, leaving him stranded
in his mind. And counting.

Rose moved through the next few days in a state of dull
bewilderment. It was denial, of course. She recognized that
without having the energy or even the desire to fight it. She
couldn't believe Drew had truly ended things between
them. Every time the phone rang, her heartbeat spiked.
Every time, she thought it might be him. And, of course,
it never was.

She hated being so pathetic, but couldn't seem to stop.
She hated that she was worrying Gemma, too, and did her
best to act normally, but all wanted to do was sleep.
On Wednesday she took a nap in the middle of the day,
telling Gemma she was trying to fight off a bug. And truly,

she felt tired, achy, as if she was coming down with the flu. But they both knew that what ailed her wasn't physical.

Although a part was. Denial couldn't stretch far enough for her to pretend she didn't ache in other ways, too. Especially at night, alone in the bed where she had always been alone.

Every day she went to the airport. What she did there might have had something to do with her fatigue. It certainly had a great deal to do with her nightmares.

On Monday she'd been escorted to the airport by a dark, quiet man who didn't give his name—one of Lorenzo Sebastiani's men. She'd been given a tape recorder and told to act like an assistant. He'd spoken briefly with all the security guards then on duty, asking them basic questions and giving her the chance to check their *èsseri*.

None of them matched the one from the bomb fragment, which she'd reported. The man had nodded as if he'd expected nothing different, and that had been it. She'd been driven home, and when she asked who they'd be checking out the next day, the answer was, "Thank you very much for your help, Signorina. I don't believe we'll have to bother you again."

Frustrated, she'd pointed out that there were a great many airport employees, including some of the security guards, that she hadn't met. Mr. Anonymous told her the others had been cleared by other means.

He'd been lying. She'd been close enough to be sure of that and irritated enough to tell him so before going inside. She could only assume that, without Drew pushing him, Lorenzo Sebastiani had decided he didn't want to waste time with her. He'd been skeptical all along—polite about it, but he hadn't expected her to be any help.

So what if he'd given up on her? That didn't mean she had to give up. Maybe, once having seen that she might be able to make a difference, she couldn't turn her back on it.

Maybe, she admitted as she sipped her third cup of coffee for the day, just because she was better at denial than letting go. Whatever her reasons, she'd gone to the airport every day, varying the time so she'd catch the different shifts.

So far, nightmares were the only result. The more she used her Gift, the more it could use her.

She wasn't sure what the other dream snatches meant, but she knew where the nightmares about the grieving woman came from—the ring her aunt had bought. Working with her Gift every day had sensitized her, and the tie, so fleetingly established when she'd touched the ring, grew stronger every night.

Which was why she was in her tiny backyard today. There was a patch of dirt beneath the three trees—Calabrian pine, cyprus and golden oak—planted in a rough triangle. Slowly Rose began to sweep the dirt, starting at the center and working out in a spiral. As she swept, she prayed.

Hail Mary full of grace…

It wasn't the same dream every night. That would have been too easy, she thought with a scowl. No, instead of a nice, clear vision, all she got was jumbled, fearful snatches.

…pray for us sinners now…

Sometimes there was a plane, a small one, and it was in trouble. That had a feel of the past to it. Sometimes there was a woman—frightened, grieving, trapped. Sometimes there was a fire. And when she dreamed about fire, she dreamed about Drew.

…the Lord is with thee…

The settings varied, the details changed, but usually there were some all-too-real elements. Like the way his hands felt on her, the way his kiss lit her from the inside out. And the way, every time, he turned and walked away. Over and over, he walked away from her. Then the fire would call her—pure, fierce, beguiling.

…now and at the hour of our death.

"Are you ready, dear?" Aunt Gemma asked, closing the kitchen door. She was wearing a moss-green dress, and her hair hung in a braid down her back, like Rose's. A white apron with deep pockets was tied around her middle.

"Not quite." It was hard to keep the denial thing working when she dreamed about him leaving her every night. She blinked the dampness away, frowned and whispered a fourth Hail Mary as she finished her careful sweeping. "Did you bring the seawater?"

"Right here." Gemma took a small blue bottle out of one of the apron's pockets. "Are you sure you're up to a seeking? You haven't been feeling well lately."

A flicker of amusement penetrated Rose's mood. "Imagine you suggesting I shouldn't work with my Gift. I'm all right, Zia. I don't have to be happy to do this. And she…she's terribly unhappy." Amusement died beneath a weight of other feelings, some of them her own. "She may even be in danger. I need to find out."

"Let's do it, then."

Together the two women completed the simple preparations. Standing inside the swept area, Gemma dribbled the seawater in a circle around them while Rose sat, cross-legged, and began centering herself.

The sun was hot. The air was moist, without a hint of a breeze and thick with the scent of lavender, thyme and honeysuckle layered over the darker smell of earth. A fat bumblebee drifted near Rose's head. She made them all part of her centering—the bee, the smells, the trickle of sweat between her breasts, the dappled sun-shapes on the ground—letting herself sink deeply into the moment.

Gemma sat across from her niece, automatically tidying her full skirt so that it covered her legs. As always, she felt the earth reach up through her, a timeless embrace of growth, death, birth and new growth, as the endless presence made her welcome.

She watched her niece, wondering, not for the first time, what it was like to have a Gift that brought disruption and change, instead of ageless comfort. The Gift of Fire was also called the Wild Gift, for good reason. Gemma's sister had told her once that connecting with fire was like embracing the dance of life, which was also death—endless possibilities, moments flickering into being and dying.

It sounded very uncomfortable.

Rose sat in complete stillness, yet Gemma could feel the life vibrating in her... *So young,* Gemma thought, love and anxiety mingling. *So young, and hurting so much...* What had gone wrong? She'd been so sure Andrew Harrington was the one for Rose.

Drat that young man, anyway. Gemma delved into one of her pockets and took out the fat, white candle and the kitchen matches. She set the candle between them, then lit it.

As always, the flame drew Rose's gaze. She stared at it for a long, dreamy moment, then held out her left hand. Gemma took it in her right one, and the connection was made. Through her, Rose was grounded, tied to the earth and the moment. She wouldn't lose herself in the fire-trance.

Then Rose held out her right hand, and Gemma put the ring into it.

Rose's hand jerked in Gemma's, then steadied. Her eyes closed and her face twisted. Grief. It poured off her in waves so strong even Gemma could feel them. Tears rolled down Rose's cheeks.

The candle flame jumped, then flared. Gemma watched it closely. It continued to grow larger, brighter, but slowly. Rose was calling on fire, but she was in control. Still, Gemma was relieved to see the flame steady when it was about one-third the height of the candle.

Wax dribbled down the side. Sweat dribbled down

Gemma's temple, and her hip ached mildly. She wondered if this would be a long session. Time passed differently for one in fire-trance. Rose might return after only moments and feel she'd been away for half the day, or she might not come back until the candle was guttering—it could last between one and three hours, depending on how heavily Rose drew on the flame—and think she'd been in trance for a few minutes.

The connection between them continued, reassuringly strong, like someone humming too low for the ears to hear. The air felt stuffy and close, like a room that needed airing. *It will storm tonight,* Gemma thought, and shifted carefully to ease her hip.

Rose didn't notice. She was too deeply in trance to be easily distracted now. The tears had dried on her cheeks, and she had that absent-yet-focused look on her face that made Gemma smile. Children usually looked so sweet and defenseless when they slept. From the time she was a baby, Rose had looked as if she took the business of sleeping seriously and was giving it her full attention.

Gemma had just decided she was going to have to shift her position again—really, this getting older was annoying at times, what with stiff joints and hot flashes and all manner of inconveniences—when the candle suddenly went out.

Rose's eyes opened. "I have to see the prince."

"I wish you'd try calling Drew again."

Rose spared her aunt a quick glance as she stepped into her black heels. They were the same ones she'd worn the last time—the only other time—she'd been to the palace. She'd changed quickly into a loose, cotton dress and pulled her hair back. One didn't barge in on royalty in dirty jeans. "It's obvious he doesn't want to talk to me, Zia."

"He probably turned off his cell phone for some reason and forgot to turn it back on."

"Maybe so." She didn't believe it for a minute. Of course, her aunt didn't know this wasn't the first time she'd tried calling Drew's private number. She grabbed her purse. "You can keep trying to call if you like. I'm going to the palace."

"I don't see how you're going to get in to see the prince! If you'd just wait until you can reach Lord Andrew..."

Rose grinned and headed for the outside stairs. "I'll make such a bloody nuisance of myself they'll fetch Drew or the prince just to get rid of me."

She heard Gemma pattering down the stairs after her. "I'm sure you're doing what you feel you have to do. But I don't see why it's so urgent—you've had the ring for over a week now, and you said yourself you aren't sure if you were picking up present, past or future."

"It's always hard to tell in a fire-trance." Rose reached the bottom of the stairs and inhaled. The air was sultry, and clouds were massing on the horizon to the east, dark and portentous.

Good. A storm would break the heaviness in the air.

"And I don't see how you're going to persuade the prince to believe your vision."

"I've got the ring." Rose's fingers tightened on the little glass box in her left hand. "And if that doesn't work..." She reached the street and glanced around, looking for the taxi she'd called. She usually took the bus if the distance was too far for her feet or the weather was bad, but a taxi would be much faster.

Gemma grabbed her arm. "If that doesn't work, *what?*"

"Then I'll just have to prove myself, won't I?"

"Rose, no! You know the rule. You must never—"

"My taxi is here." She gave Gemma a quick kiss on the cheek and turned away. "Don't worry, Zia. The prince isn't a superstitious peasant. He won't have me burned as a witch.''

Her aunt's voice reached her, quiet and intense. ''That isn't the only reason for the rule, Rose. You know that. What happens if you prove yourself and the prince believes you—without understanding the limits?''

Rose's hand checked briefly as she reached for the handle of the door. She knew the answer to that question. She didn't think her aunt needed to hear it, however.

But the question continued to echo in her head as the taxi pulled away. What would she do if the prince or the king accepted her Gift as real, and then tried to force her to use it beyond her ability to control it?

Burn, probably.

The two men walking down the grand staircase at the palace were almost of a height, but otherwise looked unrelated. One was dark, with smooth, handsome features. The other was fair, his light-brown hair too long, too curly, for the grim, narrow face.

''You've been in a weird mood lately,'' Lucas said.

''Have I?''

''You gave me advice last night.''

''That was odd of me.'' And undoubtedly a mistake, Drew thought. He listened well, but he had no experience with advising people and no qualifications for it. Last night Lucas had told Drew what was eating at him, and Drew had been moved by the need to help. That wasn't unusual. But he couldn't remember when he'd let that need spill over into the folly of offering unwanted advice.

Certainly Lucas hadn't been impressed by Drew's carefully tendered opinion. He still didn't intend to confide in his parents or ask his father to postpone the ceremony.

''You've been holed up in your room all week,'' Lucas continued. ''Working too hard, according to Mother.''

"You know the deal in Hong Kong is giving me trouble. That's why I'm leaving today." Right now he was wishing he'd said goodbye to Lucas at lunch, when he'd taken leave of his aunt and uncle.

"You always bring some work with you when you visit," Lucas agreed, "just as you always spend some time on the beach and generally drag me off to snorkel or scuba with you. You haven't been to the ocean."

Yes, he had. Which was why he hadn't been back. "If you wanted to go, you should have said something."

Lucas made an exasperated sound. "I am *trying* to find out what's wrong. I don't know how to pry people open without saying a word the way you do. Hinting doesn't seem to work, and I don't have time to get you drunk or beat it out of you. So just tell me."

For the first time in days, a small smile pulled at Drew's mouth. "You might want to work on the tact and diplomacy some more before you negotiate that treaty with the Emirate."

"I don't need tact and diplomacy with you. I need a crowbar. Or a sledgehammer."

They'd reached the bottom of the stairs. Lucas stopped and faced Drew. "You look like hell."

"Dry skin. It's hell when you forget to moisturize." He hadn't been sleeping well. Instead of crazy spells, he'd been afflicted with nightmares the past few nights, waking up in a terror sweat around three in the morning and unable to remember anything about the dream.

"My mother said you've been plagued by migraines."

"Now and then. Not this past week, however." Not since the one that had led into his last fugue spell—one week and sixteen hours ago. Soon after saying goodbye to Rose. It was hard to avoid the conclusion that she had somehow made the spells worse. If so, he might be able to go for months without another one. Since he would never see her again.

"Is there a health problem, Drew? Something you didn't want to tell my mother about?"

"Didn't your mother tell you? I had myself checked out by a specialist. He found nothing wrong."

When Lucas frowned, he had something of the stern look of his father. "If it was anyone else, I'd suspect you had woman trouble. The serious kind. But you haven't dated anyone since you came here, aside from the young woman you brought to dinner that night. Whom you haven't seen in at least a week."

"Very good. If you decide to abandon your career as a royal, you can try detective work."

"What is it with you? I spill my guts to you, and you won't tell me a damned thing, though any fool can see something's wrong. Badly wrong."

Anyone could see that? Drew was surprised, and troubled. He could see that his cousin was truly pissed off, and he understood why. It must seem unbalanced, unfair, as if Drew were unwilling to extend the same kind of trust Lucas had. Haltingly he said, "I don't know how to talk about this sort of thing."

"You just start and see what comes out."

"Nothing comes out. That's the problem." Drew dragged a hand over his hair. He really needed a haircut. He didn't know why he kept forgetting. "Look, the car is waiting. My plane leaves in less than an hour. Even without having to go through security, that doesn't leave me much time."

"She must have mattered," Lucas said quietly. "You wouldn't be acting like such a jackass if she hadn't mattered."

Drew was silent a moment. "Yes. She mattered." He gripped his cousin's arm. "You'll take care of yourself."

"Of course."

"And think about what I suggested."

"Good God, advice again." Light irony infused Lucas's voice, but his face closed up tight. "I'd return the favor if I knew enough to have some chance of hitting the target."

Moments later Drew was in the back seat of the limo as it pulled away from the palace. Off to the east, lightning flashed. He wondered if the storm would arrive before his plane could leave.

Lucas had wanted to know what was wrong. What should he have said? *I haven't had a crazy spell in a week, which is good. But I'm not sleeping. My arms feel heavy, leaden, but my legs are twitchy, as if wherever I am, I need to be somewhere else. My mind is dull, as if I were recuperating from an illness. I keep seeing her face...*

When he saw the young woman in the long, black-and-white dress arguing with a guard near the gate, at first he thought he was imagining things. That he'd found a new way to be nuts. But no. It really was Rose.

He leaned forward and tapped on the glass. "Stop." A second later he stepped out of the air-conditioned limo into the clammy heat.

She didn't see him at first, so involved was she in her argument with the guard. Drew barely noticed the man. His attention was all on the tall woman in the slim dress the breeze was teasing. Her leg showed up to the thigh on the side he could see, revealed by a slit in the dress. Her black hair was caught in a loose bundle at the nape of her neck.

He didn't know why he'd gotten out of the limo. This wouldn't help anything, and there was a good chance he'd make things worse for both of them. But he kept walking.

When he was almost close enough to touch, she turned, unsurprised, as if she'd known all along he was there. Maybe she was too angry to have room for surprise. Her eyes were flashing with fury.

"Can you fire this son of a pig?" she demanded.

The oddest thing happened when she scowled at him. He felt lighter, cleaner. He felt…happy. "I'm afraid not."

"Your uncle shouldn't have such scum working for him." She rounded on the guard. "You will give me your name, and Lord Andrew will tell me whom I should report you to."

"I haven't done anything wrong," the man growled. "We can't let in every piece of ass that comes waltzing through the gates."

Drew's attention sharpened tightly on the guard. He was short and stocky, about thirty, with a crisp crease in his uniform trousers, a good shine on his shoes and bad breath. "Excuse me. Did you just refer to this young lady as a piece of ass?"

"I…" His eyes darted from Drew to Rose. "She's been calling me a lot worse, just because I wouldn't let her in to see the prince. The prince!" He was scornful. "And when that didn't work, she wanted to send word to you or Duke Lorenzo. As if His Grace had nothing better to do than come running when she called!"

Lorenzo would know Rose was at the palace soon, if he didn't already. His men were still following her. "And what is your real name? As opposed to the ones she called you, that is."

"I don't see what—"

Drew raised his eyebrows. "I didn't ask what you saw. I asked your name."

"Edwardo Scarpa." He added defensively, "She's not on the approved list, my lord."

"And you feel free, naturally, to insult anyone who isn't on your list. I will have to ask Lorenzo if he agrees. Rose?" He turned fully to her. "Let's allow Scarpa to get back to defending the palace." He held out his hand.

She glanced from his hand to his face as if he'd offered her a dubious gift, but put her hand in his.

It felt good, right, to be holding her hand again. But the very rightness was troubling. He walked with her into the tailored grouping of trees to the east of the drive, where they would have shade and a semblance of privacy.

As soon as they were out of sight of the guard, she pulled her hand away.

Obviously seeing him didn't make her especially happy. "You wanted to talk to me?" he asked.

"You were my third choice, actually, but you'll do. I have to see the prince."

Memory moved through him uneasily. Lorenzo had said there was some kind of plot to assassinate Lucas, and that Rose might be part of it.

Ridiculous, he told himself. But his voice was harsh when he asked, "Why?"

Her head turned, held at a proud angle as she met his eyes. "I had a...call it a vision. It involves him."

"Tell me. I'll pass it on to him."

"This is too personal. He'll want to ask questions, see if I'm making this up." She chewed on her lip a moment, then opened the slim purse hanging from her shoulder and withdrew a small glass box. "Give this to him. I think— I'm almost sure—he'll recognize it. Tell him I know something about the woman it belonged to."

"A woman?" Dread balled up in his stomach. Last night Lucas had told him about a woman. "What do you mean?"

"I'll answer any questions the prince has, to the best of my ability. I don't owe you any answers."

His fingers closed around the box. He looked at it, frowning. She'd come to the palace—but not to see him. To push some kind of psychic crap on Lucas.

Or else to try to kill him.

No, dammit, he didn't believe that. But he wasn't much

happier at the idea that she was here to poke at his cousin's wounds—though how had she known? Until last night, he hadn't known Lucas was deeply worried about a woman.

Guesswork, he answered himself a moment later. Given his cousin's habits, it didn't take paranormal abilities to guess there had been a woman in his recent past. It made Drew sick to think she might be trying to take advantage of Lucas's troubles, to win money or advantage that way. He wanted nothing to do with it. But he knew what Lorenzo would say—string her along, find out what she's up to.

Even though he didn't believe Rose was connected to the terrorists, it was the right thing to do. It wasn't—surely—because he wanted a few more minutes in her company that he agreed. "All right. I'll take this to Lucas." He would notify Lorenzo first, of course. He started walking.

"Ah…the palace is the other direction."

"I have to tell my driver I won't be needing him. It looks as if I won't be making my flight, after all."

"You were leaving Montebello?" Her voice was sharp. Her eyes…

Her eyes. He looked away, giving them both a chance to recover.

Whatever she said—whatever, even, she believed—she hadn't come here just to see Lucas about some vision she thought she'd had. Or to trick the prince into giving her money or favor. She'd come to see *him.* And the pain of it staggered him. The unexpectedness of that pain left him without a compass. Why did it hurt now, when a few minutes ago the sight of her had made him happy?

He had no idea what to say to her. He couldn't explain himself to himself, so how could he explain to her?

When he reached the waiting limo, he said simply, "It was time to go."

Chapter 11

Rose's stomach still hurt when he left her in an elegant drawing room on the first floor of the palace.

He'd been on his way to the airport. If she hadn't come to the palace today, he would have left Montebello and she wouldn't even have known. At some point her aunt would probably have read about his departure in one of the gossip columns and told her about it. Rose's mind kept coming back to that simple, bare truth over and over, like a mother cat licking her dead kitten, unable to believe it wouldn't stir and walk again.

He would have been gone, and she wouldn't have known.

So much for the blessings of denial. She felt as if she'd been gut-punched. Sitting on a gilt-and-cream chair, her hands clenched tightly in her lap, Rose faced a few more truths she'd been hiding from.

She remembered that one, blinding instant when she'd touched Drew's *èssere*. From that moment to this, she'd believed he was hers and she was his. That they were fated. She'd thought of him as her ideal mate, her sexual match. The one her soul cried out to. She had refused to believe her soul could be crying alone. Surely he must have felt something, too. Even blocked as he was, he must have felt something.

How many women since the beginning of time had believed that because they loved, *he* must love, too?

But then, she hadn't thought in terms of love, had she? Looking back, she marveled at how deftly she'd dodged that particular word, never allowing herself to think it. To claim it. Now, her eyes dry, her hands white-knuckled, she faced the truth. She'd fallen in love with Drew. And he hadn't even planned to tell her goodbye.

Be fair, she told herself fiercely. He thought they'd already parted. She was the one who'd been keeping a two-fisted grip on denial all week.

She realized she was breathing too fast, like a wounded animal panting to overcome the pain. She made herself relax her hands, breathe deeply and slowly, and for the first time noticed her surroundings.

The walls were hung with gold brocade. The ceiling was high and ornately plastered; the medallion at its center was repeated on a smaller scale over each of the tall doorways. Twin sofas were upholstered in a delicate print on a cream background, the same light cream that had been used on all the woodwork. Touches of smoky olive—on one chair, and in the pattern of the carpet—kept the gold from overpowering, and subtly echoed the greens in the landscapes displayed in heavy, gilded frames.

The painting over the mantel looked like a Renoir.

Rose glanced at the sleeveless cotton dress she'd pulled on in such a hurry. It was a black-and-white print in a simple design, a slim tube that fell straight from her neck to her ankles, with slitted sides so it wouldn't hamper her stride. There was nothing wrong with the dress. It was one of her favorites. She'd found it in a little shop halfway up the coast that sold everything from magazines to scarves to psychedelic condoms.

All at once she felt as misplaced as a piece of costume jewelry that has landed by accident in a museum display.

She smoothed the dress with a shaky hand, then scowled and stood. So what if she didn't fit in his world? He didn't want her in it, anyway, and not because of where she bought her clothes. She didn't think her intact hymen was the real problem, either. Maybe it was her claim to be psychic, maybe it was a dozen other things. Problems from his past. Religious differences. The way his mother had treated him when he was little. The fact was, she didn't know him well enough to guess.

She loved him, but she didn't know him. Not the details of him, at least.

But his heart...the hot squeeze of pain made her rub her breastbone. She knew his heart.

Restlessly she paced over to the spotless fireplace and frowned at the painting above it. She wasn't sure that Drew actually owed her answers, but by God, she wanted them. Once she'd done what she came here to do and spoken with the prince...

"Lucas wants to talk to you. I'll take you to him."

She turned. Drew stood in the doorway, looking as grim as he'd sounded. She lifted one eyebrow. "You don't approve?"

"Lorenzo will be there, too."

It wasn't an answer. She studied his face. Maybe it was a warning.

He took her to the prince's personal suite. The difference between the room she'd been in, the opulence and the for-

mality of it, and the private quarters of the heir to the throne
struck her immediately.

Oh, the furnishings were still costly. But the fabric on
the overstuffed couch was worn, the dark blue faded by the
sun. This fireplace had been used recently, and a modest
pile of wood was stacked neatly in it, waiting for a match.
A fire in July was a rich man's indulgence, to be sure, but
it was a homey indulgence. There were no windows—the
prince's sitting room was surrounded by other rooms—and
the walls were richly paneled, giving the room a warm,
masculine feel. The end table beside the wing chair where
the prince lounged held newspapers, a half-empty glass and
a candy wrapper, as well as a Sevres bowl filled with more
candy. Riding boots leaned against each other beside the
chair.

This was a room that was lived in. A place where a man
could kick off his shoes and relax…as the prince had.

His socks were dark brown. There was something irre-
sistibly appealing about a sock-clad prince. Rose smiled as
she sank into a curtsy.

He'd risen politely when she entered. So had the other
man, the cousin who was head of Montebellan intelligence—and, until Lucas's return, the most likely heir to the
throne. But she didn't think manners alone drew Lorenzo
Sebastiani to his feet. To her prickly senses he seemed to
radiate suspicion. Unlike the prince, he wore a dark sports
jacket. And shoes.

"Thank you for coming to see me." Prince Lucas held
out a hand to shake.

She was struck, as she had been when they were intro-
duced, by the man's sheer physical beauty. He was far more
conventionally good-looking than Drew. And didn't move
her at all.

When she shook the prince's hand, his *èssere* met hers.
She had a quick impression of strength—a large soul, one

that wouldn't easily be trapped by pettiness. Compassionate. Stubborn. And, at the moment, troubled, though it was the subtle tension in his stance and the darkness in his eyes that spoke to her of unquiet emotions, not any empathic connection.

"Where did you get the ring?" Lorenzo asked.

"A woman brought it to the shop a week ago, wanting to sell it. I was at police headquarters. Captain Mylonas, the sneaky son of a gun, was trying to trick me into confessing by asking me the same questions over and over. My aunt bought the ring from her."

He managed to look profoundly skeptical without disarranging his polite expression. "You have documentation for this purchase?"

"Just the receipt my aunt had the woman sign, which may not be much help." She opened her purse. All three men watched her as closely as if they expected her to pull out a viper. She held out the slip of paper. "I'm afraid Aunt Gemma didn't ask for ID."

"That's a shame." It was Lorenzo who took the receipt. "We'll want to talk to your aunt."

"She's at the shop." Rose faced the prince. "You'll have been told that I'm psychic, Your Highness. Or that I claim to be," she added dryly. "I don't usually worry about whether people believe that, but in this case it's important that you accept what I tell you."

His eyes were intent on hers. "Drew said you'd had a vision. About a woman."

"Not a vision, exactly. I performed a seeking, using the ring." She spread her hands. "Never mind. The difference between a vision and a seeking is mostly technical. The point is, I was able to see the woman who used to own the ring."

"And?"

"She has long blond hair—very long, down to here."

She touched a place by her bottom rib. "Her eyes are blue and rather wide-set. She's tanned, under thirty, I think, with a heart-shaped face. She was wearing jeans and a flannel shirt, and I saw a lantern, an old-fashioned oil lantern." Rose took a deep breath. "She's trapped somehow. And I believe she's in danger."

"What kind of danger?" he demanded. "And how is she trapped?"

"I don't know. It was the impression I had." Her Gift was often stingy with details. "I think she's far away. Reaching her was difficult."

Lucas's gaze flew to Drew, standing behind Rose and to her left. He didn't speak, but seemed to be asking some wordless question.

"I didn't tell her," Drew said.

Lorenzo Sebastiani's cynical voice broke the silence. "This is all very interesting and dramatic, Signorina, but conveniently vague. A ring, a mysterious woman in danger…" He shrugged. "You'll need to give us more than that. A name would help."

"It's Jessica." The prince's voice was low, raw. "The woman…that I worked for while my memory was gone. That's her ring, and she fits the description." He stopped and swallowed.

Lorenzo's eyes narrowed. "There's no way she could know about Ms. Chambers. Not unless—"

"I've been trying to contact her. God." Lucas began to pace, taking quick, jerky steps that destroyed his usual grace. "I haven't been able to reach her. I knew something was wrong." He stopped in front of Rose and gripped her arms in hard hands. "She's all right, though? She's in danger, but she isn't…hurt?"

"I can't be sure," Rose said reluctantly. "She's hurting, but it seems to be emotional, not physical."

"You must have some idea of what the danger is."

"I don't know for sure there is danger. I'm not a tele-path. I saw her—I can describe the room she was in—and I felt she was threatened by someone, but I don't know who or how. I can't say whether the threat is physical or emotional. I did pick up some of her feelings, and…a face. I saw a face. She's…" Rose took a shaky breath. The next part was so personal for him, and so painful. "Your High-ness, I believe she's grieving for you. And your baby."

All the color drained out of his face.

There was the sound of some small, hasty motion from behind her. Drew. But he didn't speak.

Lorenzo Sebastiani did. "You are under arrest, Signorina Giaberti."

The words circled around her mind like dizzy birds. Un-der arrest…under arrest? The first trickle of alarm whirled her around, instinctively seeking Drew.

His face was stony. His eyes were a dull, cold green. Something equally cold jerked inside her, rising to her throat, then plummeting to her stomach like a yo-yo.

Drew wasn't going to help her. He was going to let his cousin arrest her. For what? Wrapping one arm around her middle where the cold had settled, she turned back to face the man who had arrested her. She made her voice hard. "On what grounds?"

"Material witness will do for now. I imagine when the ransom demand arrives, I can find something that will stick better."

Ransom demand? She shook her head, not understand-ing.

"You overplayed your hand," he said, sounding almost affable. "Coincidence can only be stretched so far before it snaps back on you, Signorina. Did you really believe you'd convinced us you saw visions? That was the purpose of letting you play with that piece of the bomb, of course, but I'm surprised you bought into our game so easily. The first rule of a good con is to fool the marks, not yourself.''

"Wait a minute," Lucas said suddenly. "What are you talking about?''

"Lucas, I'm sorry.'' There was compassion in the man's dark eyes now. "The only way she could know about Ms. Chambers in such detail is if someone fed her the information. Just as someone had to give her that ring. The most likely explanation is a kidnapping.''

Rose had both arms around her waist now, but it wasn't helping. The cold was spreading.

Lorenzo continued to explain things to the prince. "We thought at first she had to be connected to the Brothers or to a cell of them that's still hanging around. I told you about that. But there were problems with that assumption. The Brothers don't usually work with women, and she's the wrong religion. The wrong everything, from their point of view.''

Drew didn't say anything. He didn't argue, didn't contradict his cousin.

"I think now she's working with some other group that's strictly profit-oriented. Somehow she or someone she's working with stumbled on the information about the bombing. She used that to establish her bona fides as a psychic. Now the idea is to bleed you two ways—once through ransom and again by having her use her 'powers' to lead you to Ms. Chambers.''

Could Drew actually believe all this? Rose hugged herself tightly. Tiny, barely noticeable, a flicker of anger awoke.

"Assuming all of that's true," Lucas said, "is it wise to let her know how much you know?''

"Oh, I think so. I think she'll start seeing the benefit in cooperating when she realizes how little choice she has.

She's been watched constantly since the bombing. Her phone is tapped..."

Rose turned her back on the other two so she could face the silent man behind her. "Drew." Her voice was scratchy. "Do you believe all this?"

He met her eyes. His were blank, empty.

"She won't wiggle out of this," Lorenzo was saying. "Whoever her confederates are..."

Drew's throat moved once, as if he preferred swallowing his words to speaking them.

The flicker of anger in her grew. She was feeling much warmer now. "Well?" she demanded. "Don't I deserve any answers at all?"

At last he spoke. "I don't know what to say. I don't know what to think."

Lorenzo was saying, "She'll want to cut a deal as quickly as possible. The one thing she has to bargain with is Ms. Chambers's whereabouts—and her safety."

Rose ignored him, speaking to Drew as if no one else was there. "It's easier to think I might kidnap a woman, frighten and endanger her—easier to believe I would lie to you and everyone else and try to trick money out of the prince—than that I really have visions, isn't it?" Rose's hands fell to her sides, balled into fists. Her anger blazed into a rich, roaring fury. The force of it vibrated through her. "The hell with you, then. The hell with all of you!"

She turned on her heel. Drawing on that interior blaze, she called fire.

It answered. She balled the *èssere* of fire up hard and tightly with her Gift and hurled it, throwing her arm out as if pitching a ball. Hurled it straight at those waiting logs in the fireplace across the room.

With a *whoosh*, they ignited. And burned.

And the fire called her back...

Dizzy, emptied, she fought the quick, hard tug from

without, the yearning that rose from within. Always, always, part of her wanted to answer that call. Rose dug her fingernails into her palms and used the pain to try to cut off the call. Then she looked at the three men.

They were staring at the fire, at her. All three faces showed some blend of horror, disbelief, shock. Drew's face had gone paper-pale, as if he might faint.

Good. She hoped he fell on his face and bloodied his nose. Propping her hands on her hips, she said, "Fit that into all your clever little theories, Your Grace."

Chapter 12

Drew had been fighting nausea. As he listened to Lorenzo's reasoning, so damningly clear and logical, the sickness had spread from the pit of his stomach until he wondered if he was going to disgrace himself.

Then she cracked reality wide open.

Nausea vanished. So did thought. She spoke, but he didn't hear what she said. After several blank seconds, he realized he'd finally gone completely around the bend.

But his head didn't hurt. Reality hadn't slipped into the terrible sensory dislocation of one of his spells. Except for the fire. There was a fire burning where there couldn't be a fire. She hadn't been anywhere near the fireplace, hadn't thrown any kind of device at it. She'd pointed, and the wood had ignited.

He lifted one of his hands and looked at it. His body was obeying him.

He wasn't crazy. And she wasn't deluded or a terrorist or a kidnapper. What *was* she?

"Son of a bitch," Lorenzo said reverently.

She was staring at the fire. No, she was leaning toward it, her body rigid and unmoving. Sweat beaded her brow. Her hands, spread wide at her sides, were as still and taut as the rest of her—yet they made him think of someone scrabbling for purchase on a steep slope. A chill went up his spine. "Rose?"

"Put it out." Her voice was hoarse. "Put the fire out."

Drew reacted instinctively to her voice, grabbing a tall vase that held gladiola and racing across the room with it. The fire was blazing now, higher than seemed possible from the modest pile of wood. Heat hit him in the face as he dashed the contents of the vase on the blaze.

There was a hiss, a sputter, but the water from the vase wasn't enough. He glanced around, saw Lorenzo running into the bedroom with Lucas right behind. The bathroom was off the bedroom.

Rose was swaying. Her eyes were dark and fixed in her pallid face.

The others could take care of the fire. Rose needed him. An irrational conviction seized him that the fire was dangerous to her. He didn't stop to analyze, but ran back to her and pulled her against him, turning them both so that he stood between her and the fire. He brought her head down into his shoulder. "Don't look at it," he said fiercely.

Her hands gripped his shirt and she burrowed into him, holding on as if she stood in a gale and he was all that anchored her. He heard water running, and a second later glimpsed Lorenzo with a huge, dripping bath sheet. He flung it over the fire and was answered with an angry hissing. A moment later Lucas emerged at a run, carrying a metal waste basket. Water sloshed over the rim and he dumped it onto the towel.

The fire was out.

Rose's body relaxed against Drew's, her hands sliding

down his chest to rest at his waist. And Drew realized he was completely hard, with heat of a different sort pulsing through his body.

Fortunately she didn't seem to notice. Probably in shock, he decided, and eased her away enough to make his condition less obvious. "Come on. You need to sit down."

She let him steer her to the couch. He sat beside her, keeping one arm around her shoulders. Her face was still pale.

Lorenzo appeared in front of them with a glass in his hand.

"Brandy," he said. "It should put a little color back in your face."

Her lips quirked up as she took the glass. "Do you treat all your prisoners this well?"

"Consider yourself unarrested." He glanced over his shoulder at the smoldering fireplace, back at her. "That…was amazing."

Lucas stood in front of the fireplace, his back to them, his hands thrust in his pockets. "If you're ministering to those in danger of fainting, I'll take whiskey. Neat." He turned slowly and walked across the room, stopping in front of Rose. Drew had the impression that his cousin wasn't aware of much except her at that moment, that even the sudden reality of magic, so dramatically demonstrated, was mainly important because it meant Rose had been telling the truth about the woman Lucas had loved.

Rose sighed and straightened, pulling away from Drew. "Sorry about the mess. I'm better at starting fires than putting them out."

Drew exchanged a glance with Lorenzo. Lucas, however, was more single-minded. "You believe everything you told me. That Jessica is trapped somewhere. That she's in danger. And…you said there was a baby."

Rose nodded. "I'm sorry, Your Highness. I don't know what happened to the baby, just that she lost it."

Lorenzo had moved over to the small bar, where he was filling glasses. "I take it you have reason to think a baby is possible," he said carefully.

Lucas looked haggard. "I've always been careful. Lord knows how many times my father drummed that into me—use protection. Mustn't catch nasty bugs or let the royal sperm wander around loose and confuse the succession." His laugh was hard and short. "But I wasn't myself for several months. I was a drifter named Joe. Joe was a pretty nice guy in some ways, but he wasn't always careful."

Lorenzo brought the glasses over, handing one to Lucas, one to Drew and keeping one for himself. "How much time do we have to find her?" he asked Rose.

"Time gets funny in fire-trance. What I saw could be happening now, in the recent past or near future."

Lorenzo got a pained look on his face. He glanced down, shook his head slightly and pulled a little notebook out of the inner pocket of his suit jacket.

Drew knew how he felt. It was hard to take what she said as the literal truth. She saw things she couldn't possibly see, but they were real. She started fires with a gesture. Yet she couldn't tell the difference between present, past and future?

Rose had no idea what was going through Drew's mind. They questioned her for some time, of course—once they persuaded the prince he couldn't fly to the U.S. immediately. That argument waxed fierce for a while. Lucas was unimpressed when Lorenzo said that if there was danger—which was by no means certain—the prince had no business stepping into it. He listened more patiently when Drew mentioned the strain his father had been under and the duties Lucas had recently assumed to ease that strain. He scowled when Lorenzo pointed out the need of the people to see the succession secure. But Rose didn't get the impression he'd resigned himself to staying in Montebello, though he did fall silent.

Lorenzo asked her all kinds of questions then, jotting things down in his notebook. Lucas paced restlessly. While Lorenzo took Rose over her story again and again, the prince drank more than a medicinal amount of whiskey.

Drew didn't contribute much.

Outside, unseen, the storm hit. Here, in this interior room insulated by thick walls and other chambers, even the sound of the rain on the roof was barely noticeable. She'd long since taken her hair down, and it hung in messy waves along her shoulders and back.

Lorenzo asked her to describe the room where she'd seen Jessica—for about the fifth time. She leaned forward, her elbows propped on her knees, and massaged her temples. She was tired all the way down to her bones. "I want to help. I came here to help. But I don't think I can tell you anything more."

"Can you try again?" Lucas stopped his pacing to crouch down in front of her. "I've got the ring. Maybe if you did this seeking thing a second time, you could learn more."

A little spurt of fear had her straightening. "I can't. I'm sorry. Not tonight."

"You're exhausted." The words came from Drew, the first he'd spoken in some time. "Lucas, she'll need to stay here tonight. She's too tired to see straight."

"Tomorrow, then?" Lucas persisted. "Whatever you need to do this, you'll have."

"I don't know." She tossed her hair back out of her face. "If you want the truth, I'm scared to try. I had to go very deep to reach Jessica the first time, and my control isn't that great. You saw what happened with the fire."

It had claimed too much of her. A relatively small fire

like that one didn't exert the pull of a big one, yet she'd been unable to cut the connection, to stop feeding it. She didn't know why. Exhaustion, she supposed. And, of course, she hadn't had Gemma to be her Ground.

Yet when Drew had stepped between her and the fire, the call had ended. As if his big body was glass, a shield, impervious. That had never happened before. She glanced at him, wondering.

"What does this seeking business have to do with the way you played Puff the Magic Dragon earlier?" Lorenzo asked. He looked sour, as if offended by his own question.

For some people, she knew, the very existence of the irrational was an affront. She suspected Lorenzo Sebastiani would have preferred to deny the evidence of his senses, but he had a core of honesty that wouldn't let him.

"They're not entirely separate abilities. It's like the difference between walking, dancing and running. You need legs for all of them, right? Well, to call fire, see visions or enter a fire-trance, you need to be touched by the Fire Gift. Each Gift has its own dangers," she ended neutrally. "If my control is shaky with fire right now, my control in trance is apt to be nonexistent."

Drew closed a hand around her arm. His eyes were clear again, sharp, his expression intent. "What does that mean? What happens if you don't control it?"

She shrugged. "I might forget how to come back."

"That's out, then." His eyes narrowed. "You said it was hard to reach her. That there seemed to be a great distance between you. Does distance make it more dangerous?"

"Well, yes. The farther I have to travel, either in time or space, the trickier it gets."

"If you were closer to Jessica, then, there would be less danger. You might be able to pick up more." He turned to the others, keeping his hand on her arm as if holding her in place for when he wanted her. "Jessica is probably being held in the U.S. She lives in Colorado, doesn't she?"

"Yes!" For the first time, hope lit the prince's face. "We'll need American currency. I'll take care of that."

"Wait a minute," Lorenzo snapped. "You're not going."

Lucas lifted one eyebrow, every inch the prince. "I don't require your consent."

"Lucas." Drew moved in front of him. "What will she think if you turn up suddenly on her doorstep? Unless you plan to resume the relationship, it will be kinder to let me go in your stead."

Rose couldn't see the prince's face, but when he turned away the movement was jerky, his usual grace destroyed by emotion. He was silent for a long moment. "Very well. Lorenzo, which will be faster—commercial transport? Or should I have the jet readied?"

"The jet to London," Lorenzo said crisply. "The Concorde to cross the Atlantic."

Rose's mind was whirling. "Wait a minute."

Drew gave Lucas a level look. "You'll need your father's permission to use the royal jet. You'll have to tell him why."

"I realize that." Lucas's voice was flat. "I've given him and Mother enough grief the last year. I don't want to add to that, but speed may be important."

"Fortunately," Lorenzo said, "Rose's family elected to maintain dual citizenship when Britain granted our independence. She has a British passport, so she won't need a visa to enter the U.S. That will speed things up."

She eyed him without appreciation. "I suppose you know what my grades were like in middle school, too."

"And what kind of profit your business has shown since you opened it," he agreed cheerfully. "Among other things."

Drew turned to her. "Speaking of business, you have a shop to run. Can your aunt and that young woman who works for you take care of it for a week or so?"

"Yes—at least, I imagine so, but—"

"Or will you need your aunt with you? You said she helps with the trances."

"Hold on." She pushed to her feet. "Everyone just hold on a minute."

Lucas stood very still and looked at her. He didn't say anything. He didn't have to.

"I'm willing to go," she said. "That's not the problem. I just don't want you to expect too much, Lord." She shoved both hands into her hair and stood there cupping her skull as if she could force clear thought with the pressure of her palms. She couldn't help thinking of her aunt's warning and the third reason for the rule. "How do I explain? I'll go there, I'll do my best, but I'm not a Finder. You need to notify the U.S. authorities—their police or FBI or something."

Drew and Lucas exchanged a look she didn't understand. Drew spoke. "The American police aren't going to take psychic predictions seriously, and we don't have evidence that anything is wrong with Ms. Chambers. If we contact the authorities, the media are likely to find out."

Lucas raked a hand through his hair. "I don't want to expose her to that."

"That's another reason for you to let Drew handle this," Lorenzo said. "If you go, you'll draw newshounds right to her."

Lucas slanted him an angry glance. "I've already agreed to sit on my hands here. Don't push it." He looked at Rose. "What's that Finder business you mentioned earlier?"

"It's a rare Gift, kind of like being an idiot savant— Finders find things, but they're psychically deaf otherwise. Those of us who aren't Finders can't do what they do, any more than a normal mathematician can multiply five-digit numbers in his head instantly. If Jessica isn't at her ranch, I won't be able to track her like a dog following a scent. My Gift doesn't work that way.''

"What will you be able to do?"

"I might see who is with her. Or pick up details about where she is being held."

"You said you can see into the past. Why can't you look back and see what's happened to her?"

"I don't have that kind of control." Rose struggled for patience—but patience wasn't her best thing even when she wasn't so achingly tired. "Think of the cliché about time being a river. Most people are like twigs floating on that river. They go wherever the current takes them. One who's Fire-Gifted can swim, but the current is strong and tricky. I have more control over where the river takes me than you do, but I'm not a blasted motorboat."

"What the hell good is this Gift of yours if you can't use it better than that? You may be great at starting fires, but I can do that myself with a match!"

"What good is it?" she snapped. "Damned if I know. It's just a trait that runs in my family, like a cowlick or blue eyes. If the Gift made me all-seeing, I'd be sitting here in the palace running things, and you'd be selling pitchers to tourists."

The beat of silence lasted long enough for Rose to realize she'd just told off the prince of her country.

Then Lorenzo chuckled. "You would at least be amassing an impressive portfolio by predicting the stock market, which I can assure the others you haven't done. We accept that your, ah, abilities have limits, Signorina."

"For heaven's sake, call me Rose." She paused. "Oh, hell. Now I'm telling a duke we should be on a first-name basis."

Lorenzo grinned, his gaze flicking to Drew for a second,

then back to her. "I believe I can live without being Your Grace'd constantly. And since you are no longer under arrest, I would be pleased to call you Rose."

She was beginning to think she might end up liking Lorenzo Sebastiani. Amazing. Her gaze, though, had followed his, and she didn't like what she saw. "Drew, you don't look well."

"It's nothing. A headache." He made a dismissive gesture. "We are agreed, then? Lucas will arrange for American currency and the royal jet, and Rose and I will leave in the morning."

Protests rose to her tongue, but she closed her lips on them. Gemma couldn't go with her. Her aunt was earthbound, quite literally. Flying not only made her sick, it disrupted the very tie that let her act as Ground for her niece.

Drew had stopped the fire's call when he held her. Maybe he could take Gemma's place.

Drew started for the door. "Someone should call Rose's aunt, let her know what's going on and ask her to pack a bag for Rose. She'll need the passport you mentioned."

"I can pack my own bag."

One hand on the doorknob, he paused. There was a blurred look to his eyes, as if he was in pain. "You're so tired you're about to fall down. You'll stay at the palace tonight."

"You should call the woman," Lucas said. "You've met her. You'll be able to reassure her."

"*Dio!*" Rose exclaimed. "Can't you see he's the one about to fall down? I'll call my aunt myself. Drew—"

He interrupted brusquely. "I have medication for my headache, but I'm afraid it knocks me out. The three of you will have to settle the remaining details among yourselves."

She watched, bewildered, as the door closed behind him. He'd rushed out as if dogs were snapping at his heels.

"He doesn't want you to see him like this," Lucas said. "Hurting, I mean. Male pride."

Turning, trying to master her expression, if not her feelings, she said, "His headaches must be severe if he carries medication for them."

"I didn't know he had headaches," Lorenzo said. "Or any human weaknesses."

"Not ordinary headaches. Migraines," Lucas said tersely. "They've returned. My mother wormed it out of him, or I wouldn't know, either."

Lorenzo snorted. "He's not exactly a confiding sort. This situation has to be hard on him, but he'll never let it show."

The two men exchanged one of those knowing looks. It irritated Rose intensely. Why would the situation be hard on Drew? He didn't even know Jessica Chambers. "He's suffered from migraines in the past?"

"When he was a child. We all thought they'd gone away when...well, when he outgrew them."

He'd started to say something else. Frustrated because she didn't have any right to demand answers, Rose gestured at the phone. "Should I call my aunt or a taxi?"

"No, Drew was right about that. You're exhausted. I'll arrange a room for you as soon as I've spoken with the pilot. My father will have to confirm my orders, of course, but I can set things in motion." Lucas picked up a phone and punched in a number. "Signorina, my apologies for keeping you so late."

"You're worried." That much she was sure of, though she didn't know how deep that worry went. Jessica—it was good to be able to put a name to the woman she knew so intimately in some ways and not at all in others—was in love with the prince. If he was in love with her, too, surely he would have done more than try to call her a few times?

Lorenzo handed her a cell phone. "Does your aunt know where to find your passport?"

"If she doesn't," Rose said sourly, "I imagine you could tell her."

He grinned. "You really should keep such important documents in your safety deposit box, you know. The cash drawer of your store isn't terribly secure."

Her part in the arrangements was soon over, and not long after that she stood under the shower in the lushly appointed bathroom connected to one of the many guest chambers. It was far too grand, she thought as she toweled dry, to be called a mere bedroom.

The palace staff had even provided a nightgown—cotton, floor-length, with fine lace trimming the neckline. It had been ironed and smelled faintly of violets. She wondered if she was wearing one of the princess's nightgowns, or if the staff kept an assortment of sleepwear on hand to offer unexpected guests the way hotels stocked toothbrushes.

She also wondered if Drew's cousins had found it odd that he hadn't suggested she stay in his suite, if not his bedroom. They knew he'd been seeing her. Maybe this was the way things were done in a palace, though, and even if they had been sleeping together they would have been given separate quarters. God knew she'd no experience with life lived at this level.

The thought depressed her. She was too tired to pretend it didn't or deny the reason. Drew was comfortable with this life. The palace was like a second home for him.

When she turned off the light and pulled up the covers, she expected to drop off quickly. The bed was comfortable, she was exhausted, and the lightweight comforter added just enough warmth. But her noisy mind wouldn't let her poor body have its way.

Gemma wasn't happy about the trip. She thought Rose was getting in over her head. In the elegant privacy of her temporary quarters, Rose had to agree. She rolled onto her side and closed her eyes, trying to empty her mind.

He hadn't even tried to defend her. When his cousin had placed her under arrest, Drew hadn't said a word.

Her eyes opened.

He didn't know her. That's what it came down to. He didn't know her, didn't believe in her, and he certainly didn't love her. She'd felt the connection between them, but he hadn't…or, if he had, he didn't accept it.

If she hadn't shown up at the palace gate today, he would have left the country without a word to her. Yet he'd insisted on accompanying her to the United States tomorrow.

That was for his cousin's sake, she thought, and rolled all the way over to her other side. It was so quiet, so deadeningly silent in this room—no traffic noise, no voices calling on the street, no sound of a neighbor's television or radio. No windows in this interior chamber. Even the storm couldn't make itself heard, muffled by all this opulence. How did people sleep in such silence?

She sighed. Drew thought she'd need help on the trip. He was probably right about that, though it wasn't the intricacies of international travel that worried her. She'd need him to be her Ground—if he could. If he was willing to try.

She didn't even know that much. How did he really feel about her Gift? He'd left so quickly…but it had been a migraine, not her, that had sent him out the door. She'd seen that he was in pain, but she hadn't known he suffered from migraines. Were they connected to his blocked Gift?

His cousin Lorenzo hadn't known about the migraines either. *He's not exactly a confiding sort,* Lorenzo had said.

No, he wasn't. She stared bleakly out at the darkness. She was in love with him, but knowing his heart was no prescription for bliss when she knew so little else about him. She didn't know his mind or his body, nothing about his childhood or his friends, little about his business. She'd never been to his country. Most of all, she didn't know his world—a monied world, one where people casually flew across continents for a business deal, a party or to help a friend.

Maybe Drew was right to turn his back on what was between them. But if he did...

Her eyes closed. He'd held her so tightly when the fire threatened her control that one of his buttons had dug into her cheek. She remembered the faint scent of starch, the strong arms covered in cotton and the hard beat of his heart.

Oh, how she'd wanted him. In that instant she had been desperate for him. And he'd wanted her, too. His body had made that clear.

But he'd stepped back. Always, always, he pulled back from her.

Follow your heart, her aunt sometimes said. But was that wisdom or a slick cliché? Women had been falling in love with the wrong men for centuries. Being in love was no ticket to happiness. Rose had always known that, and deep down, had always felt a touch smug. She would recognize her perfect mate if she ever found him.

She hadn't realized that finding a soul mate offered no more guarantees than falling in love the usual way—blind and dizzy and scared, with no promise of a soft landing.

Rose lay awake a long time. Finally exhaustion won, dragging her down firmly as her mind slowed, spinning into silence. Her last clear thought was that it didn't matter what she decided to do. Drew wasn't likely to give her a chance, anyway.

The alarm jerked him from nightmare into cold.

Drew lay still with his heart racing as if he'd been running. He'd kicked the covers off, he realized dimly. He was damp with sweat, chilled from the air-conditioning... Air-conditioning. Not the bitter seep of winter through the walls of an unheated warehouse.

This time he'd brought pieces of the nightmare back with him.

He sat up slowly, as if balance was a precarious negotiation between himself and gravity. But there were no ropes binding his hands or ankles. He could have light whenever he wanted, at the flip of a switch.

God. He rubbed his face and was embarrassed to find it wet, too. But not with sweat.

Well, he'd been eleven when it happened, he thought wearily, reaching out to silence the shrill alarm. And was eleven again, it seemed, when he dreamed of it. Though God knows why, after all these years... No, wait. He could see why the nightmare had returned, he thought with relief as he hit the light switch. He was dealing with a probable kidnapping. Naturally that resurrected some scraps of memory.

He put those scraps away again, mentally packing them up in the past as tidily as he might pack for a trip. He was in the shower, grateful for the heat and steam, when it occurred to him that the nightmare had returned several days before he knew Lucas's lady was missing.

Chapter 13

Twelve hours later Rose was sleeping in yet another bed owned by the king—this time at thirty thousand feet. She awoke all at once and disoriented. A strange woman was smiling down at her.

Oh. Memory returned. It was the stewardess, Mareta.

"We will be hitting some turbulence soon," she said pleasantly. "There's a bit of a storm over London. You'll be more comfortable in the forward section, with a seat belt."

"Of course." Rose sat up and swung her legs off the bed, dragging a hand through her hair. Her fingers hit snarls and she grimaced. "Do I have time to visit the lavatory before I strap down?"

Having been assured that she did and should find whatever she needed to freshen up in the drawers in the vanity there, she stepped into her sandals and headed for the door at the rear of the sleeping compartment.

This bathroom was nothing like the cramped cubbyholes

in commercial airliners. The water taps were gold. The tub was larger than the one Rose bathed in at home. She grimaced at the sight the mirror over the sink offered. She'd tossed around on the bed as much as she'd slept on it. Her hair looked as if she'd been dragged through a bush backward.

The rest of her was presentable, she thought. She wore black slacks with a full-sleeved black shirt, cinched at the waist by an ornate belt. Her earrings were her favorites, chosen because the tiny gemstones that formed the pattern picked up almost any color she might wear. Both the earrings and the clasp on the belt were her own design, and gave her confidence.

The first drawer she opened held several new toothbrushes, three brands of toothpaste, three kinds of lotion, a small manicure set and two brands of mouthwash. The second drawer contained a surprising assortment of unused cosmetics. The third, deepest drawer held three hairbrushes, two sizes of curling irons, a blow-dryer and various gels, sprays and hair ornaments.

Shaking her head at the courtesies the ultrarich routinely extended their guests, Rose selected a brush and started working on the tangles.

After awhile you reached a point, she thought, when any decision was better than indecision. Besides, she didn't care to let Drew have everything his way. She would make him discuss their relationship and his reasons for ending it. She'd promised herself that over a hasty breakfast before they left for the airport.

But all day he'd been perfectly, infernally pleasant—a lot like the stewardess, damn him. He'd told her about the plane they were flying in, a Gulfstream V the king had had specially fitted. He'd talked about politics, business, music, art.

Had she once thought he wasn't charming? Today he had been. Endlessly charming. She'd never seen such an unscalable wall erected from pure charm. It had proved impossible to intrude on that flawless formality with anything personal. When he'd excused himself—ever so politely—to go to the workstation, where a desk, two phones and a computer made it easy to bring the office along, she'd given up and napped.

A sharp jerk of the brush made her wince, and she used her fingers to tease out one especially large tangle. At least she'd caught up on her sleep.

That was all she'd accomplished.

The plane's interior was divided into three sections, in addition to the cockpit, the kitchen and the bathroom. Drew wasn't in the middle section, where they'd eaten coq au vin on gold-rimmed china several hours ago. The teak table had long since been cleared. She continued to the first section, walking on carpet so thick she could have curled up on it for her nap if she hadn't been afraid of shocking the stewardess.

Drew wasn't working now. He sat in one of the oversize armchairs with his seat belt fastened. He was sound asleep.

Rose stopped. He'd taken off his suit jacket. His tie hung loose and the top two buttons of his shirt were unfastened. His head tilted back, exposed the strong line of his throat. She could see the pulse beat in the tender pocket beneath his jaw.

Her heartbeat picked up at the sight of him. This, too, had driven her from his presence. She'd been too aware of his every movement, like a cat tracking a robin on a branch. The more time she spent with him, the more sensitized she seemed to grow to his physical being.

He'd watched her, too. But only when he thought she wasn't looking.

She looked at his hands now, lying open and lax in sleep, one on his thigh, one on the arm of the chair. Clean, strong, masculine hands. His fingers were long, the nails neatly tended but not professionally manicured. He wore no rings.

When she looked back at his face, his eyes were open, regarding her steadily. He looked tired. The creases beneath his eyes were flat, mere lines now.

She said the first thing she thought of. "You never wear any jewelry."

His mouth crooked up. "Does that offend you professionally?"

"You'd look good in an earring."

"A pearl, perhaps," he murmured. Amusement touched those green eyes, then faded, leaving them bleak.

The reminder of their flirtation at her shop didn't make him happy. What did? she wondered. And all at once said, "You never asked me why I'm still a virgin."

His eyes rounded.

The plane dropped. She staggered.

He had his seat belt off and was steadying her before she quite got her feet back under her.

"It's nothing to worry about," he said soothingly. "We've apparently hit some bad weather and the ride may get a little bumpy. But you'd better sit down."

For an instant she actually considered pretending to be frightened so he would go on soothing her. Touching her. Annoyed with herself, she said, "A little turbulence doesn't worry me." She glanced at the windows as she spoke. It was dead black out there. Suddenly lightning flashed somewhere in the clouds they were flying through. She flinched.

He slid one arm around her shoulders. The comfort he offered may have been meant impersonally, but she sighed and relaxed against him. *At last,* she thought. At last. His arm around her felt more right than anything ever had.

If he felt what she did, it didn't show. "I'm glad you're not a nervous flier, since we do seem to be in for some turbulence."

"Jet fuel makes big fire. I'm sure there's no big fire in my near future, so the plane isn't going to crash." She paused. The plane pitched, dropped and steadied. Drew shifted with the motion easily, still holding her with one arm.

"If it's possible for planes to crash without burning," she added, "I don't want to hear about it."

He chuckled. "Your Gift provides some assurances, but no guarantees?"

"No. No guarantees." She met his eyes. She couldn't read anything there...but his hand, the one on her shoulder, was toying idly with her hair as if he wasn't aware he was doing it.

The heck with trying to find a smooth way to bring the subject up. She'd go for the direct approach. "I'm considering getting rid of my hymen."

He choked. Since he wasn't drinking anything, his sudden coughing fit was rather satisfying. Then he looked at her and her grin faded. "Don't expect me to believe you're going to pick up some man in a bar."

Now he was easier to read. Fury was hard to hide. "No, I was thinking a trip to the doctor would be the best way to take care of it. That's sensible, isn't it? No pain that way, the first time."

"Rose." He looked away, but the view outside the small, rounded windows didn't please him, either. "Don't trivialize something that obviously means a great deal to you."

"Don't make assumptions. You never gave me a chance to talk about this—you've been too busy avoiding me. I'm not a virgin because I want to be."

"You've undoubtedly had plenty of opportunities to change your state if you'd wanted to. You're beautiful."

It was said so flatly, as if referring to a long-established fact, and not one that especially pleased him. She still liked hearing it. "I'm picky. Very picky. Not exactly by choice." She hesitated. He seemed to have accepted the reality of her Gift, but the very ease of his acceptance bothered her. It seemed a social construct, like his charm. "For some of the Gifted, sex can be difficult. Especially for those tied to water and fire."

"Fire and water don't mix, I suppose." Absently those long fingers continued to sift through her hair.

She shook her head impatiently. "Don't joke. Please. This is...harder than talking about hymens. More personal."

His eyebrows lifted. "*More* personal?"

They'd turned more fully into each other, their bodies acting on a quiet, mutual gravity without their conscious notice. She laid a hand on his chest. "It's..." She smiled suddenly. "Trying to explain is like talking about sex to a virgin. A truly inexperienced virgin, that is, not one who is only technically intact."

"I'm beginning to find the word 'technically' quite erotic." He rested one hand on her shoulder. With the other he scooped up her hair, brushing the back of her neck with his fingers and raising shivers. Carefully he brought the mass of hair forward, over her shoulder. "Are you talking about your Gift again?"

"Yes." There was a faint line between his eyebrows. She couldn't tell if it indicated concentration as his fingers drifted slowly through the length of her hair...or discomfort with the subject. "In sex, you see, not just bodies join. The *èsseri* mingle, too." Her quick upward glance was half shy, half pure mischief. "A little mingling here and there can be fun, but there's a terrible dissonance if bodies join, but the *èsseri* don't fit well.''

His fingers continued to tease her hair. They didn't brush her breast. They didn't touch her body at all. She wondered, with an odd little ache, if he felt the need, too—the need to touch. It wasn't sexual. Not purely sexual, at least. She was aroused. But her need to touch him went beyond the giddy delight of desire.

There was bemusement in his voice, a quiet, absorbed pleasure in his face. "Are you saying our, ah, essences fit?"

"Yes, but…to be honest, the first thing I liked about you was that you're completely blocked. I can't feel your *èssere* at all right now."

His hand stilled. "You said something along those lines before."

"You're Water-Gifted, Drew. An empath."

His head moved in a quick, definite negative. And the plane moved in a sudden drop and shudder, ending with the nose pointed steeply down. He put both hands on her shoulders. "We need to sit and fasten our seat belts. This is foolishness."

She had a feeling he referred to more than the stupidity of standing up in a plane that was jolting its way through a storm. As the captain's voice came over the speakers just then, advising them that they would be landing shortly at Heathrow, she couldn't argue. But her skin felt cold when he took his hands away.

Rose sat in one of the cushy armchairs and clicked the seat belt into place. Drew sat in the one beside hers, close enough to touch had she stretched out a hand. But she didn't. His face was closed again, all signs of that quiet pleasure erased.

The landing gear had been let down when he spoke

again. His voice was tight. He wasn't looking at her. "I shouldn't have led you to think... I meant to keep my hands to myself on this trip. I will from now on."

"And I mean to change your mind."

He met her eyes. His were grave and weary. "I'm asking you not to. I can't afford you, Rose."

Heathrow was as familiar to Drew, in its way, as the Copse or the Old Knoll at Harrow. Crowded, cavernous, smelling of hot grease and chips as they passed a fast-food section, it was no more unpleasant than most airports.

He hadn't cared much for Harrow, either, as he recalled.

Passengers clogged the waiting areas around the gates, spilling out into the breezeways. Summer storms seldom disrupted air traffic for long, but two storm cells had collided over London with unusually violent results, and planes were stacked up over the airport. Some incoming flights had been diverted, many were delayed and a few had been canceled.

No one was happy. Drew found the airport more than usually oppressive.

"It's strange not to have to do anything," Rose said. "No luggage to worry about, no check-in... Are you *sure* we don't have to check in personally?"

"Quite sure," he said, amused. She'd been fretting over that ever since they landed. "The jet's crew are quite accustomed to handling this sort of thing. Everything will be taken care of. We have a bit of a wait, though." They'd made unusually good time, pushed along by one of the storm fronts on the last part of their flight.

"Three hours." She sighed. "Not enough time to leave the airport and do anything. Not that I could see much, anyway, I suppose, with the way it's pouring rain out there.

It's selfish of me to even think about sightseeing, considering why I'm here."

"You've never seen London?"

She shook her head. "Athens, Istanbul, Cyprus, Venice—I've traveled in my own little corner of the world on buying trips for the shop. But I've never been this far north."

"We can get a drink in the lounge, if you like. Or gasp at the prices they charge in the airport shops." Women and shopping. He had a feeling he knew which activity she'd choose.

Drew reached behind him to rub his neck, where the muscles were tense. He felt tired and jittery all at once, as if he'd drunk gallons of coffee to stay awake. That, he thought, was probably the result of sexual frustration. He was worried about Lucas, and he kept having to remind himself not to grab Rose's hand. Yet he wasn't unhappy.

"We'll have to come back through security if we visit the shops."

Got it in one. He grinned in spite of his weariness. "We've got time."

She wouldn't let him buy her anything. It would have frustrated Drew if he'd been a gentleman, since a gentleman wouldn't force an unwanted gift on a woman. Since he was happily free of such scruples, he merely arranged things without her knowledge. His gift would be waiting for her when she returned to Montebello. It was a small satisfaction, considering he wouldn't be around to learn whether the gift pleased her in spite of her scruples, but he enjoyed the planning of it.

Perhaps some sly part of him was hoping she'd be angry enough or pleased enough to contact him, even after he'd walked away. He wasn't proud of that. Walking away clean was best for both of them.

After last night there seemed little doubt that she somehow triggered his spells.

Absently he rubbed his neck again as they stood on line at the security check. Slightly ahead of them, a tired toddler was whining at her mother. The man directly behind him kept crowding him, as if he could speed things up by stepping on Drew's heels. At the moment he was complaining loudly to his wife about the delay, blaming the long line on Labour immigration policies, incompetent personnel and his wife's brother.

Drew's head was beginning to throb. He kneaded the tense muscles and wished the man would shut up.

"Headache?" Rose asked.

He glanced at her. Her tone was light, but her eyes were worried. Lucas, he realized, must have said something to her about his "migraines." Why couldn't people keep things to themselves? "I must have slept crooked on the plane. My neck is stiff."

"You have that same white look around your eyes you did last night."

"I'm all right. I'm not a bloody invalid."

"You're not too bloody polite, either."

He grimaced. "Sorry. I've been told I'm the world's worst patient. I truly don't have a headache, though—just tense muscles and a crick in the neck." Not to mention that the idiot behind him was getting on his nerves.

"Common wisdom says that men are always bad patients, illness being such a shock to the machismo."

It occurred to him that she wouldn't know, from personal experience, if that was true. She'd grown up without brothers or a father. All sorts of normal male rituals, from shaving to arguing with the sports announcer when one's team was losing, had been left out of her childhood. "But how can we trust common wisdom? It insists on clichés. Like the one about women loving to shop."

"And we all know how false that is," she replied seriously, shifting the bag with her purchases from one hand to the other.

"Obviously. Then there's the one about—" The loudmouth behind him stepped closer, so close his shoulder brushed Drew's back. The muscles along Drew's neck and shoulders tightened like a dog with hackles raised. "The cliché about men not asking for directions," he said, trying to ignore the idiot and his own rising irritation.

The man bumped him again. Harder.

Clamping down on the urge to snarl, Drew turned to the loudmouth. "I will cede these few inches of floor to you as soon as I am able, but I really don't believe we can occupy them at the same time."

The man glared up at him—bloodshot eyes, a pug nose, bad breath and a belly that hid his belt entirely. "Look wot we got 'ere, Muriel—a pretty lord standing on line the same as us 'umble folk. Don't like being around yer inferiors, yer lordship?"

"Dear God," Drew said, his eyebrows lifting. "Yet another cliché. This one speaks."

Ahead of them, the whining toddler started to cry. Or scream, rather. The loudmouth's wife made ineffectual hushing noises at her husband. The loudmouth himself planted his feet well apart and sneered, "Did I get 'is lordship's pretty suit all dirty? Let me clean it up for you." He swiped one hand down Drew's shoulder.

Drew felt as if he couldn't breathe—no surprise, since with every breath, he inhaled the fermented gases from the bastard's last few meals. "Get your hand off me."

The loudmouth buffeted Drew's shoulder this time.

The wife bleated. Rose said Drew's name firmly. Drew's lip drew back. "Flattered as I am by these delicate little advances, old chap, it really isn't at all the thing, with your wife standing right here."

The man's face turned purple. "Why, you—"

The pain hit without warning, blinding, white-hot. Drew staggered as if he'd been struck.

Voices—loud, converging, melding into a senseless cacophony—*I didn't do it! I didn't…oh, my God…can't see, Mama…he dying?…get back, everyone get…poor man… miss my flight for sure now.*

Too close. Too loud. He closed his eyes, both hands clasping his head, trying to squeeze a thought through past the agony. Then an arm, steady and familiar around his waist, urged him forward and he heard one voice, quieter than the others. "You'll sit down now. Just a few steps this way…come on, Drew, you can make it."

Rose. His legs were rubber, all the strength drained out by the agony in his head. "Get me…" He had to stop and breathe. Something touched the back of his knees—a chair. He collapsed into it. "Get me away from here," he said through clenched teeth. "Alone. Need to be alone."

"I'll take care of it."

He heard her tossing off instructions to someone—migraines, she said, and something about his medicine and their luggage. The fictitious medicine wasn't going to do him much good. How long did he have? God, for it to hit like this—all these people around, everyone close, too close… "I need to be alone," he gritted out.

"Soon." She squeezed his hand. "The paramedics should be here soon. They can give you a shot at the hospital, Drew, to take the pain away."

"No." He forced his eyes open so he could see her,

make her know how important this was. "This will pass. No paramedics. No hospital."

Her eyebrows were drawn down in a sharp, worried frown. She studied his face a moment. "All right. No hospital. But—"

It hit. As he'd known it would, reality jarred itself loose. Sound was the first of his senses to go this time, mutating into texture instead of noise. Voices became sandpaper scraping his skin. "No," he said, or thought he did. But it was too late. It was happening.

Vision went next, shapes sliding into shapes, normal geometry corkscrewing into impossibilities. He tried to close his eyes, but it was already too late. Too late...

But one sense hadn't gone. He felt Rose's hand smoothing his hair, front to back, smoothing his head over and over...it didn't hurt. For some reason it didn't hurt at all. And words. He heard words...

"Be still, be calm...that's it, you're safe now, no one can get in, Drew. I've got you."

The words were nonsense, but that he could hear them at all soothed him. Miraculously his eyes did close.

The next half hour was hell. He kept sliding partway into a spell, but Rose—her touch, her voice—would somehow pull him out again. Only he couldn't get all the way out. At the edge of madness, the pain waited to seize him. Bits of reality filtered in between bouts of pain and madness— the pilot's voice, men in uniforms, Rose telling them what to do... She wanted him to walk, so he did, or thought he did. Bend down, climb in...a limo, he was sitting in a limo. But he wasn't alone, not yet—God, he needed to be alone. Rose was there, and others—he felt them beating at his mind, pressing in on him, and the pain trebled impossibly, like a giant crushing his skull in two huge fists.

This time when the madness rose, he didn't resist. Time

passed in the prison of his mind as he counted. And counted. He counted very high this time...

Cool air along his left side. Warmth on his right, and warmth on his face...Rose's breath on his face. Her lips brushing his, then nibbling. The damp touch of her tongue. Her hand sliding over his chest, pausing to tease one nipple.

His breath drew in sharply. He inhaled roses and musk and woman.

What came over him then wasn't the deadly fatigue that always followed a spell. It wasn't anything he could have predicted or fought against. As if it were a beast that had been crouched, waiting, all his life, it came roaring up out of his belly.

Hunger.

Chapter 14

Rose sat on the hotel bed beside Drew. The drapes were drawn. The light by the door created a lopsided darkness with the bed in the center of the room, sitting somewhere between twilight and a yellow, artificial dawn.

His skin was clammy. He was entirely still, barely breathing. His eyes were half-open and entirely unseeing.

But he wasn't entirely gone. Even though she couldn't reach him, some part of him lingered, dimly accessible. Even after he'd gone away inside himself, he'd answered her instructions, delivered with voice and mind and heart. Walk. Turn. Lean on me. Lie down. With the help of the copilot and stewardess from the plane she'd gotten him here, but she was desperately unsure if she'd done the right thing. Maybe he should be in a hospital, regardless of what he'd said.

But there would be people, bright lights, intrusions both physical and mental at a hospital. Doctors weren't prepared to deal with a nearly catatonic empath.

She wasn't sure she was, either. His shields had fluctuated wildly at the airport—failing, she thought, due to the pressure within and the press of people without. She'd been terrified. Heathrow was not the place for a blocked empath to suddenly lose all his barriers—the flood of otherness from the crowds would have destroyed him.

But neither could Drew afford to remain blocked. The pressure from within would eventually destroy his mental dam, and might take his mind with it.

Unless he had help when that deluge hit.

Rose took a deep breath and cupped his face in her hands. "Time to come back, Drew." Bending, she feathered kisses over his face. "It's safe now."

Nothing. She hesitated, then drew her hands along his chest. His bare chest. She'd unbuttoned his shirt.

Her breath quickened. She hated that, hated knowing she could arouse herself by touching him while he lay helpless. It felt like rape. He was unconscious, or something very like that state—but he had to be called back. Somehow. He was too far away, closed up tightly inside his mind, no longer responding to her voice, his psychic barriers so strong she couldn't touch him except with her hands and her body.

If she couldn't call him back now, he might never return.

Careful kisses weren't working. He needed to be aroused—literally. She bit her lip. Do it, she told herself. And unfastened her belt, tossing it to one side. Then her shirt went. And her bra.

After a brief hesitation, she left the bed and opened her suitcase. Gemma had packed a few things she hadn't specifically requested, including a souvenir she'd brought back from the little shop where she'd bought the dress she'd worn to the palace. That purchase had been made half in humor, half wishful thinking.

She opened the box and put a couple of the foil-wrapped packets on the bedside table. Just in case.

Then she settled alongside Drew, pressing her body against his, putting skin to skin. Her nipples hardened at the contact. Her breath sucked in. This time she didn't just kiss him—she teased with lips and tongue. She slid her hand up his chest and tickled one flat nipple with her fingernail.

His chest moved. He shuddered. And two hard hands seized her arms and rolled her over onto her back.

He sprawled on top of her, heavy and male. His mouth crushed down on hers, and there was no teasing, no exploration, no gentle melding. He forced her mouth open and took.

Shock held her still. He kissed her as if she was all his hope of heaven, every muscle of his body taut with need—kissed her as if he wouldn't, couldn't, stop. Something—she refused to call it fear—trickled through her, but it was dwarfed by sensation. His shield was tight and she couldn't *feel* him, but his scent filled her. His skin was hot now, and she sent her hands racing over it, cherishing the feel of his back, then stopping to dig her fingers into his shoulders. He'd brought his thigh up between her legs, pressing up against her.

She wrapped herself around him, holding on to him with her arms, twisting one leg around his as if she could press him inside her entire body. He shuddered. She said his name, then said it again—Drew was with her, he was back. And he wanted her. She felt him—her love, her lover—not with her Gift, but with senses more primitive and basic, and everything in her answered.

But was it right? Should she make sure he was all the way back, that he knew what he was doing? If he made love to her now and regretted it... She pushed on his chest, but he groaned and kissed her harder, his tongue tangling with hers.

Finally she grabbed his hair and pulled his head away so she could look at him. His eyes were dark, pleasure-filled and just this side of desperate.

"Rose, beautiful Rose." He cupped her breast, his thumb drawing shivers from her. "Don't ask me to stop. Please. I need you."

"All right. But if you regret this later, I'm going to kill you."

His eyes gleamed, their color lost in the static shadows that wrapped them. "There is nothing about you I could regret," he said, and brushed his lips lightly over hers. "No matter what happens."

Before she could muster enough thought to wonder what he meant, he'd turned his attention to her breasts. The dampness, the heat, the tugging made contradictions in her. She wanted to lie there and let him make magic on her body for hours, but she wanted equally to explore his body, to taste and sample and find the places that made him wild. The needs built and clashed until she felt him unfastening her pants.

Naked was a good idea. But if she was going to be stripped, so was he.

They tumbled together on the big bed, hands reaching for zippers, tugging cloth, each of them easily distracted by the opportunities presented by newly bared skin to lick, touch, savor. At the last minute Rose remembered the condoms she'd put on the bedside table. She stretched out an arm, snagged one and handed it to him.

Seconds later they came together again, skin to skin, and the shock of sensation stole her breath. He nudged her legs apart and braced his arms on either side of her head. His gaze was on hers. A drop of sweat rolled down his cheek, and she leaned up and licked it off. He turned his head, catching her mouth with his.

While he was kissing her, his hips moved, a tentative thrust that stopped with him barely inside her.

He was big. The teasing, stinging feel of him was foreign to her. She shifted, trying to find an angle, a position that would help her accommodate him.

He gasped and his head went back, the tendons in his neck standing out. "Rose," he said, hoarse. "Be still a moment so I don't…I don't have much control left."

Again he moved, testing. Pushing against the barrier, that scrap of flesh she'd claimed didn't matter. It hurt. It felt wonderful. She needed to move but didn't know what to do. Then the muscles in his buttocks bunched and he drove inward.

"That *hurt!*" Her surprise was outsize, unreasonable. She'd known it would hurt, but the pain had chased away the other feelings and it was that loss she was unhappy about. Her fingers dug into his hips, but she was trying to keep him from moving now, not urging him on.

"I know. I'm sorry." He bent and, instead of kissing her, licked her lips. Slowly, carefully, as if he wanted to lick where it hurt, but he was lodged there and couldn't. Some of the tension sighed out of her.

As soon as it did, she noticed other things, like how full she felt. He was throbbing inside her, or was she pulsing around him? The other feelings weren't gone, after all, she realized, and experimentally pushed up with her hips, which pulled him in even deeper.

Oh, my. That felt…incredible.

He began to thrust, slowly at first. He was being careful of her, and she loved it, loved the closeness, the heat, the sensations shimmering through her. The pain wasn't entirely gone, but behind the lingering sting lurked shadowy feelings she was hungry for, a huge, wanton excess of possibilities. She matched his careful strokes and ran her hands down his back, letting her fingertips linger just above the cleft in his buttocks. On her body, that spot was particularly sensitive.

Apparently it was a sweet spot for him, too. For a second she felt *him*—his essence, his self, touching hers. But it was the merest flicker, and then his shield was back. And then he was kissing her.

This kiss was greedier, not so careful. He licked her ear and rocked against her. "I'm beginning to understand why I found the idea of a purely technical virgin so exciting."

She laughed, low and husky.

He pushed her legs a little wider, making more room for himself and changing the angle, and he began to move faster. With each shift, each change in tempo or pressure, she discovered new sensations. She had the dreamy thought that she could do this forever and never be done, never stop finding some new and marvelous feeling.

Of course she knew better. She knew what a climax was. But she didn't know what it was to climax with her lover— with Drew—inside her. This question was beginning to gather some urgency.

Her hand slid over his buttocks and down between his legs to the bit of skin stretched tight there. She scraped it lightly with her fingernails.

His whole body arched as a low sound tore from his throat—then he was slamming into her. Hard, too hard— pitching her into a realm that was all body, no mind. If it hurt, she couldn't separate one sensation from another enough to know—all were tangled up together, subsumed in urgency.

He gasped, paused and put a hand between them, his thumb finding the sweetest spot on her body. As he thrust hard into her, his thumb pushed on that spot and she convulsed.

Having lost thought in the moments before, she now lost her grip on time, as if it were a thread wrenched from her suddenly lax hands. After a while she drifted back into herself, smiling.

He was heavy. His breath came fast and hard in her ear. He kissed it, wrapped his arms around her and rolled so that she was on top of him. The air was chilly on her damp back and bottom. She considered lifting her head, but it was so comfortable to let it rest there on his chest. She could hear his heartbeat.

And she felt horribly alone.

Now, every instinct shouted, now was when she should feel him, heart to heart, open to her. But she couldn't feel him, not in the way she needed to.

He was petting her again, stroking a hand along her hair. But the silence was deafening. She stirred, shifting more to his side with one leg over his, and winced.

His hand paused. "Sore?"

"A little." She propped herself up on her elbow so she could see his face. Sleepiness and satisfaction had his eyelids drooping, but the eyes beneath them were sharp with thoughts and feelings she couldn't guess.

Rose touched his cheek, finding the hint of beard she'd felt against her breasts earlier. "You promised not to regret this."

His mouth crooked up. "Surely that's supposed to be my line."

Their eyes met, and the silence grew louder.

Does he hear it, feel it? Is there a place inside him that aches with emptiness where I should be, the way I'm empty now where he belongs?

"I told you," he said softly, "I couldn't regret you, no matter what." He tucked her hair behind her ear. "And now, much as I hate to leave you for even a moment, I'd better…'' His gaze drifted down the length of his body. His eyes widened. ''Good Lord.''

He was still semierect and sheathed in the condom she'd handed him.

It was green. And glowing.

''Oh, my,'' she said weakly. She'd forgotten the special properties of this box of condoms. ''Not exactly your usual English overcoat, is it? My aunt, um, apparently decided I might need them. She included them when she packed for me.''

''Your aunt packed condoms for you.'' It wasn't a question. His eyes were still wide, fascinated by a part of his body that didn't normally glow a radioactive green. He shook his head. ''I have seriously underestimated that lady.''

Drew disposed of the glowing condom in the bathroom. Then he stood with his hands braced on the counter on either side of the sink, his shoulders tense and his head hanging.

He was in a hotel. That much was obvious. A fairly nice one—the door to the bathroom was heavy and paneled, and the counter he leaned on now was an expensive synthetic that looked like brown marble. Everything looked familiar, but in a generic way. He didn't think he'd stayed here before, but he'd been in hotels much like this one.

With a quick, almost violent gesture he turned on the tap and splashed water on his face. He didn't know where he was or how he'd gotten here. Or why Rose had decided to seduce him instead of having him taken someplace quiet, with padded walls and burly keepers.

No hospital, he'd told her. For some reason she'd agreed. How many people had seen him flip out?

The face in the mirror returned no answers. He shut off

the water and the lights, then padded back into the bed-room.

She'd turned on the lamp by the bed. Her shoulders were smooth and erect, the black hair tumbling over them in messy extravagance. Her eyes were dark and wary.

He tried to soften his expression as he sat beside her. "I'm not sure how to handle this except by plunging in. We need to talk about what happened. Not what happened between us exactly." He captured her hand. "Though God knows that comes into it. What happened…at the airport." He paused. "You'll have questions. I have some myself. I guess I'll start with the obvious. Where am I?"

"The Robertson Hotel at Heathrow. The stewardess and copilot from the plane helped me get you here."

The swift wash of humiliation made his jaws tight.

"I told them you had epilepsy. A rare form that caused lingering disorientation."

That loosened his jaw. "Ah…epilepsy?"

"Well, I had to tell them something. The migraine story worked when you were all pale and bleary with pain, but migraines don't turn people into zombies."

A zombie. So that's what he looked like when one of his spells hit.

"A friend of mine has petit mal seizures. She blanks out from time to time. Sometimes she goes entirely out and falls, and when she comes to she's confused for a while. Sometimes she just gets a blank look in her eyes for a few seconds and loses a little time. You had the same not-there look on your face, though your attack lasted longer than her seizures do."

"I suppose it's better than telling the truth." He rubbed his thumb along the back of her hand. "The story will get back to my aunt and uncle, though."

"You haven't told anyone at all, have you?"

"Told them what? That every now and then I go nuts"

He dropped her hand and wished, suddenly, he'd pulled on some clothes before beginning this discussion.

The sheet slipped as she leaned forward, revealing the upper curves of her breasts. "You are not crazy."

"I did see a doctor, Rose. A specialist. There's nothing wrong with me physically, which means the problem is mental."

"Sure, if you consider all forms of psychic ability some kind of mental problem."

His lips tightened. "I'm not psychic. I can't read minds, and I would have noticed at some point if I were prone to trances. Unless you think that's what happens to me—that I go into some kind of trance."

"I'm not sure what to call what happens to you, but it isn't a trance. A fugue state, maybe. And you're an empath, not a telepath, so you don't read minds, you pick up feelings. Or would, if you weren't completely blocked. That's what is causing your problem, Drew. Your shields."

He stood and reached for his pants and underwear. "You don't know what you're talking about."

"I'm the only one you're likely to find who *does* know what I'm talking about on this subject."

He pulled on the boxers. "You may be, as Lucas said, great at starting fires. That doesn't mean you're right about me."

She made an exasperated noise. "So, because I can start a fire without a match, you trust me enough to fly across the ocean. You believe what I say about a woman I've never met—a woman I know about only because I held her ring in my hand. But you don't think I'm right about the man I love?"

He froze with one foot stuck in his slacks.

"Dio, come stùpida," she muttered. "I didn't intend to say that."

He let the trousers drop and turned to face her. She was

pale. Worse, she'd braced herself, expecting to be hurt. "I don't know what to say."

Her mouth curved up. It didn't affect the look in her eyes. "You don't exactly have a problem with your mouth running away with you, do you? I wish I could say the same. Drew...I know you aren't thinking in those terms and your first instinct is to head for the hills. I'd planned to keep it to myself for now, but my mouth snuck up on me."

She was right. His first reaction was to run. To put distance between them as quickly as possible. Moving carefully, as if his center of gravity had shifted and he had to learn how to balance all over again, he came and sat beside her on the bed. Feelings swirled in him—a dry torrent, windy and wordless.

"Rose." He couldn't find any way to make what he felt clear to either of them.

"I'm warning you." Her voice aimed at wry but wobbled. "I don't think my ego can handle a 'let's be friends' speech right now."

"I have *never* wanted to be just a friend to you." He touched her cheek, then let his hand fall. "You scare me, though."

She swallowed. "I'm scared, too."

"Not, I think, for the same reason." He had to look away. "You seem to be triggering my crazy spells."

A beat of silence fell, followed then by her demand, "Why? How? And you are *not* crazy."

"I don't know how. But until I met you, they were mercifully rare. Now they're hitting constantly. And...the week I didn't see you. I didn't have any spells that week."

She thought that over, her teeth worrying her lip. "We need Gemma."

He couldn't imagine discussing this with anyone else. He didn't like discussing it with Rose. "If my spells are triggered by being around one psychic, I don't think bringing in another one would help.''

"She isn't powerful, but she's Earth-Gifted, not fire. A healer. Of course, another empath might be able to help, but..." A worried V formed between her eyebrows. "There are only two empaths in my family. My great-uncle Alfredo is Water-Gifted and functions very well, but his Gift is slight compared to yours. He couldn't get past your walls to show you anything.''

"Wait a minute. I thought you said it was the women in your family who were psychic.''

"Gifted male children are born occasionally, but it's rare—at least in my family—and the men aren't able to pass it on to their children. That's why we've always tracked our lineage through the female line. I have a theory that passing on the Gifts has as much to do with psychic bonds formed between a mother and the baby in her womb as it does with genetics, but—" she waved a hand dismissively "that's another subject.''

"You said there were two empaths in your family." Dear Lord. Was he actually taking her idea seriously? Deep inside, something uneasy quivered, like a guitar string plucking itself.

"Um...Pia wouldn't be much help, I'm afraid.''

He found a note of grim humor. "Pia doesn't function well?''

"She talks to aliens. Looks like you're stuck with me.''

He wanted to be. The knowledge hit him like one of his spells, unstoppable, unreasonable and almost as debilitating. He clenched his jaw.

Was he falling for her? Was he...in love?

His head went light and dizzy, like a helium balloon trying to escape its tether. His fingers tingled as if he'd been hyperventilating, and his heart pounded. And he looked at her sitting so close, her skin dusky gold in the lamplight, her eyes worried and trying not to be. He saw the shape of her beneath the sheet and smelled the musky scent of sex, and he wanted, badly, to make love to her all over again.

But she would be sore, and one thing was certain in the midst of his vast confusion: he wasn't going to hurt her.

Not any more than he had to, at least.

"Drew? You have the oddest look on your face. Did you think of something important?"

It wasn't so hard, after all, to smile. "Oh, yes," he said, and brushed a kiss across her forehead. His head didn't hurt. Whatever she'd done when she called him back from limbo, the effect seemed to be lingering. Maybe sex really was a cure, albeit a temporary one.

Besides, some risks were worth taking. "But you can't do what I'm thinking of. Not tonight, at least. I'm going to draw a bath for you," he said, and touched her cheek, her throat, her shoulder, because she was here and he could touch her, and that was a delight all by itself. One he needed to savor while he could. "And then I'm going to wash your back. Among other things."

Chapter 15

Drew seemed suddenly possessed of a great need to take care of her. He wouldn't even let her walk into the bathroom when the bath was ready, but scooped her up in his arms and carried her there.

He also, she thought, had a need to play, to push everything else aside for a time and just be lovers. New lovers, who had just discovered each other and the delights of sharing their bodies. She understood. Until yesterday he hadn't believed real psychics existed; now he was supposed to accept that he was one. It was a huge mental leap. They would have to return to the subject of his attacks, but she could give him a little time to adjust.

At least, that's what she told herself. But it might have been simply that Drew, in a playful mood, was irresistible.

He'd filled the tub with warm water and bubbles, and he climbed into it with her. He lathered her back, as he'd said he would, and massaged it, too. And other places... Her body, she learned, had sweet spots she'd never known about. Toes, for example. Shoulders. Who would have thought the scrape of a whiskery cheek on a soapy shoulder would make her shudder? By the time they got out of the tub, her entire body was one big, throbbing erogenous zone.

They took an inordinately long time drying each other, but when they reached the bed, he seemed to want to cuddle under the covers. And that was all. When she pointed out that his body had a different program in mind, he informed her that she was too sore.

"Since it's my body we're talking about now," she said, sliding a hand down his chest, "I don't think you have the final say on how sore I am. How would you know?"

"I'm psychic," he answered promptly, and stopped her hand short of its destination.

She laughed and said there were ways to avoid making her sore that would do wonders to help them relax. She couldn't help noticing that he was a bit...tense.

"I have no idea what you're talking about," he said with an admirably straight face. "You'll have to show me."

She did, but her demonstration didn't get very far before he insisted on applying the lesson to her, and she would have mentioned her suspicions that he'd had previous instruction along these lines if she had been able to form complete sentences at that point. When they were through, they were both extremely relaxed.

His shields didn't flicker once. She wished she knew what that meant.

Afterward, they cuddled. She lay along his side, her head on his shoulder, one of her legs twined with his. He'd turned the light out, and the night hung heavy and dark against her open eyes. By all rights, she should have been dozing. She was sleepy, sated, limp. But she wasn't sure how many more such nights she would have. She wasn't sure if she would have any more at all.

He thought she triggered the attacks. And she couldn't say for sure he was wrong.

When she moved her hand over his chest this time, her impulse was only to touch, to connect. "Drew, why did you come with me on this trip if you thought I was triggering the attacks?"

"Because I'm an idiot." He turned his head and brushed a kiss across the top of her head. "Because I wanted to be with you."

That made her glad of the darkness. She didn't want him to see how easily he brought tears to her eyes. "We have to talk about your attacks."

"I like your word for them better than mine. It does feel as if I'm under attack." He began playing with her hair, his fingers teasing out the tangles he'd put in it earlier.

"It's being blocked that causes the problems. We need to know what caused you to block everything off so completely."

"You do realize I haven't the foggiest idea what you're talking about, don't you?"

"Back to Psychic Studies 101. Or maybe we're up to 201 now." She needed a moment to gather her thoughts, which were trying to drift toward sleep. The feel of his hand gently sifting through her hair was delicious, but it didn't help her stay awake. "Everyone, even the non-Gifted, is shielded to some degree. People grow shields as naturally and unconsciously as they grow skin, and for the same reason. Protection." A yawn interrupted her.

"Then shields are necessary."

"Yes, but they can be a problem, too, for empaths. Because they're so sensitive to others' emotions, empaths sometimes develop really thick, strong shields. Like yours. It's almost unheard of for a shield to be so complete a Fire-Gifted can't touch the person's aura, however."

His voice held a lazy smile. "You can touch me anywhere else you like."

"Thank you, but you're missing the point." On purpose, she thought. Frustration chased away some of the sleepiness. "For an empath, going through life completely blocked is sort of like sleep deprivation. It makes the mind do strange things."

"What kind of things?"

She rubbed her thumb absently over a rough place on her fingernail. "Well, it varies. A lot. I mentioned my cousin Pia? She can't process everything she picks up when she's open, so she spends most of her time shielded, which is almost like being blocked. As a result, she's a little confused."

"I don't talk to aliens." There was a hint of humor in his voice. "What other problems do, ah, blocked empaths have?"

She didn't want to tell him. She really didn't, not now. She picked at her fingernail. "Oh, all sorts of things."

"The way you're dodging answering, the problems must be pretty serious."

"The point is, the treatment is the same regardless of the symptoms. You have to learn to control your shields."

"What kind of symptoms are we talking about? Crazy spells like mine?"

"You're not crazy."

"Rose."

She sighed. "Okay, worst case…a few become psychopaths. They like to hurt others, maybe because of an unconscious need to feel something from outside themselves. Pain is easy to pick up, you see. Even the non-Gifted are sensitive to it to some degree. But that isn't the way you're headed," she added quickly, laying one hand on his leg. "That only happens when the empath becomes blocked while still very young, probably as a baby. He never develops right.''

"I'm glad you don't think I'm psychopathic,'' he said dryly. "I tend to agree with you. My crazy spells don't make me want to hurt anyone. What else aren't you telling me?''

"Some blocked empaths…a few…become catatonic.''

He was silent for several heartbeats. "That fits.''

She propped herself up on her elbow and tried without success to make out his expression in the darkness. "Drew, think back. It would help if you could remember a time before you were completely blocked. Did you sometimes know what people were feeling when no one else seemed to?''

He shifted uneasily. "I had a pretty normal childhood. I don't remember anything like that.''

He didn't *want* to remember. She gritted her teeth and tried coming at it from another angle. "I'll bet people consider your mother unusually kind and intuitive about others.''

"What does that have to do with anything?''

"You say you had a normal childhood. Young empaths born to non-Gifted parents don't, generally. I'm guessing that your mother is mildly empathic and instinctively helped shield you when you were very small, so that you learned how to shield from her. She probably wouldn't know about her Gift,'' Rose added. "But I'll bet she's known for being good with people.''

"She is,'' he said reluctantly.

Rose smiled and teased her fingers through his hair. "Such pretty curls. I'll bet you were an adorable little boy.''

"Hardly.'' He sounded appalled.

"So what kind of little boy were you?''

"Quite ordinary. I pestered my sister, fought with my

brother and climbed trees I'd been forbidden to climb. Fell out of one once, too. When I was twelve I wanted a motorcycle desperately, but my mother wouldn't hear of it. She…went through a period when she was overprotective."

Not surprising, if she was empathic. "Are you close to her?"

He shrugged. "When I was small, I was. A lot of things changed after the kidnapping."

After the… Her mouth went dry. She had to swallow twice before she had enough saliva to speak, and even then her voice came out funny. "Drew, what kidnapping?"

"I thought you knew." There was surprise in his voice. "With your tabloid-reading aunt around…they managed to keep it all out of the papers until after I recovered, though, so while it made a splash it was a brief one. And it's ancient history now."

Her throat was tight. "Tell me."

"I was kidnapped when I was eleven. Held for ransom."

"That's the headline. I'd like the story."

"I don't remember most of it." His voice was flat. "What I do remember, I prefer not to."

Slowly she lowered herself, finding the curve of his shoulder again. He put his arm around her, but his muscles were stiff and unwelcoming now. *No wonder,* she thought. An empathic child in the hands of people willing—possibly intending—to kill him…his sanity had probably depended on being able to block out his captors completely. "Were you held captive for long?"

"About three months."

Three months. Dear God. *A lot of things changed after the kidnapping,* he'd said. He didn't remember most of it. Didn't want to remember. "That's when you became blocked."

"Perhaps." His voice was cool, neutral. And very tired.

"If it's all the same to you, I think we'd better get some sleep now. You said we're booked for a nine-thirty flight in the morning."

She wanted to push, force him to give up the answers she needed—the answers he needed, too, if only he could be made to realize it. But she heard the deep weariness behind the crisp syllables, and she couldn't do it. "All right." She twisted so she could leave one last, soft kiss on his mouth. "Good night, then."

His arm tightened around her briefly. Then he sighed, and the terrible tension began to drain out of his body. Within minutes he seemed to be asleep.

Rose lay awake for a dark, endless time, held close in her lover's arms. Thinking. Trying to plan. Wondering exactly when he was going to leave her—and trying not to imagine what had been done to a young boy all those years ago.

The rag, the rag in his mouth, they'd jammed it down too far. He couldn't breathe, couldn't— Oh, please, no! God, no—

Drew's eyes flew open. He was gasping for breath. The nightmare fell away in pieces, breaking up more with each ragged breath, until all that was left was the need to get away. To be alone.

Beside him, Rose slept peacefully, one of her legs between his. He glanced at the clock. Almost six.

He eased away, careful not to wake her, and went to the chair near the window. There he sat with his head in his hands. For the first time in twenty-one years, he tried to remember.

But it was no use. The pieces were too small. His mind slid around them as if it were greased, unable to pluck one and fit it to another. He'd been tied up. He'd been cold. Those pieces he'd always had, and a single image—a window, high on a dingy wall. A grid over that window, and outside only another wall, brick, of some adjacent building. Drew knew he'd been found in an abandoned warehouse because he'd been told that afterward. He'd been told about other things, too. Afterward.

The window undoubtedly belonged to the warehouse, but he couldn't conjure any scrap of memory to say this was so. No more than he could claim any memory of the other things he'd been told.

One piece, though—one small piece—that was new he managed to hold on to, as much from sheer surprise as from any effort of will.

He'd counted then, too.

Chapter 16

The first-class section of the Concorde wasn't as luxurious as the royal jet, of course, but it was still far roomier and more comfortable than economy, which was how Rose had always flown before. There was plenty of room for Drew to spread out an assortment of files from his briefcase in lieu of the meal he'd just informed the flight attendant he didn't want.

Rose, too, had refused the meal. After crossing two time zones yesterday, her body wasn't at all sure what time it was now, but she'd had breakfast before leaving the hotel.

And if she were completely honest with herself, her stomach was too uneasy to welcome food. She glanced at the man beside her. "They'll have to hustle to get the meal served and the trays picked up before we land. It's strange to think we'll cross the entire Atlantic Ocean so much faster than we flew from Montebello to London."

"The Concorde flies faster than sound." He took some papers from one of the files without looking at her. "The king's jet can't match that."

The flight would be so short, in fact, she wasn't sure she was going to have time to pry Drew out of the mood he'd fallen into overnight. He might as well have stamped Keep Out on his forehead, she thought unhappily. Not that he'd been unpleasant. Oh, no. He was back to being considerate and charming.

A rip-roaring fight might help. But it was going to be uphill work getting that much emotion from him this morning.

Cocking her head, she studied the papers he was laying out like a shield in front of him. The letterhead on one page caught her attention. "I've heard of the Warren Foundation," she said. "They help refugees find homes and jobs, don't they? I can't imagine what that would have to do with your real-estate investments."

"I'm on the foundation's board," he said curtly. "And we've a quarterly meeting coming up next month. I need to familiarize myself with the agenda."

"Oh, yes, and you have only a month to do it in. I understand. And this?" She tapped another folder. "Are you on the board of the International Red Cross, too?"

"No, I promised to evaluate a property that was recently donated to them. The location makes it unsuitable for their use, and they need to know whether to sell it now or allow it to appreciate. If you're bored, Rose, I believe there's an in-flight movie available."

"I was making conversation. You've heard of the practice?"

"Sorry." Grooves bracketed his mouth, making him look austere and tired. "I'm not good company right now. I hope you don't mind if I work for a while."

"Yes."

He blinked.

She elaborated. "Yes, I do mind. And I don't need to be entertained. You're my lover, not my host."

"You surprise me. I hadn't thought you the type to demand a man's attention every second at the expense of his work."

Temper shot her eyebrows up. "Really? Well, you seem to me exactly the type to use work as an excuse when you want to avoid something scary, like feelings."

His mouth flattened. "Of course I am. As my former fiancée could tell you, I'm a poor bet for any kind of serious relationship."

Anger drained away as quickly as it had flared up, leaving her chilled and...not exactly nauseous. Or at least not in her stomach—it was more as if her whole body was queasy. Her hands curled into themselves. "One mistake does not mean you're hopeless. And she must have had problems of her own. A healthy woman doesn't try to kill herself over a man."

"No doubt that's true. But so was what she said. I *am* a cold, distant man."

"Oh, yes, that would be why you donate your time to the Warren Foundation. Because you're so cold and uncaring. Or maybe you have ulterior motives. You serve on the board for the valuable business contacts it provides?"

"No, but you're—"

"And no doubt you're charging a hefty fee for evaluating that property for the Red Cross."

"I take your point," he said dryly. "But it's possible to be a decent human being in a general sense and remain a cold bastard in personal relationships."

"It's also possible to care very deeply and not have the faintest idea how to express it. Especially in words." Words would seem hopelessly awkward compared to the kind of understanding he instinctively craved and was cut off from.

"Rose." He was holding a plain gold pen in his right

hand and began to turn it over and over, not looking at her. "Don't expect too much of me."

"I know you intend to tell me goodbye when we return to Montebello." The sick feeling spread when she said that aloud, but she managed to keep her voice level. "I can't blame you, since you think I trigger your attacks. But I don't like being shut out while we're still together."

"I shut everyone out." His eyes were bleak. "That's the problem."

Yes, he did. Last night, when she'd been completely vulnerable to him, he'd been barricaded against her. That was outside his control, she knew. She just wished it didn't hurt so much. "A blocked empath would have trouble letting down his guard," she said carefully. "Drew, you have to learn how to control your shield."

He sighed and set down his pen. "You're determined to have this conversation, aren't you."

"We have to figure out what to do. Yesterday, just before you had your attack, I felt your shield wobbling. You were insisting you didn't have a headache, then all of a sudden you were white with pain and your shield was oscillating."

"Say you're right. Say you're one hundred damned percent right about all this. What good does it do? I can't sense these bloody shields you keep harping on. Can you tell me how to fix something I'm completely unaware of?"

"I can help you become aware." She hoped she could, although there was nothing in the lore about teaching an adult empath to control his shields. She didn't, in truth, know if it was possible. "The traditional way empaths are taught in my family requires the shields to be down, so I'll have to improvise. Meditation may help."

"Great. I'll buy a book on Zen the first chance I get. In the meantime, it doesn't do any good to talk about it."

She reminded herself to have patience. "The specialist

you consulted probably wanted to know all sorts of things about the circumstances surrounding the attacks, right? Well, we can do the same thing. We can start by examining what you were doing, thinking, feeling just before every one of your attacks.'' The sickness was growing. She dug her fingernails into her palms to fight it. ''Maybe something about me is a trigger. Maybe not, though. You had attacks before you met me. And you haven't had one now for...''

''For about thirteen hours.'' He paused, looking down as if gathering himself for some great effort. ''I have thought about all that,'' he said quietly. ''About what was going on before each of my attacks. I...woke very early this morning.''

''I noticed.'' She'd reached for him. Before her eyes had opened that morning, she'd reached for him and found him gone. He'd been sitting by the window, fully dressed. And distant. Horribly, pleasantly distant.

''I did a lot of thinking while I was waiting for the sun to come up. I believe I've found the common denominator.''

He sounded calm, matter-of-fact. But the grooves in his cheeks cut deeply now, as if even his flesh were pulled in on itself, and his breathing was faintly uneven. Instinctively she reached for his hand.

His fingers closed around hers instantly. Tightly. And the weird all-over queasiness began to fade. Not that everything turned rosy and wonderful—she was still worried. Her throat was still tight, as if she'd been holding back tears for some time. But her world swam back into focus when he held her hand.

Then he began to talk. ''It occurred to me that at the airport yesterday I'd been feeling tense. Crowded.''

''Empaths don't like crowds,'' she said quietly.

''Yes. Well, when I considered that in terms of these shields I'm supposed to have, it made a certain sense. So

I looked for similar stressors at other times when I'd had an attack. For example, one of my spells hit shortly after I arrived in Montebello. I'd been at the airport for hours after the bombing, surrounded by people in a state of high emotion, so that fit. Looking further back, I remember staying late at a nightclub that was especially crowded shortly before one attack. Right before the first one, I'd attended a soccer match. And then you…when I'm with you…"

Her throat ached. "I stress your shields, too. Because I want in."

"Not just that. I…want you in."

It was hard to speak past the lump in her throat. "There. Was that so difficult to say?"

"Yes," he assured her dryly. "But not as hard as what I must say now. My desire for you seems to weaken my shields. Only I can't handle it, Rose, when my shields go down. That's what triggers my attacks. Not my shields, but the lack of them."

She couldn't speak. Her head felt stuffed with thoughts, all of them jammed up at some threshold so tightly none could get through and be heard. And inside, deep inside, a voice was crying, *No, no, no…*

"I suppose, like your aunt's cousin, I simply can't process what happens when my shields falter," he was saying in that cool, dry voice. "There are steps I can take to manage my disability. I'll need to avoid crowds as much as possible, obviously."

"And me." Her mouth was as dry as her eyes, dry and burning. "You'll have to avoid me." Then, because she couldn't help it: "But I brought you back!"

His hand tightened on hers. "I think I would always come back for you if there was anything of me you can reach. There's…a connection. But that connection damns me as much as it saves me. I can't live with constant attacks, Rose."

"No." She couldn't look at him now. "No, of course you can't."

The logjam of thoughts was breaking up, and every one of them supported what he'd said. Oh, she'd wanted to believe the answer lay in his learning to be open. Of course she'd wanted that, she thought, bitter with herself. And she still believed it was dangerous for him to remain wholly blocked—the lore was quite definite about that—but he'd lived for more than twenty years in that state. The danger there was less acute than the one she posed.

He had very nearly not come back from his last attack.

So naturally he'd pulled back this morning, establishing his usual distance. He couldn't afford to do anything else. And she had to help him maintain that distance. She had to be cool, dispassionate, unemotional.

It was like asking the fire not to burn.

Oh, God, she thought, suddenly remembering the other reason she'd wanted him with her on this trip. She'd intended to ask him to help ground her when she searched for the prince's Jessie. He had stood between her and the fire in the prince's rooms and cut off the fire's call. Somehow he'd used his Gift to shield her.

And right after that, he'd been stricken with a "migraine." "That last night at the palace," she said. "You had an attack that night."

"Yes." Humor, dark and self-derisive, coated his voice. "I practically ran out of the room so no one would see me when it hit."

She couldn't ask him to help her. She felt a flutter of panic. She would just have to keep it a light trance, she told herself. Being physically close to the object of her search should help.

"You still have to learn to control your shields. How to soften them, even release them from time to time. Even if I have been triggering your recent attacks, the underlying problem is that you're blocked. You have to deal with that.''

''How?''

She had no answers for him. For either of them.

His thumb was making slow circles on the back of her hand. He hadn't let go. In spite of everything, he hadn't let go of her hand. ''I should never have come with you,'' he said abruptly. ''I'm more likely to be a burden than a help.''

''You said you couldn't regret me, no matter what.'' Now she looked at him, willing him to meet her eyes. When he did, though, she almost wished he hadn't. The despair she saw there broke her control. She looked away, swallowing all those tears she couldn't cry. Not now, not yet. ''I can't regret you, either. Or this time with you. No matter what.''

They landed in New York at ten-thirty local time. Because they'd missed their original flight the night before, they'd also missed the connecting flight to Denver. The prince's people had adjusted their itinerary accordingly, but it meant they had to change airports to make the next leg of their trip. Kennedy Airport, where the Concorde landed, didn't have a flight for Denver with seats available until the next day.

LaGuardia wasn't as crowded as Heathrow had been, but Drew had been with Rose constantly for twenty-four hours. She assumed his shield was already stressed and so watched him closely—with her eyes, yes, but even more with her other senses. They ate lunch in a generic sort of airport lounge, then went to the security check.

The line was long. She put a hand on his arm. ''Go to the men's room.''

His eyebrows lifted. ''It isn't necessary at the moment.''

''Your shield feels...not down, but a little mushy.

You're Water-Gifted. Splash some water on your face. Hold your hands under running water. It should help.''

Without another word he left. It must have worked, because his barriers were solid again when he returned, and he didn't suffer an attack.

The flight to Denver was long and exhausting. For the first part of it, she instructed him in other ways he could protect himself. The color black offered some protection for an empath, as did dark blue, but they shouldn't be overdone. She recommended he wear those colors when he knew he would be in crowds. Also, he should avoid wearing synthetic materials. Wool, cotton, silk, linen—all helped buffer the emotions around him, which would help keep his shields from being stressed. He would be best off with clothes that could be laundered, she added. Immersion in running water cleansed the psychic dust better than cleaning with chemicals.

And whenever possible, especially if he was tired and stressed, he should get away to the water. Ocean, lake, river—he needed to be around water as much as possible. A tabletop fountain in his bedroom would be a good idea.

He listened carefully, only commenting at the end that it sounded frightfully New Age-ish. ''Are you sure I shouldn't invest in some crystals?'' The creases under his eyes deepened with amusement.

''It wouldn't hurt,'' she retorted. ''Another thing you can do if you're feeling crowded and there's no nearby body of water—go to a church.''

That startled him.

''Or a synagogue or mosque, but you'll probably be more comfortable in a place of your own faith. Prayer really does work, you see—on a psychic level, it cleanses. Some of the older churches are incredibly pure. Oh, and you should wear turquoise—the gemstone, not the color. It has healing properties, and seems to resonate especially strongly with the Water-Gifted.''

"Still trying to get me to wear jewelry? I prefer pearls," he said thoughtfully.

Her throat closed up altogether.

For the rest of the flight, Drew worked—this time, without her interference.

He would have to remember to compliment Lucas on his people's discretion, Drew thought as the bellboy returned from putting Rose's suitcases in one bedroom. A two-bedroom suite was a tactful solution when making arrangements for a couple who might or might not wish to share a bed.

Necessary, too, he thought savagely as he handed the man a couple of bills. Damnably necessary.

Rose was looking out the large window at one end of the sitting room when the door closed behind the bellboy. The draperies were open, displaying a magnificent view of Denver at night.

She hadn't looked at him since he told the bellboy to put her suitcases in one bedroom, his in the other. "We'll check in with the police in the morning," he said, wanting to go to her. He ached for her, body, mind—and soul. "It's too late to accomplish anything tonight, and you're too tired. You didn't sleep much on the plane."

"My body thinks it's after three in the morning." She yawned. "I guess I'd better turn in."

"You should eat something first, even if you don't feel like it. It will help you adjust to the time change. I'll call room service."

She turned away from the view, saying lightly, "Determined to take care of me, aren't you?"

She was smiling. And she was pale, her eyes shadowed by pain. "Don't," he said, his voice thick. "For God's sake, don't keep smiling and smiling. I'd rather you screamed and threw things.''

Her lips quivered as the smile slid away. "Maybe tomorrow. I'm too tired to muster a decent tantrum tonight. You must be wiped out, too.''

"I'm not too tired.'' The words were out before he could catch them. "I'm sorry. I don't have any right...I need to be alone, but that isn't what I want.''

"The risk is too great," she said quietly.

Without meaning to, he took a step toward her. And stopped. "Sex...seems to break the rules. You brought me back that way, and without the exhaustion that usually hits. And the first time I kissed you—that's the only time I started to have a spell, but it stopped.''

"Drew." Her voice shook. "If we make love, I'll push at your shields. I—I want that kind of joining too badly. I won't be able to help myself.'' She turned away. "Maybe...maybe when I'm rested I'll have more control.''

"Of course. I shouldn't have said anything. I'll call room service now. Something light—soup and a salad, perhaps?'' Good God, he was babbling.

She gestured a vague refusal without looking at him. "I'll acclimate tomorrow. I'll deal with everything—tomorrow.'' She hurried to the room where he'd had the bell-boy put her things and closed the door.

Drew stood where he was while something inside him ripped and ripped, as if he could be endlessly torn. At last, moving slowly, he went to his room, stripped and claimed the shower. He stood under the pounding water for a very long time. Because without the aid of any senses, rational or irrational—unsupported by logic or reason—he *knew* she was crying. If he heard her, he would go to her. If he went to her, they would end up joining their bodies.

And then one of two things would happen. Either she'd succeed in breaking down his shield and he'd go catatonic on her. Maybe she would be able to bring him back if that happened; maybe the spell would fade on its own. Probably, he thought, he wouldn't be trapped like that permanently.

Or else he would manage to make love without opening himself up to her at all the way he had last night. And it would be her heart that broke.

Chapter 17

Rose woke with her head clogged and aching. For the first few bleary seconds, she couldn't imagine where she was. Or when. She blinked groggily at the clock, frowning. Ten-thirty. Was it a.m. or p.m.?

Then she saw the crumpled tissues on the bedside table. And she remembered.

With a grimace, she threw back the covers. Crying herself to sleep—how stupid. No wonder she had a headache. A crying jag, after breathing the dessicated airplane air for hours, was a good way to give herself sinus problems. If Gemma had been here... But she had more pressing reasons than a stuffy head for wishing her aunt was there. She grabbed her clothes and headed for the bathroom.

How long had she heard the shower running last night? She bit her lip, her hand on the tap. Misery was such a liquid business. It didn't help to know he was suffering, too. Rose preferred anger to tears, but there was no one to be angry with. Not even herself. Action, she thought fiercely, was better than either anger or misery, and she stepped under the water. She was in Denver for a reason. She needed to remember that.

The steam helped clear her head. She washed her hair and combed it out, pulling it into a quick braid without drying it. Then she went to face Drew, and the day.

He was sitting at the round table near the window, already dressed and shaved. He wore neatly pressed slacks and a white shirt with tiny blue stripes. No tie or jacket. Sunshine gilded his hair, making it almost golden.

What did the pain matter? she thought. What did it matter, when the sight of him could lift her heart and make the world sing? "I smell coffee," she said. "And food, though it looks as if you ate without me. I can't believe I slept through the arrival of room service. I don't know if there's time to order me some breakfast before we go—"

He pushed his chair back and stood. "I'm afraid I have bad news."

She stopped. Her insides played roller coaster.

"After I went to bed last night I felt a headache coming on. I…" He looked away. "I decided to get out of the hotel. Away."

Away from *her,* he meant. "And if you'd had an attack while wandering around Denver? I did pull you back last time."

"I didn't wander around Denver. And my headache went away as soon as…soon after I left the hotel." He shook his head slightly. "Never mind about that right now. Rose—I drove out to the Chambers ranch and spoke with the caretaker."

"Caretaker? I thought ranchers had foremen. Wranglers."

"Not when the owner is dead."

"No." She shook her head. "No, I felt her—she was grieving for her child. She wasn't—she isn't dead."

"You weren't sure if your vision was past, present or future," he said gently, coming to her. "You couldn't tell. You couldn't have changed this, Rose. From what the man told me, it was already too late when we left Montebello."

She was still shaking her head. Her knees felt weak. Drew took her shoulders in his hands and pushed.... Oh, the couch was behind her. She sat, dizzy with guilt. "It wasn't too late when I first touched the ring. Gemma was right. Oh, God, if I'd tried then, as soon as the ring came to me..."

"No, she was already dead then." He sat beside her, his arm around her. "It's not your fault, Rose."

Rose thought of the sad woman with the strong, gentle heart, and grieved. "But the baby. I don't understand. If I touched Jessie at some point before her baby was born, she wouldn't have been grieving for it. She wasn't pregnant when I reached her, Drew. I'm sure of that."

He was silent a moment. "Are you sure she was grieving for her baby? Not Lucas?"

"She...both of them." Rose put her hand on her stomach, remembering the emptiness. "She'd lost them both."

"Maybe," he said gently, "you were picking up the most intense emotional experience of her life, right after her baby was stillborn. When she knew she was dying. That would explain the sense of loss, and the feeling she was in danger."

It would. It did, but it didn't feel right. And... "I *saw* her, Drew. She wasn't in a hospital."

"Apparently she chose to have the baby at home, with a midwife in attendance. The man I spoke with—the care-taker—is the midwife's brother, a friend of the family. He's mildly retarded, I think—"

"Maybe he told you wrong, then. Maybe he didn't un-derstand, and—"

"Rose." He touched her lips with his, silencing her.

"The cattle have all been shipped off. The hands have been let go. And the caretaker showed me her grave, freshly dug in a small family plot out on the ranch."

She closed her eyes and tried to accept it. "Does Lucas know?" She rubbed her chest, where an ache had settled. Grief for a woman she'd never met…and for the man who had cared for her. Maybe loved her. "The ring," she murmured. "How did I end up with her ring?"

He frowned. "I hadn't thought of that. There's a sister— the caretaker mentioned her. She's the only family from what he said, and she had been staying with Jessica. She left when Jessica died."

"She came to Montebello." Rose pushed to her feet. "She must have. She's the one who sold the ring to Gemma. Jessica must have told her about Lucas, and she flew there to see him, to tell him. But she hasn't." She started to pace. "She probably can't get past the guards, everyone surrounding the prince. He'll want to talk to her, Drew. Even if it hurts, he'll want to see her."

"I'll tell him about her." Drew stood. "You're right. He'll want to know."

"I've hardly thought of her at all. We came here for her, and she's barely crossed my mind since we got on the king's jet. Oh, God."

"Thinking about her more often wouldn't have saved her."

"But it's typical. So typical. I've put myself first all along. For so many years…" She moved jerkily, stopping by the window. "For so long I've avoided using my Gift. I presented myself as an expert to you yesterday." Her short laugh was derisive. "Oh, such an expert I am. I've been careful to learn the bare minimum, myself. What I had to know to control my Gift and not a whit more. Because I'm afraid." She hugged herself.

"Rose." He crossed to her, lifted a hand as if he meant

to touch her—then let it drop. "You can't blame yourself. Being psychic doesn't make you omnipotent or all-knowing."

"But if I'd learned how to use my Gift better—if I'd practiced it daily, the way Gemma wanted—I would have known she was dead. Instead I scared Lucas, but I let him think things were mostly okay. That whatever was wrong, there was still time to do something to help her."

"Lucas is hurting, but you didn't cause it. And you couldn't have prevented it."

She swallowed and hugged her arms around her middle, feeling cold. So cold. "If I'd been working with my Gift all along, I'd be able to handle it better. Maybe I'd be able to help you. Maybe we wouldn't have to live apart."

This time he didn't hesitate. He put his arms around her and pulled her gently against him, her back to his front. "The flaw is in me. You know that. You know it, Rose."

"If I could control myself better—if I didn't push at your shields—"

"It's me pushing at them, I think, that does the damage," he said quietly. "I want you. In every way, not just the physical. I didn't realize how alone I was until…" He stopped. "I can't feel these shields you keep talking about, but I can feel myself trying to—to reach for you. I can't control that any more than I can the damned shields, but I can tell I'm doing it."

His shields were being stressed from within and without, just like at the airport. He'd nearly gone catatonic then. She'd pulled him back, but what if he went farther, deeper inside himself, next time?

She swallowed hard, stepped out of his arms and faced him. "I think your shields must go soft sometimes when you're alone. Otherwise the pressure would have over-whelmed you before now. Drew, you need to get away by yourself soon." It wasn't a cure, but it might help. It had to help.

"I'm doing all right. I haven't had an attack since the one at the airport."

"Your shields flickered a lot that night. That may have relieved some of the pressure, but it's a temporary relief. You had a headache last night, Drew." One that had gone away when he put distance between them.

His eyes were bleak. "Who in the hell decided to call this psychic crap a Gift?" He shook his head and reached for her.

She stepped back. "You shouldn't touch me. The risk—"

"To hell with the risk," he growled. "I need to hold you."

While I still can.

Rose didn't have to be a psychic to hear his unspoken words echoing between them, and she couldn't deny either of them the contact. Quietly she moved into his arms. It felt so good, so right... *I'll be careful,* she thought. *If his shields start to weaken, I'll pull away.*

"Why are you afraid of your Gift?"

She stiffened, and hoped he wouldn't notice. "I told you. There's a danger of getting lost in the fire trance."

"When you started the fire in the prince's fireplace, you were afraid. That had nothing to do with a trance." He paused. "Your mother died in a fire."

It was hard to hide anything from an empath, she thought. Even a blocked one. She nodded.

"She was Gifted, too, wasn't she?" he asked softly. "Like you are. Fire-Gifted. And it killed her."

"It's not... I may have been too careful. Too afraid. Because of what happened."

"What did happen, Rose?" He stroked her hair. "I need

to know. I need to understand how your Gift puts you in danger.''

Rose closed her eyes tightly, trying not to see it again, feel it all over again. ''My mother was open about her Gift. She'd trained with it all her life and used it to tell fortunes—to earn a living, yes, but also because she wanted to help. She said it was up to us to make our Gifts a blessing, not a curse. She believed the times of ignorance and persecution were over.''

His hand was warm and soothing. ''Unfortunately, ignorance never really goes out of style.''

''No, it doesn't. Neither does fear. Or evil.'' She swallowed. ''She warned a woman, a client, to leave her husband, because that's what he was. Evil. You could feel it on him, as if he were coated in pestilence...she'd Seen that he would kill his wife if she didn't get away. Well, the woman did leave him. And he blamed my mother. Called her a witch.'' Memory swirled, dragging at her. ''She knew. When she warned the woman, she knew he would come for her.''

''She foresaw her death?''

''No. She Saw him setting fire to the house. Our home. She sent me to stay with Gemma.'' The pain of that burned in her still. ''I didn't want to go, but...but I was only eleven.'' The same age as Drew had been when he was kidnapped. The eerie coincidence held her mute for a moment.

''She didn't leave the house herself?''

Rose shook her head. ''She thought she could handle it. She thought...calling fire, starting fires—that's easy. It comes naturally to us. But to control the fire—to put it out—we have to go *into* it. That takes training, and it's hard. Because we don't just call fire. It calls to us, too, makes us want it, crave the dance...and if we go into it and it's stronger than we are...'' She shuddered.

"What happens?" His voice was low, intense. "What happens if you go into the fire?"

"You burn." Tears came. "Oh, Drew, she burned. Not the house. *Her.* She called the fire to her and couldn't come back out. And I know, you see, I know how it happened. I Saw it, felt the fire calling—and it didn't hurt." The tears were falling freely now. "There should be pain, there should be, but there isn't. There's this terrible exultation as it burns you and burns you, and it doesn't hurt. It doesn't hurt at all."

"God." His arms tightened, then eased. "Dear God, Rose, you felt it all?"

"Not the way an empath would. But I Saw. Gemma told me I woke up screaming. I don't remember that."

"How could your aunt ask you to use your Gift? After that, how could she ask it of you?"

"Because safety lies in practice. In learning control. She's right about that, but the Gift grows stronger with use. The stronger the Gift, the greater the danger, and I—I'm already stronger than my mother was. So I've tried to use it as little as possible, just for trancing, and that rarely. I've never gone into the fire," she finished, suddenly, absurdly tired, considering all the sleep she'd had. "I've never dared."

His fingers were cool and gentle on her cheeks, wiping away the dampness. And she felt his shield flicker.

Instinctively her heart reached for his—and she wrenched herself back. Out of his arms, away from that dangerously uncertain shield. She retreated several feet. "Drew. Your shield."

He froze, his face blank. "What am I supposed to do—dash under the shower?"

"You need to be alone. Away from me. I'll go. I can…the restaurant. I'll go there and have breakfast." She could manage coffee, at least.

"No, I'll leave." He made a curt, chopping motion. "I'll go back to the ranch, talk to the caretaker again. Maybe I can find out how to reach Jessica's sister. It's little enough to bring Lucas, but I can at least do that much."

Her throat was tight with pain. And though she wasn't an empath, she wasn't sure how much was hers, how much his. "We flew halfway around the world for nothing."

"Not for nothing."

His voice was cool and level. His face...wasn't. His eyes blazed with emotion. His face was tight with it, the grooves in his cheeks dug deep.

She struggled to keep from going to him. If they hadn't followed her faulty vision, they wouldn't have had even these few days together. Even though she couldn't touch him, even though she might never touch him again, it had been worth it.

"No," she said when she'd won the battle for control. "You're right. It wasn't for nothing."

He hesitated. "I'll be gone all day, I expect."

"I'll be fine. Go."

After he left, she sat on the couch, hugging her knees to her chest, curled in on her pain. They couldn't go on like this. It hurt when he pulled away, closed himself off from her. Even knowing why he had to do it, it still hurt. But she could handle that. Except now...now she realized it hurt him, too. In a different way and maybe more deeply. To keep from reaching out, in comfort, in love... She shuddered. This morning she'd had a taste of how that felt.

Neither of them could stand hurting the other. Neither of them could keep from it. Not as long as they were together. She'd been steeling herself for the time he would tell her goodbye. She'd even thought she was being strong and selfless because she stood ready to sacrifice whatever she must for his sake.

But she'd put all the responsibility on him. Leaving

Drew the pain and guilt of telling her they must part was
not an act of love, but cowardice.

Feeling old and weary in her soul, Rose reached for the
phone. There was one more thing she could do for him.

Drew rode up in the hotel elevator, rubbing the tight
muscles at the back of his neck. He'd gotten a description
of the sister, a few facts, but the caretaker hadn't any idea
where she was.

He'd visited Jessica's grave again. This time, he'd left
flowers.

It wasn't much, balanced against his cousin's grief. But
it was all he could do.

He walked a little faster as he approached their suite,
knowing that Rose was waiting for him. He would be more
careful, he promised himself. He wouldn't touch her, but
he'd be able to look at her, talk to her.

He had the key card out before he reached the door. It
was late—maybe she'd already eaten. He hoped not. They
could go out. That would be better than the intimacy of the
suite, he thought, shutting the door behind him. He
wouldn't be so tempted in public, and...

The suite was dark, except for a single lamp beside the
couch.

He knew. Even before he went to her bedroom and found
her letter, he knew.

After the first few sentences, the flowing handwriting
blurred. He shut his eyes, trying to pretend something other
than tears was ruining his vision. An urge to crumple the
paper, to kick something, break something, swept over him.

It passed. He carried the letter to the couch and sat there,
holding it. Smoothing it with his fingers while he waited
for his eyes to clear.

She'd written it on hotel stationery, filling the first side
and half of the other. Her handwriting was like her—

slightly spiky, with dramatic peaks and lush, rounded curves. She wrote of love.

He sat there for a very long time, touching the paper she'd touched. Knowing that this, even this, had been an act of love, taking on herself the burden of parting.

She'd called Lorenzo and had him arrange her return to Montebello, sparing them both a parting that would undoubtedly have been emotional enough to wreck his shield. She said they could write each other if he wanted. Or he could call—she would always be happy to hear his voice, no matter what. But she would understand if he found it better to do neither.

For a long time, all he could hear was her name. Over and over, her name rose in his mind, a cry from the heart. *Rose.*

When his eyes were clear again, he went to the desk and took out another sheet of stationery. There was one more thing he could do for her—something he would have done before, had he not been so much a coward.

I'm not as strong as you, he wrote. *I don't think I could stand to hear your voice, knowing I couldn't see you, be with you. Perhaps, in time, I'll be able to write you, to hear from you this way. I hope so. I can't right now.*

He hesitated long over the next part, struggling with his old enemy—words. Nothing he could write would come close to what he felt. But she deserved his effort, however flawed the result. So eventually he continued: *I've been more alive in the time I've spent with you than I thought possible. It's pathetically inadequate to say I'll never forget you—that would be like saying I'll not forget my arm, or the colors of sunset, or the smell of spring. I love you. I always will.*

Chapter 18

Montebello, four days later

Rose turned the sign on the door to Closed with a sigh of relief. She'd made it through another day—or this part of it, at least. There were still hours to go before bedtime.

Not that she expected to sleep much. Gemma, she thought with a grimace, would probably make her drink one of her teas again.

Before the long hours of the night arrived, though, she had another chore. One she'd taken up after she returned.

With her aunt's help, she would practice using her Gift.

Her steps were slow as she climbed the stairs. She wasn't fooling herself. Her decision to work consciously with her Gift had something to do with a woman who had died, but it had just as much to do with hope. Stupid, irrational hope. The odds against her being able to learn enough control to keep from stressing Drew's shields were vanishingly small. And even if she did, he might not have the control *he* needed. Or he might have changed his mind by then.

But she didn't believe that.

I love you. I always will. That was what he'd written, and that was what she believed, heart and soul.

Her throat ached. Something, it seemed, was always aching these days. She hadn't realized heartache could be so physical.

Gemma greeted her cheerfully when she entered the living room and watched her anxiously. Just as she had ever since Rose had come home. "I'm almost finished with this sauce," she said. "Give me another ten minutes and I'll be done."

"That's fine. I'll change."

Rose went to her room and pulled on her jeans, then went to the closet for a shirt.

Right in front, in pride of place, was the gift she'd found waiting upon her return—the absurdly expensive evening coat she'd admired in Heathrow. It was ankle-length cashmere, soft as sin and red. Incredibly bright red. She adored it. Not that she had anywhere to wear such impractical elegance, but that didn't matter. She stroked one soft sleeve. Seeing it, touching it, gave her pleasure. So did the idea that when he'd bought it for her, Drew had been thinking of the places he wanted to take her. Places that were part of his world.

When the ache in her throat threatened her control, she grabbed a T-shirt and closed the door on her beautiful, impractical token. Time to get to work.

Gemma was waiting outside. She handed Rose the broom, and Rose performed the ritual cleansing of the area. They sat, as they had before, with a candle between them and she took her aunt's hand.

This time, though, Gemma didn't light the candle. Rose did, with a wave of her hand and a call. And then—hesitantly, carefully—she opened herself to fire.

* * *

Drew hesitated at the door of the little café. The last time he'd come here, he'd attended the *fioreanno* with Rose. He wondered if it was a sign of incipient masochism that he'd mentioned this café to Lorenzo when his cousin had suggested they have a last drink before Drew left the country.

But there was pleasure, along with pain, in being here. Perhaps he was merely pathetic, he thought, threading his way through the tables to the one Lorenzo had chosen, at the back. He'd gone to the beach, too. As if he could hold on to her a little longer by visiting the places where he'd known her.

"How's Lucas?" Lorenzo asked when Drew sat down.

"Pretty much the same." He'd just come from telling Lucas everything he could about Jessie. It had been a difficult conversation. "Unhappy. Grieving. Blaming himself and trying his damnedest not to let anyone know about any of it."

"You'd know about that."

"I didn't even know her."

"I'm not talking about Jessica Chambers. What will you have?" Lorenzo asked as the waitress arrived, smiling brightly at both of them.

"Beer will be fine." Drew had gotten drunk once, the first night after she left. He hadn't dared repeat that. Drinking his way into oblivion was entirely too tempting.

"So why are you leaving?" Lorenzo asked after the waitress brought them their glasses.

"Business calls. I'll be back for the crowning ceremony. Speaking of which," Drew said in an effort to direct the conversation away from himself, "have you heard anything more about, ah, any potential problems?"

"Nothing. If anyone is planning something, they've kept it almighty quiet. I'm wondering if we were fed that tip to distract our attention from their real goal. What happened with you and Rose?"

So much for directing the conversation. "It didn't work out. But that's nothing unusual, is it?" He took a healthy swig of beer. Like everything else these days, it lacked flavor. "I'm not known for the longevity of my relationships."

"You were different with her. She mattered."

Drew looked down at the amber liquid in his glass. "Yes. She did." And still does, he thought. And always will. "Lorenzo…"

"Yes?"

"Never mind." He wasn't sure what he wanted to ask. How do you go on when you can't have the one person you need? Her absence was a hole in his gut, gnawing at him constantly. He was leaving Montebello because he didn't trust himself to stay away, and she'd been right—neither of them could stand the way they kept hurting each other.

Lorenzo leaned back in his chair. "In my experience—and I do have vast experience in this area, having screwed things up royally with Eliza before she took pity on me—the hardest thing for a man to do in a relationship is surrender control."

"Surrender?" Drew's mouth quirked up. "I can't believe you said that."

Lorenzo shrugged one shoulder. "We want to be the ones on top. And I mean that in more ways than literally," he added, a glint of humor in his dark eyes. "Letting ourselves go, being out of control, doesn't come easily."

It didn't come at all for Drew. He put down his glass. "Thanks for the drink and the advice to the lovelorn. I should be getting to the airport."

"I'll drive you."

"That's not necessary."

"Sure it is. You can even things up by giving *me* advice."

Drew stood. "Buy low, sell high and be sure to look both ways before crossing the street."

Lorenzo laughed and clapped him on the back. "Come on. Let's go."

Rose had lit the candle, gone into the tiny flame and put it out three times in fifteen minutes. Sweat beaded on her forehead.

"You're getting better at this," Gemma said encouragingly.

"Faster, anyway." The first time she'd tried, it had taken her the entire thirty minutes to extinguish the flame. Of course, she'd spent much of that time in a pure funk, terrified, unable to bring herself to open to fire.

The fear was still intense, but she was learning. "One more time," she said. "But I'll feed it a little first."

"Are you sure?" Gemma's forehead wrinkled. "You're still new at this."

"It's a very simple fire. And it can't get too large—even if I lose control, it has only the candle to draw from." And herself. But she wouldn't let it have her. Rose took a deep breath, centered herself and called fire. The wick flamed. She fed it—just a little—and it flared higher. She opened herself...

Flame, mild and hot, dancing in the air. In her mind. Calling her as she had called it...and she let herself answer. And join. Ah, the dance! The heat, the fiery chaos swam over her, through her, became her...

Flames. Orange-hot, sucking the air from her chest, shouting smoke at the sky. Flames, drawing her skin hot and tight over the rapture within, the coiled secret at the bottom of her soul. Flames, calling her...fire crackling merrily over the bones of its prey, a familiar mass of dark shapes and angles. There were people, too—she saw them as movement, their outlines blurred by possibilities.

And there were bodies, dark and still and horribly visible.

Rose jerked back, her head stiff, her eyes wide with horror. "The airport. Oh, God, Zia, they're going to bomb the airport—again!"

She scrambled to her feet and took off for the kitchen at a run.

"Are you sure?" Gemma called from behind her. "Rose, love, maybe you slipped in time, went back—"

"No." Rose's hand shook as she shoved open the phone directory. "No, this was a future vision, not past. Near future, very near... Oh, God, where's the number for the police?" Her fingers were so clumsy she had trouble turning the thin pages, but finally she fumbled to the right one and punched in the number.

The corporal who spoke to her was an idiot. No, he didn't know where Captain Mylonas was, or when he would return. So sorry, but don't worry, *signorina*, he would tell the captain about her call. No, no, it wasn't at all necessary for her to speak with his superior—be sure he would pass on her warning to the appropriate people.

He wouldn't. He didn't believe her. The only person he might tell would be some buddy so they could both laugh at the weird calls they got sometimes.

It was up to her.

She disconnected and thrust the phone at her aunt. "Here. Try to reach Duke Lorenzo at the palace. He'll believe you if you tell him the warning is coming from me."

"But...but where are you going?"

"To the airport," Rose called, already out the door. "They'll listen. They've seen me there with the duke."

Drew was puzzled when Lorenzo parked the car—illegally, but rank hath its privileges—and came into the airport with him. He supposed his cousin was worried about him. Hell, everyone was. It was annoying, especially when all he wanted was to be alone.

No, what he really wanted was Rose. But he *needed* to be alone. He'd learned to notice when his shield began feeling stressed. After the talk with Lucas, after Lorenzo's well-meant probing—after the endless, gray days without Rose—he felt frayed.

So he wasn't as pleased as he should have been when he realized his entire family—most of the ones here on Montebello, anyway—had shown up at the airport to see him off. Surrounded by palace guards, of course.

The show of support and caring made his throat tight. It also made him feel precarious. Vulnerable. But he couldn't tell them that or let it show. So when the guards admitted him, he smiled and hugged his aunt, shook hands with his uncle, kissed Lorenzo's pretty new wife and asked who was running the country while they made the airport guards nervous.

Lorenzo was smiling, pleased with himself. "Was this your idea?" Drew asked, low-voiced.

"No, the king suggested it. Everything was arranged very quickly—no chance for word to leak, except—"

A flash went off. Then another one.

"Except to the press," Drew said dryly. "We're making a show of family solidarity, I take it?"

"The king believes it's important for his people to see him in public, carrying on a normal life. Lucas didn't come, because I insisted they shouldn't both be in the same place at the same time, but the risk is very slight. No one could have anticipated this."

Drew nodded, accepting the political necessity and trying to ignore the pushing journalists.

"Drew," Lorenzo said, "it isn't all for show. He wants you to know your family cares."

And that was undoubtedly true. King Marcus had always

had to balance his duty to his country with his love for his family. Drew understood that.

But there were too many people crowded around him. Family, loving and close. Guards. Reporters. Strangers—a whole airport full of them, passengers, their friends and family and associates.

His head began to pound.

Rose threw money at the driver and bolted out of the cab, not taking time to shut the door. She hit the airport sidewalk at a run, but was forced to a near stop at the central door—it was one of those revolving doors that moved at its own pace. Desperately slow.

She entered the concourse and paused, looking around frantically for the nearest guard. There was a knot of people at the west end of the concourse, and guards— Oh, God! Those were the uniforms of the palace guards! And with them…yes, that was Lorenzo!

She started running. Another guard, one in the blue uniform of airport security, grabbed her by the arm before she got far. "Here now. What's the rush?" His eyes were dark with suspicion.

This one she'd never seen in her visits to the airport. He wouldn't know who she was. "I know it looks funny, me running toward—toward whoever the palace guard is protecting." She tried to see around him, to see which of the royals was at the airport with Lorenzo, but the guard blocked her, his fingers tightening on her arm. "Please," she said, "you have to believe me. There's a bomb. You have to get everyone out."

He grabbed the walkie-talkie off the belt at his waist and spoke into it, using some kind of numerical code-talk. But he didn't let go of her.

Another guard hurried up to them. A chubby man, he

was sweating slightly in spite of the air-conditioning. "What's the problem?"

"Bomb threat. I've called it in."

"It's not a threat. It's a warning. Please," Rose begged, "get everyone out of here. It could go off at any time."

The second guard rubbed at the watch on his wrist, shifting from foot to foot. "I know who you are. That woman who thinks she's a witch or something." He laughed nervously. "Must be a false alarm, eh, Frederico? Unless you believe in witchcraft."

"Tell the duke," Rose pleaded. "Duke Lorenzo. Call him—he's at the other end of the concourse. Tell him Rose Giaberti said there's a bomb."

The chubby guard kept fiddling with his watch. "Wait," he said suddenly, "I see the sergeant outside. I'll go get him."

"You're not supposed to leave now," the first guard protested. "That's not procedure. We have to wait for instructions."

"I'll get the sergeant," the chubby one repeated, and pushed past Rose.

When he did, his *èssere* brushed against her. And she knew him. "You," she whispered, her eyes big with horror. "It was you."

She threw her body frantically to one side, breaking the first guard's grip.

Drew's headache was rapidly getting worse. He was going to have to make a break for the men's room and try splashing water on his face and hope that would be enough. He excused himself to his aunt, who had been telling him about a doctor in Paris she wanted him to see.

Though no one had said anything about his supposed epilepsy, he was sure his aunt and uncle, at least, had been informed.

It was Lorenzo's posture that alerted him. His cousin stood at the outside of the cluster of guards and royals, watchful as ever. And he was watching something farther down the concourse with the attention of a bird dog on point.

Drew stopped beside his cousin. There were too many people in the way to see clearly, but he caught a glimpse of a couple of the airport's security people. They seemed to have someone in custody—a woman.

"What is it?" Drew asked. A reporter spotted him and thrust a microphone in his face. He pushed it away.

"I don't know," Lorenzo said, and began to walk quickly.

Drew went with him. He felt each step in his skull, a harder, hotter throb of pain. But something about that woman—

She suddenly pulled away, and he saw her. Rose.

He started to run.

"Lorenzo!" she screamed. "There's a—"

The guard grabbed her again, yanking her arm behind her.

"A bomb!" Rose yelled. "There's a bomb!"

A couple of people screamed. Others scattered, while some stood staring and some tried to wrestle their luggage with them in the suddenly panicked crowd. Behind him Lorenzo cursed and began calling quick instructions to the palace guard. "Form up! Get them out of here!" Drew ran, shoving past whoever got in his way and sending a jolt of pain from his soles, up his spine to his head.

Rose!

The loudspeaker came on, advising everyone to be calm. "No bomb has been found. Proceed in an orderly manner to the doors and let the police investigate. Repeat—no bomb has been found...."

He was about fifteen feet from Rose when there was a

loud popping noise and a blinding flash. Fire leaped out at Drew from a ticket counter—

And vanished.

Rose's head snapped back, her spine arching. The guard holding her made a startled sound and stepped back, holding his hands out as if he'd been shocked.

She began, faintly, to glow.

A sound tore from Drew's throat. He hurled himself at her, dizzy with pain and terror, and wrapped his arms around her. But there was no getting between her and this fire, because it was inside her.

She was hot. Dear God, she was burning hot—and she didn't see him, didn't respond at all. Through the sluice of agony he tried to think—he couldn't go away now, he had to fight it, but to get inside, where the fire was, he had to drop his shields.

He didn't know how. Squeezing his eyes shut, he began to pray, fast and incoherent...and images fled before his closed eyes. A face, cruel, pockmarked—*he's going to hurt me again, please don't, please*—but pleading didn't help. They'd hated him, his kidnappers, his keepers, hated what he stood for—wealth and privilege, rank—everything they lusted after and didn't have. Especially the man with the cruel eyes, whose hatred swamped him as he...

Drew shuddered. And stopped remembering—because he hadn't been there when the rest of it had happened. He'd gone away. He'd counted and he'd gone away, far away inside himself. Just like he'd gone inside himself at Heathrow. Fear sweat stood on Drew's skin, but he didn't feel it, didn't hear the fire alarm or the crowds or the screams. He knew what he had to do. Surrender.

Letting ourselves go, being out of control, doesn't come easily, Lorenzo had said. His cousin didn't know the half of it. This time when the dizzy dislocation hit, Drew didn't fight it. Instead he let go—of sanity, reason, his senses. Of everything except Rose.

And as reality twisted into screaming colors and he fell into darkness, a single thought—a memory—plummeted into the void with him. At the age of eleven, he'd come back. He'd gone far away inside himself, but when it was over, when the man with the cruel eyes and hands had gone and left him alone once more, he'd brought himself back.

By counting backwards.

Fire. It roared inside her, around her, huge and devouring and unbearably beautiful. Rose stood outside normal space and time, in a place where only *èsseri* could exist. She'd slipped a few scant seconds away from the instant the bomb had exploded and *called*—and the fire had answered, following her to this glowing non-place where she stood immobile.

Five.

She stood utterly still because she was in the heart of fire now, a raging inferno that sang to her and around her, calling her to dance—and if she moved at all she would dance, would join in the rapturous destruction.

Four.

She fought to hold on to the order that was self—fought with fire and with her own longing, as chaos raged through her, around her.

Three.

Fire everywhere. The world was fire. It was too much—too perfect, too beautiful—*Dance with me, dance!* She was breaking up, losing her hold on herself—

Two.

The shimmering orange glow parted. A shape appeared where there could be no shape, only change. Yet it was there—darkness formed into a man-shape. Moving toward her.

One.

A hand. A man's hand reaching out through the flame, closing around her arm. Cool and solid and real. A hand—an essence—that she knew. And had never thought to feel again.

She cried his name in the silence of the fire and felt his arms wrapping around her, holding her tight to his cool, solid body. Here, where there was only flame and dissolution and her, Drew was here. Pouring his strength into her, wrapping his body around hers, sheltering her. Standing with her against the flames.

Drawing on his solidity, the core of him that was impervious to fire, she rediscovered order and command, and she cooled. As she did, so did the fire. The glow dimmed. The wild dance calmed...and settled...and died.

She opened her eyes. And smiled, and touched his damp cheek.

He was holding her in this world, too.

Three hours later Drew still had his arm around her. They were sitting on a gold sofa in the king and queen's private suite. He'd pulled her snugly up against him as soon as the king's personal physician finished with her, and after a brief protest, she'd subsided contentedly. This was exactly where she wanted to be.

As he knew. She glanced at him. His shield was up again, but it felt softer now. Less of a barrier, more simple protection. Faintly she sensed his *èssere* and was happy.

He would know that, too. With his shield so soft, he couldn't help picking up her feelings when they touched this way.

Drew might have been content to hold hands, but hers were burned. Not badly—there were a couple of small blisters, but the other spots were simply red and shiny. The doctor, who hadn't asked a single question about how she came to be burned, didn't think she would scar.

She glanced at her aunt, sitting in a chair beside the queen. Gemma was quite sure Rose wouldn't scar. She'd seen to that.

The prince stood near the fireplace, listening, as they all were. Lorenzo was reporting to the king.

"The guard's name is Artesio Dipopulous," he said. "He's talking his head off. We have two of his confederates in custody and hope to have the third before morning." He named the other conspirators and gave a brief précis of their parts in the plot.

"Remarkably accommodating of him," Lucas said. "We usually don't have much luck getting the bastards to talk."

Lorenzo grinned. "Whatever Rose did, it put the fear of God into Dipopulous. He seems to think divine retribution is at hand and is eager to confess."

Several interested glances came her way. Drew chuckled. "Somehow I don't see him mistaking you for a priest."

Lorenzo smiled, satisfied as a cat with a mouse beneath its paw. "Another bit of good news—for some reason every inch of film in the news hounds' cameras was overexposed. They may print a bunch of nonsense about what happened, but they won't have any photographs to back it up."

Rose breathed a sigh of relief. She had not looked forward to being a nine-day wonder. However Lorenzo had managed that trick, she was grateful to him.

"How did Dipopulous get past the background check?" King Marcus wanted to know. "Guards at the airport are investigated rigorously."

Lorenzo grimaced. "He passed because there was nothing to find. It seems his motives were personal, not political or religious. He had a grudge against the royal family. His father killed himself several years ago, and for complex and irrational reasons, he blamed the Sebastiani family. The connection existed mostly in his mind, so his background check turned up nothing suspicious.''

"He planted the first bomb,'' Rose said. ''That's how I recognized him.''

"Yes.'' Lorenzo met her gaze. There was, she thought, an apology in his dark eyes. If he'd made sure she met all of the guards when he was pretending to believe her, none of this would have happened. ''Dipopulous's goal this time was to plant an incendiary device in the royal jet. He'd brought it to the airport a few days ago—it looked like a box of candy—but security has been too tight for him to get it into any of the restricted areas.''

"When all of you showed up at the airport,'' Lucas said, ''it must have seemed like too good an opportunity to miss.''

Lorenzo nodded. ''He decided to trigger it as soon as he could leave the building. Then Rose showed up. When she started talking about bombs, he panicked.''

More curious glances came her way. Rose spoke. ''He fiddled with his watch right before... Was that how he set it off?''

"Yes. A sophisticated bit of electronics, that watch. Probably didn't keep time well, but powerful. He could trigger the device from half a kilometer away.''

"We're lucky they decided to go with an incendiary charge this time,'' the king said. He was sitting in a rather shabby armchair that had the look of an old favorite, cherished for comfort, rather than appearance. ''If they'd used straight explosives again, there would have been great loss of life. As it was, I think no one was hurt.''

"Just Dipopulous's girlfriend at the ticket counter,'' Lorenzo said. ''She'll be hospitalized awhile, but her injuries, though painful, aren't critical. She told my man she had no idea what was in the box of candy her boyfriend asked her to keep for him. I tend to believe her, since she would undoubtedly have died if Rose hadn't done—ah, whatever she did. As it was, she sustained second-degree burns in that split second after the device went off and before the fire…disappeared.''

There was a moment's silence, then the king stood. ''The rest will wait for morning. You've done an excellent job, Lorenzo, as usual.''

Taking the king's action for dismissal, Rose started to get to her feet. Drew tightened his arm around her, preventing her. She turned to him in surprise.

''Not yet,'' he murmured.

King Marcus came to stand in front of her. ''I won't pretend to understand what you did or how it was possible. My son has explained as much as he is able about your abilities, but my nephew has been quite close-mouthed. Particularly concerning whatever part he played. But from what little Drew did say, I understand that your act was much like throwing yourself over a grenade, sacrificing your own life to save others.''

''Oh,'' she said, flustered, ''it wasn't like that. I mean, with a grenade there's no chance of survival. Obviously I did survive, so—''

''Rose.'' Drew squeezed her shoulders. ''Shut up. I was there. I know how poor your chances were.''

''For what you have done for your country, you will be thanked at the appropriate time, with all due honor. For what you have done for my family…'' With a surprising grace for a man his age, the king knelt on one knee. ''For saving the lives of my wife, my nephews and myself, my lady, there are no thanks possible.''

''Oh, don't!'' Distressed, embarrassed, she reached for him—and winced the moment she touched him. ''Please, Your Highness, don't kneel. It isn't right.''

''It is entirely right. As a sovereign, I kneel to no one.

As a man, desperately grateful—'' He broke off, clearing his throat. His eyes were damp. "Grateful for the lives of my family, I can and will kneel to the one who was willing to give her life for theirs. But since it makes you uncomfortable—'' he chuckled and stood, reaching for her upper arms and pulling her to her feet, too "—I will finish on my feet, and as a king.''

"I'm a countess,'' Rose said some time later, dazed. "Or will be, as soon as the paperwork is completed.''

"So you will.'' Drew twirled the strand of her hair he'd been playing with, then tickled her breast with it. "I hope I didn't forget to show the proper respect, my lady, in my enthusiasm for relieving your pain.''

Her grin was slow and sleepy. They were entirely naked, sprawled together in his big bed. Her hands still throbbed, but for a while she hadn't noticed them at all. Of course, she hadn't used them. Drew had informed her she was to lie back and think of England while he made use of her helpless body, then had made it impossible for her to think at all.

She rolled onto her side, snuggling close. "I enjoyed your enthusiasm. As I think you noticed.''

He was silent a moment. "It's going to take some getting used to, this being able to sense feelings.''

"And a lot of work.'' His shields were soft now, weakened by the fire they'd both passed through, and not truly under his control yet. But the terrible pressure that had built up behind them was gone. He had time to learn what they both needed to know.

They both had time. "Eventually you'll be able to thin or thicken your shields to suit yourself and the situation.''

"Good. In some situations, shields would be a crime. Like right now.'' His grin was sleepy, male and smug. "The side effects were remarkable.''

She thought so, too. Being made love to by a man who knew *exactly* how she responded to everything he did...it was a wonder she was still breathing.

He'd stopped playing with her hair and was running a fingertip around and around her nipple, which responded just as if she had the energy to follow through. "I hope this title business won't go to your head. I'm a younger son so mine is a mere courtesy title. You'll outrank me now. Yours will be passed on to our children."

Her heart thudded once, hard, in her chest. As soon as she had her breath back, she slid him a sideways glance. "You're taking a lot for granted."

The creases beneath his eyes deepened. "Am I?"

She was annoyed to feel herself blush. He'd undoubtedly read her shock of delight. Shifting carefully so that she took her weight on her elbow, not her hand, she raised herself so she could look at his face. "I know you have trouble putting things into words, Drew, but there are times when nothing else will do."

"We have a great deal to work out, I know," he said soberly. "Where we'll live, for example. We might try dividing our time between England and Montebello. My business is flexible enough to make that work. Of course, you may not be happy leaving your shop in your aunt's hands for long periods of time—"

She stopped that list of issues with a quick kiss. "All of that needs discussing, but those aren't the words I'm waiting for."

"Oh," he said innocently, but with a suspicious gleam in his eyes. "You want *those* words."

She waited.

He smiled, and his whole face was part of the smile this time. His whole being. His eyes were green and clear and warm. "I love you, Rose."

She smiled back at him and settled once more into her

place, her head on his shoulder, her hand over his heart. "In that case…yes, I'll marry you."

He waited, and when she didn't say anything more, he prompted her. "And?"

"I love you, Drew," she said softly. "I always will."

* * * * *

ROMANCING THE CROWN
continues next month with

**SECRETS OF A PREGNANT PRINCESS
(IM #1166).**

Don't miss it!

Chapter 1

From the moment they boarded the private jet, Farid Nasir knew that something was up with Princess Samira Kamal. Throughout his years of working for the Kamal family, he'd watched Samira grow from a shy, unimposing young girl into a gentle, caring woman known for her warmth and openness.

But on the plane ride, he'd seen a tension develop in this woman he was assigned to protect, a tension that had nothing to do with her dislike of flying. Her dark, long-lashed, almond-shaped eyes had snapped with secrets...and secrets worried Farid.

She'd told her father, Sheik Ahmed, that she was coming to Montebello to visit Princess Anna Sebastiani, but her exclamation of surprise upon learning that Princess Anna was absent from Montebello hadn't rung true.

He now sat in a chair in a corner of the living room of their temporary home on the Montebellan palace grounds waiting for Samira to finish freshening up and unpacking.

It was just after nine, and he'd had to turn on a lamp against the encroaching darkness of night.

Looking at his watch, he frowned. She'd now been in the bedroom for more than twenty minutes, and he'd heard no sound from the room in the past fifteen.

He knew she hadn't gone to bed. The only thing he'd learned in the past two and a half months as her bodyguard was that Princess Samira liked to stay up late and then to sleep in.

Again a disquieting unease crept through him. Instinct told him something was wrong, and Farid never ignored his instincts.

He got up from his chair and went to her bedroom door. He hesitated a moment, then knocked. "Princess Samira?"

There was no reply. No sound whatsoever came from behind the wooden door. No light seeped from beneath the door, either.

She couldn't be unpacking and freshening up in the darkness, he thought. His unease kicked up a notch, transforming into real concern.

He knocked again and when there was still no answer, he twisted the knob and eased open the door.

The room held a stillness that indicated emptiness. "Princess Samira?" he said softly, then turned on the overhead light.

Immediately he spied the open window with the screen removed. Horror riveted through him. He raced to the window. Had somebody ripped the screen away to kidnap Samira? Was she now being held someplace for ransom? For political purposes? Farid knew that there were terrorist groups that always posed a threat to all the members of the royal family.

Fear, icy cold and sickening, filled him. A fear that turned to rage as he realized the screen could not be removed from the outside, but only from the inside.

That meant Samira herself had removed the screen and disappeared into the shadows of the night.

Why? The question rang in his head as he raced out of the house. He hesitated on the sidewalk, unsure of which direction to go. He had to find her. As a princess of Tamir, she should not be wandering around alone.

Dammit, she knew better than to go off on her own, he thought as he hurried down the sidewalk. His gaze swept left then right as he ran, searching for any sign of the princess, who was supposed to be under his protection.

Sheik Ahmed would have his head if anything happened to his beloved daughter. And Farid would not be able to live with himself.

He knew the palace grounds were huge, and he had no idea if he was going in the right direction. As he hurried along, he encountered two palace guards. The first one had seen nobody all evening long. The second guard told him he'd given Princess Samira directions to Desmond Caruso's quarters, and now gave the same directions to Farid.

Farid ran, knowing that as long as Samira was alone, she was in danger. As he raced in the direction the guard had indicated, he felt a new burst of rage.

What had possessed her? Had this entire trip to Montebello been about a romantic liaison? If so, it was the most irresponsible thing she'd ever done.

He breathed a sigh of relief as he spied her petite form standing on the sidewalk just outside Desmond Caruso's residence.

Although her back was to him, he recognized the bright coral dress that hugged her slender shape. He grabbed her by the shoulders and whirled her around to face him.

"How dare you compromise my position and your own safety by sneaking out!" he exclaimed angrily.

Her beautiful eyes widened at the sight of him, then she

burst into tears. He instantly dropped his hands from her shoulders.

"And don't think your tears will temper my anger with you," he continued irritably. "I will not be manipulated by your tears. What you did was foolish and irresponsible."

"You have no idea just how foolish and irresponsible I've been!" she cried, and before Farid knew her intent, she threw herself against him, sobbing as if her heart were breaking in two.

* * * * *

CODE NAME: DANGER

The action continues with the men—and women—of the Omega Agency in Merline Lovelace's *Code Name: Danger* series.

This August, in TEXAS HERO (IM #1165) a renegade is assigned to guard his former love, a historian whose controversial theories are making her sorely in need of protection. But who's going to protect *him*—from her? A couple struggles with their past as they hope for a future....

And coming soon, more *Code Name: Danger* stories from Merline Lovelace....

Code Name: Danger
Because love is a risky business...

Silhouette®
Where love comes alive™

**Where royalty and romance
go hand in hand...**

The series continues in Silhouette Romance
with these unforgettable novels:

HER ROYAL HUSBAND
by Cara Colter
on sale July 2002 (SR #1600)

THE PRINCESS HAS AMNESIA!
by Patricia Thayer
on sale August 2002 (SR #1606)

SEARCHING FOR HER PRINCE
by Karen Rose Smith
on sale September 2002 (SR #1612)

And look for more Crown and Glory stories in
SILHOUETTE DESIRE starting in October 2002!

Available at your favorite retail outlet.

If you enjoyed what you just read,
then we've got an offer you can't resist!

Take 2 bestselling love stories FREE!
Plus get a FREE surprise gift!

Clip this page and mail it to Silhouette Reader Service™

IN U.S.A.
3010 Walden Ave.
P.O. Box 1867
Buffalo, N.Y. 14240-1867

IN CANADA
P.O. Box 609
Fort Erie, Ontario
L2A 5X3

YES! Please send me 2 free Silhouette Intimate Moments® novels and my free surprise gift. After receiving them, if I don't wish to receive anymore, I can return the shipping statement marked cancel. If I don't cancel, I will receive 6 brand-new novels every month, before they're available in stores! In the U.S.A., bill me at the bargain price of $3.99 plus 25¢ shipping and handling per book and applicable sales tax, if any*. In Canada, bill me at the bargain price of $4.74 plus 25¢ shipping and handling per book and applicable taxes**. That's the complete price and a savings of at least 10% off the cover prices—what a great deal! I understand that accepting the 2 free books and gift places me under no obligation ever to buy any books. I can always return a shipment and cancel at any time. Even if I never buy another book from Silhouette, the 2 free books and gift are mine to keep forever.

245 SDN DNUV
345 SDN DNUW

Name	(PLEASE PRINT)	
Address	Apt.#	
City	State/Prov.	Zip/Postal Code

* Terms and prices subject to change without notice. Sales tax applicable in N.Y.
** Canadian residents will be charged applicable provincial taxes and GST.
   All orders subject to approval. Offer limited to one per household and not valid to current Silhouette Intimate Moments® subscribers.
   ® are registered trademarks of Harlequin Books S.A., used under license.

INMOM02   ©1998 Harlequin Enterprises Limited

COMING NEXT MONTH